Raise Me Up

Abigail Glenn

Contents

Playlist

Emergence – Sleep Token
2008 – cleopatrick
A Bar Song (Tipsy) – Shaboozey
Hypnosis – Sleep Token
Animals – Architects
bernard trigger – cleopatrick
Hurt You – Spiritbox
Too Sweet – Hozier
Opera of the Urchin – Grim Salvo
Stone Leader Falling Down – VOLA
Perfect Soul – Spiritbox
Are You Really Okay? – Sleep Token
To Be Alone – Hozier
Only Pain – Gojira
Wings For Marie (Pt 1) – Tool
10,000 Days (Wings Pt 2) – Tool
TALK DOWN – cleopatrick
Provider – Sleep Token
Spotify Link

Author's Note and Content Warnings

While *Raise Me Up* absolutely *can* be read as a standalone, you may have a greater appreciation for the characters if you read *Drag Me Down* first. This is a MMF romance that slightly overlaps the timeline for *Drag Me Down*.

Content warnings include mentions of child abuse (both physical & verbal), a difficult medical diagnosis, homophobia from parents, brief mention of suicidal ideation, and a whole lot of f-bombs.

Eleven Years Old

I'm half asleep, buried under a heavy knitted blanket, when boots thud up the stairs to my bedroom.

My stomach lurches on instinct. Jolting upright, I force my sluggish brain to run through the day. The house is spotless. Dinner is sitting on the stove, covered in foil. I tackled my dad's laundry as soon as I got home from school.

Raking my fingers through my long hair, I tug hard at the roots. What did I forget? Where did I mess up?

Thud. Thud. Thud.

Dread tumbles around in my gut, and I bite down on a scream of frustration. I was so lost in a daze on my walk home from school that I forgot to pick up beer from my dad's shady friend at the convenience store.

How could I let myself get so distracted? How could a few strummed chords turn into an hour of playing guitar with the new kid in music class after the bell rang?

This is why I can't have friends. Not that my dad would let Hail come over anyway, and even if he said yes, I wouldn't want to expose Hail to the hell I live in.

Sometimes I wish I didn't want to live so badly because the effort of surviving is exhausting.

Footsteps pause outside my door. I catch the shadow of boots beneath it. The coppery tang of blood fills my mouth as I sink teeth into my cheek, weighing my options. Is it a hide under the blanket or a run to the bus stop kind of night?

My gaze flicks to the DART card on my nightstand that my mom left. Do I have any money left on it? I'm not even sure the buses are running this late.

As far as my mom goes...

Yeah, she's done helping me. She's been gone for three months. Up and vanished after I got suspended from school for fighting. I've started having nightmares that my dad murdered her and tossed her bones in the woods behind my school.

Ice sheets my body when the door handle rattles. "What the fuck did I tell you about locking this door, boy? You stupid like your mother?"

I clench the blanket in my hands. I may not be able to forgive my mom for leaving me, but I know she's a lot smarter than him.

She never laid hands on me.

A fist bangs on the door, hard enough to make me wince in anticipation of pain. Leaping out of bed, my foot gets caught in the blanket, and I tumble to the floor, head and elbows first, with a sharp cry.

"You think I can't hear you? Get your ass over here and unlock this damn door. You know you made a fucking mistake. You're gonna pay for it."

My heart slams against my ribcage, desperate to escape. I know it's not possible to die from fear, but in times like these, I question what's real.

This can't be normal. This isn't how things should be.

Scrambling over to a pile of dirty clothes near my closet, I yank on dark jeans and a black hoodie. Frantically, I search around for my boots.

Where the fuck did I leave them?

The lock on my door gives out. I cringe as it slams against the wall and trembles from the force.

I don't get to watch much TV, but I've seen enough to know my dad could star as the serial killer in a slasher movie. His eyes are pools of midnight, vast and cold as a desert at night. His giant body fills up the doorway, blue-collared shirt unbuttoned and sweaty black hair curled over his forehead.

Alarms blare in my head. *Pain. Pain. Pain.*

I think about calling the cops, but it wouldn't matter. I'll be dead before they get here. Even if they do make it in time, I doubt they'll be able to pull him off me.

Chancing broken limbs, I leap out of my second-story window. Crickets fall silent as I land in the overgrown grass with a grunt. Rolling to my bare feet, I take off through the gap in the neighbor's worn fence.

I fight back tears as I run. I don't understand. Why does my dad keep me around? Why not dump me on someone else?

Or am I that unlovable?

Is that it? Is that the real reason I'm stuck here? No one else wants me? My mom clearly didn't.

As I claw my way through a thick wall of hedges, the aggressive rumble of my dad's muscle car fills the night. My heart is pounding so hard, I'm scared it's going to break free from my chest.

My mom used to tell me that my dad wasn't a happy person. Sometimes those bad feelings overflowed, and we just had to ride them out. She told me if we ever left him, he'd starve himself or drink until his organs shut down.

Those words haunt me every time I try to run away. I don't want to be responsible for my dad's death. But I don't want him to hit me either.

Racing across yards, I see his rusted beige car blinking in and out of existence between houses and trees. He's cussing and jabbing his finger in my direction.

I *hate* him. I hate how brittle he makes me feel. Like I've got paper bones. Like one strong gust of wind would crumple me.

I know I'm not going to outrun him, but I refuse to let him drag me back to hell tonight.

I need a better plan.

Pumping my arms and legs harder, I turn in the direction of the new kid's house. I'd thrown the scrap of paper he'd given me in the trash at school, but I memorized his address. Almost like I knew I'd need him.

Will he be awake this late? Do I trust his kindness?

I don't even care at this point. I'm so tired of being alone.

Climbing over the brick wall of a gated, wealthy neighborhood, I tumble into a freshly mowed yard. I do my best to stay away from cameras as I creep to the sidewalk.

A few streets in, the faint plucking of guitar strings reaches me. Lured by the melody, I hide behind a parked car. I peek around at two small figures in the dark sitting on the concrete steps off the side of a garage that could fit my entire house. The fancy gold numbers on the brick exterior match those in my memory.

Overwhelming relief rushes through me. I run toward them so fast, I scrape my toes on the curb. As I hiss in pain, two similar faces lift at the same time to look at me. I stumble to a halt.

I didn't know Hail had a twin.

Blinking back at them in shock, I compare their soft features. He's got lighter blonde hair and amber eyes, where his sister's eyes are a richer, honey brown like the bourbon my dad sometimes drinks when he has extra money and doesn't feel like paying the electric bill.

"Liam," Hail whispers. "What are you doing here so late?"

Bloody toes curling into the grass, I struggle to form words. I hadn't thought this far into my plan. What do I tell him? That my dad's chasing me in his car because I forgot to feed his stupid addiction?

What if he comes here and hurts the only person who has ever wanted to be my friend?

"Hey." Hail rests his Ibanez against the house and hurries over to me, all traces of his earlier sunshiny mood gone. "Are you alright?"

My gaze darts to his sister, still sitting on the stairs. *Am I scaring her?* That's the last thing I want to do.

"Sorry," I mumble, tears burning my eyes.

I should be over this crying shit.

Hail wraps a hand around my wrist. He doesn't give me a chance to freak out over his touch, quickly pulling me into the garage. His sister follows on silent feet.

A shadow of him.

Instantly, I hate the thought. I hate that she seems *less* present. Hate it because I know what it feels like to be invisible, too.

At least, until my dad loses his temper.

"Stas, can you take Liam upstairs? I'll make sure the coast is clear," Hail says.

I get stuck on the pronunciation of his sister's name. An "ah" sound followed by a "z". I repeat it in my head several times as Hail vanishes inside the house.

Nervously, I meet her gaze and get lost in her big brown eyes. She looks...soft. Her voice is even softer when she speaks. "Let's get you cleaned up, okay?"

All I can do is nod. I don't know why tonight is hitting me so hard.

Signaled along by Hail, I follow Stasi up the spiral staircase in their giant house. They operate like a practiced team, making me wonder if it's normal for them to sneak around at night. I've always been a night owl. Late hours are when my dad passes out in his recliner, and I can pick up my guitar to practice music.

She motions me into a bright yellow bedroom. Curiosity mixes with adrenaline as I step inside, and she shuts the door.

It's the first time I've been in another kid's room. I imagined there'd be posters and sports medals on the walls. *Some* kind of display of who she is or what she likes. But there's no trace of personality anywhere. Just a thick stack of textbooks on a plain white desk by the windows.

Stasi turns on the light in a connected bathroom, and Hail appears from the other side. He sets neatly folded clothes on the counter. "These should fit. I think we're the same size."

He doesn't mean it as an insult, but his words poke at an open wound, anyway. I was held back twice in school, and I'm still too small for my age. Too bony and weak.

Hail slips away like a ghost again. I get the sense he doesn't like to sit still.

"Do you want to rinse off?" Stasi asks, eyes dropping to my bloody, dirt-covered feet.

Worried she'll get in trouble if I mess up the clean carpet, I give her another nod.

She leaves me in the middle of her bedroom to start up the shower. When I don't follow, she comes back to get me, gently tugging on my baggy sleeve. "It's okay."

For some reason, those two words settle me. Or maybe it's her sweet smile. I don't think I've ever been around someone who didn't make me feel like hiding. Whose touch didn't make me want to cower.

She guides me into the bathroom. I'm not thinking clearly because I start to peel off my hoodie with her still in the room. Her eyes go wide as they fall to the yellow and purple bruises splattered like paint across my skin.

"Please," I whisper, frantically shaking my head. "I don't want to talk about it."

Her little nose scrunches, but she eventually nods. "I'm a good listener, Liam."

Instead of pushing me for more information, she closes me in the bathroom. Suddenly, I'm deflating. Pushing all the air from my body like I've been holding it for years.

I dare a glance at my reflection, frowning at the stringy, dark-haired, dark-eyed kid staring back at me. He doesn't look like someone I'd want to be friends with.

Turning my body, I examine the bruises and scars across my back from steel-toed boots, beer bottles, and cigarette burns. Hot coffee when I burned breakfast one time.

Stripping out of the rest of my clothes, I step under the hot spray of water and stand there like a statue until the water runs clean. Then I dress in the clothes Hail left for me—a black band tee and a pair of sweats with a drawstring I have to tie extra tight.

I startle when I open the door and find the twins waiting for me on the edge of Stasi's bed. They both seem genuinely worried about me, and I don't know what to do about it. Part of me wants to assure them I'm good now. No harm done this time.

The other part wants to break down and ask them to hide me in their rooms forever.

Stasi peeks at her brother.

"Rooftop," he agrees. "I'll grab the stuff."

Do they share thoughts like they share features?

Hail darts from the room, and I'm left to stand awkwardly in front of his sister. She hops to her feet and moves over to the window. Cracking it open, she climbs up onto the ledge.

"Hey—" I lurch toward her, terrified over the height of her window in comparison to mine.

Perfectly calm, she turns and holds out her hand to me. "I won't let you fall."

Swallowing in the face of those warm, confident eyes, I place my shaky hand in hers.

I don't think I breathe again until we make it over the peak of the roof. We're not super high up, but a fall from this height would do some damage, so I cling to her hand like I'm the one saving her life tonight, not the other way around.

We sit beside each other, hidden behind the tall trees in their backyard, gazing up at the endless night sky. It's hard to make out any stars with the light pollution, but a few shine through, desperate to be seen.

I sneak a look at her. Is it weird to think she's pretty when she looks like her brother? Is it weird to think he's pretty, too? Do I only feel that way because they're being nice to me?

My stomach does a flip when she meets my gaze. I'm not sure what this feeling is expanding inside me, but it feels like something big. It feels like something that could fill the hole in my chest.

Shuffling on the roof has me ripping my hand out of hers. I turn my head in time to see Hail coming over the peak with a red plastic net of popsicles swinging from his hand. He sits down beside me and rips a blue popsicle open with his teeth. When he hands it to me, I end up sucking it down before he gets a red one open for his sister.

"Good, huh?" Hail grins, fetching me another one.

Can a broken soul be healed with sugary flavored ice? Or is this the magic of the Koval twins at work?

"Hey, Liam?"

"Hmm?" I glance over at Hail, a lime green popsicle still dangling from my mouth.

"You should sleep over tonight."

My chest tightens at his serious expression. I don't think I've ever wanted anything more. If I could, I'd stay in this bubble of peace with them forever. I'd never go home.

I peek at Stasi as she tips her popsicle wrapper above her head to suck out the remaining juice. It almost gets a laugh out of me. Almost.

"Yeah," I answer quietly. "I'd like that."

ONE
LIAM

There are dozens of local gyms in Uptown. Why the fuck did I have to pick the most distracting one?

As I curl a thirty-pound dumbbell in each tattooed hand, my gaze instinctively seeks out the swish of a long blonde ponytail in the wall of mirrors.

It's hotter than hell in here tonight. Even with the industrial fans battling the Texas heat, sweat rolls down my spine, sticking the thin fabric of my sleeveless black tank to my chest and abs.

Yet Stasi showed up in thick, baggy layers. If I didn't know any better, I'd assume she'd scooped up some random guy's clothes off her bedroom floor to rush to the gym.

According to her twin brother, Hail—my best friend and ex-bandmate—Stas is single. And honestly, it's fucking me up.

I want her in *my* clothes. Want her naked in *my* bed.

Stasi hasn't noticed me among the hulked out gym crowd, and it's a bit of a hit to my ego.

As the retired lead guitarist of the popular metal band, Atonement, I can't remember the last time I had to work to gain anyone's attention. Not that I'm actively trying to ruin my friendship with her by adding sex to the equation.

But she hasn't reached out once since I became a permanent resident in the Dallas area.

A cackle of laughter has my attention drifting from her to a group of muscled regulars. The three guys smirk and nod at Stasi as she adds another steel plate onto a barbell.

I set my dumbbells back on the rack. She isn't lacking sass when it comes to conversations with Hail, but sometimes she gets stuck in her head and questions her voice.

The shorter guy from the group with a leaner build and too much swagger moves in, tugging on the end of her ponytail to get her attention. Anger swims through my veins.

Not your business, Liam.

Last time I intervened in a situation, I almost beat the shit out of some nobody harassing Hail's boyfriend in a hotel lobby while we were on tour. Took me weeks to shake the fear of who I almost became in those heated seconds. My piece of shit dad is six feet under now, but I still feel his presence looming over me, pulling invisible strings to manipulate my thoughts and emotions.

With my headphones in, I can't make out what the guy says, but the furrow between Stasi's brows tells me she's not interested.

Body language, fucker.

Her expression twists further when he points at the plates on the barbell. So what if he can't see the strength she hides under all those clothes? He doesn't have any right to step in. She's weathered enough condescending bullshit from her parents for one lifetime.

Oblivious gym rat struts to the end of the barbell and starts pulling off plates.

Yep. I'm done watching.

Popping out my earbuds, I leave them blasting Atonement's latest recording as I drop them into a pocket of my sweats and saunter over to them. I've listened to the track a hundred times. I'll listen to it a hundred more until I figure out what's not working.

Positioning myself right behind the guy interrupting Stas's workout, I tug on his hair. He whips around, eyes narrowed and nostrils flared, but as his eyes dip down my body, he naturally eases a step back. "Can I help you?"

"Definitely not," I reply darkly.

The guy rolls his shoulders like he's mentally working himself up to a confrontation. I can tell he's fighting the instinct to run. I know the gut feeling well. Spent my teenage years lifting weights so I'd never have to experience it again.

He has the audacity to look at Stas for backup. I wait for her to tell him off, but she drops her head and starts picking up the plates he removed.

Concern prickles in my chest. Where has her fire gone, and who the fuck extinguished it? Is she struggling with family stuff? Would Hail know, or is he too wrapped up with the new album and calls to his long-distance boyfriend to notice what's going on with her?

I step into the gym guy's view. "No chance, bub. That's her signaling you to fuck off."

He huffs. "She could have told me that."

"Oh, she did. You're not *listening*."

"Whatever. Not on me when she gets hurt," he mumbles, strutting off to rejoin his flock. I keep my gaze on them as I catch mutterings about the "situation". Of course he's the benevolent gym hero who was approached by an asshole.

I *am* an asshole. I don't give a shit who thinks it.

Forcing a deep breath, I squat to pick up a plate and return it to the barbell. Stas gives me a calculating look. Did I overstep?

I fall victim to one of our staring games, melting into her pretty brown eyes framed by an unholy amount of darker lashes.

We stare so long, the years we've shared unfold around us. Suddenly, I'm eleven years old, accepting the hand of a quiet but strong friend helping me through her window.

Time warps, and I'm seventeen, laid out on Hail's bedroom floor, my fingers tangled in the silky hair of a pretty girl who didn't know her worth as her brother plays guitar in the background.

I'm twenty-six, fighting to keep my gaze from taking in long, toned legs and flashes of rebellious smiles that quicken my pulse.

Stasi breaks eye contact first, crashing me hard into the present where I'm set to spend the rest of my years alone.

Doesn't mean I can't admire her. She's caught me looking more than a few times. It's quickly becoming an addiction trying to make her sun-kissed, freckled skin flush and her eyes glint with something wild.

"You've got your scary face on," she whispers, brushing against me to slide the clamp in place on the barbell.

I *should* give her space. However, I can't find the willpower to move away as I breathe in the scent of her citrus body wash.

My gaze runs down the soft curve of her neck, visualizing my hand wrapping around it. I'd tilt her head to the side and bring my tongue and teeth to her skin so I could taste her.

She'd be too sweet for me.

Regretfully, I ease back. "Most people would say that's my normal face."

When she spins around to face me, she has to lift her chin high to meet my eyes. The impulsive thought is there to grab her by the thighs and hoist her up against my body so we can be on the same level.

"That's not you, Liam," she says firmly.

Something tightens in my chest. "No?"

"No." Her conviction is enough to snuff out the lingering anger from the gym guy messing with her.

Sighing, I reach out to tug at the hem of her baggy sweatshirt. "What's with the get-up?"

She purses those full lips at me. "It's not a get-up. It's called comfort."

I fight back a grin, pleased to have her sass back.

Without thinking, I ask, "You coming to the party at my house this Saturday?"

"I wasn't sure if I was invited."

"Why wouldn't you be?"

She frowns. "Because no one asked me."

"You don't need an invite, Stasi."

She sinks her teeth into her bottom lip, and I have to shove my hands into my pockets to keep from tugging it free. It's rare that I have to practice restraint anymore. My success in the metal music world has earned me a ticket to *take* what I want in most situations.

"Do you need help getting ready?" she asks.

"Not unless you want to help."

An audible breath escapes her. "It's like talking in riddles with you. Yes, Liam. I'd like to help."

We get stuck in another dangerous staring game. As much as I want to close the distance between us, I won't be the one to make the first move. She knows what I'm about. I earned my reputation as a heartbreaker.

I try to think back to when my thoughts about Anastasia Koval shifted. If I had to pinpoint a moment, it might have been the night I gave her the keys to my 1969 Firebird as a joke while I wrangled a drunk Hail out of a music venue after a show. We were nothing more than a popular local band at the time. Kids still obsessing over a dream.

I knew Stas couldn't drive a stick, but I also knew she wasn't one to turn down a challenge. With a quiet stubbornness, she'd climbed into the driver's seat.

By the time we made it to Hail's apartment an hour later, she was shifting smoothly enough to have me hard. Fuck, if *that* didn't make for a confusing night.

It was the first time I'd thought about kissing her.

Stasi turns away from me and drops onto the bench. I watch her tighten her ponytail, imagining the drag of her polished red nails down my bare back.

My jaw clenches. This desire for something *more* with her was so much easier to avoid when I was touring. It's definitely a mistake inviting her over. The last thing I want to do is hurt her. I've only experienced a connection like this with one other person, and I haven't spoken to him in seven years.

Pushing aside thoughts of Beau and then visions of Stasi in tempting positions, I move behind the barbell and give it a smack. "You gonna show everyone up or what?"

TWO
STASI

How am I supposed to lift this weight with Liam Beckner, sex god and legendary metal guitarist, standing over me?

Muscles flex as he crosses his arms over his broad chest. His dark eyes sear into the very center of my being. They're not *actually* black—I've had the luxury, and the travesty, of seeing them up close for most of my life—but in certain lighting, combined with his devastating looks, *all* of him looks like he was forged in hell itself.

Okay, so he can be scary.

He *would* be scary had I not known him since the fourth grade.

Sure, I didn't get to stay close to him like Hail, but sometimes they took pity on me and let me tag along when they played shows at rundown graffiti'd venues or snuck out for a late meal.

Most of the time, though, I admired Liam from a distance. I watched him transform from a scrawny, bruised up kid who struggled to read to this beast of a man, tattooed, pierced, and shrouded in intimidating energy.

He's got his black hair tied up in a messy bun today. Shorter layers of it have fallen out to frame his face and hide some of the elaborate black and gray tattoos along his thick neck. His brows slightly arch up at the ends, adding to his overall image that screams danger.

And possibly the best orgasm you'll ever have.

That's just my assumption, though. I wouldn't know from experience.

Rolling my body down onto the bench, my gaze snags on the pointed canines he reveals with a flash of a wicked grin. Hot blood rushes through my body.

Not helping my workout.

Had I dealt with that gym bro faster, Liam wouldn't have even bothered walking over here. For the most part, he leaves me alone. Occasionally, he confuses my brain with flirtations I know don't hold any weight because Liam doesn't date.

He *fucks*.

I should have picked a different gym. I knew the vibes were off as soon as I walked in, but considering this place is across the street from my apartment and getting anywhere in Dallas is a pain in the ass, I thought I was doing myself a favor by saving time and gas.

Liam leans over the bar, putting his face right above mine. "You good?"

And there goes my heart rate all over again. I'm gonna need medical intervention soon.

I do my best to shove him from my mind, but it's hard when his powerful thighs are right beside my head and his sleeveless black shirt is cut wide enough on the sides to show off what he's working with—a thick trunk of a body cut with too many abs for him to be human.

Don't look at his dick. Don't do it, Stas.

Swallowing, I grip the bar and adjust my body position. If I can't lift this, I'm proving those guys right and Liam wrong.

Liam stands back and tucks his hands into his pockets, not even pretending to spot me. Better him than a stranger stepping in trying to tell me what I'm capable of. I'm already well aware of my limitations. There's no need for anyone else to add to the negativity circling like vultures in my head.

Speaking of vultures, I haven't heard back from my mom. She'd asked if I planned on attending dad's family work event at the country club this coming Sunday, and I'd explained that my appearance depends solely on whether or not they invited Hail. Not that I expect him to go, but if they can't accept my brother for who he is, then I need to reconsider if I want them in my life. I've given them plenty of time to adjust to the news of him dating a man.

Sensing multiple pairs of eyes on me, I lift the bar from the rack. I don't know what it is about me that screams "weak" to others, but I'm getting kind of sick of it.

The bar glides down to my chest easily enough. It's pushing it back up that has my arms quivering and my teeth clenching.

God, this is heavy.

Five reps in, and I'm breathing hard. Toxic thoughts creep out of the cages I've shut them in, seeking purchase in my mind.

Life was supposed to get easier when I finished my DPT program, passed my NPTE, and completed a neurologic physical therapy residency. I'm several months into a career at a renowned inpatient rehabilitation center.

But now there's student loan debt to pay back. And family drama. And finding a house that doesn't cost my soul to afford. Rent is bad enough as it is...

Eventually I'm going to have to figure out dating because I don't want to spend my life alone.

"Three more. You got this. Shut those fuckers up," Liam murmurs.

Fire sparks in my chest. I don't care about those guys anymore. I only care what Liam thinks. I care about him more than I'm willing to admit.

The weight gets stuck a few inches above my chest. Liam uses one hand to take some of the pressure off my arms. With his other hand, he slips a wireless headphone into my ear. I recognize the chugging guitar instantly, having heard it through my bedroom wall almost every night growing up.

"New stuff?" I ask, eyes widening.

His mouth quivers, teasing me with a grin. "New stuff. Get to it."

He removes his hand, and I push through the last three reps, letting the heavy guitars and pounding drums power me through the pain in my muscles.

Maria, the vocalist who replaced my brother when he shifted into Liam's empty spot as lead guitarist, absolutely *destroys*. She may not have the lower register like my brother, but her highs are bone-chilling. *Demonic.*

I sit up and give the song the attention it deserves as I catch my breath. When it ends, I pop the earbud out and hand it back to Liam. He keeps those eyes on me, heavy and expectant. "Well?"

"It's good."

His dark eyes glint before he narrows them at me. I can't help a little laugh and a soft eye roll. "You know I'm not your target audience, right?"

"You telling me we subjected you to over two decades of metal music and you don't even like the genre?"

"I'm supportive, but yeah. It's not for me."

The side of his mouth twitches. "Fair enough."

I don't want him to feel obligated to babysit me at the gym, so I give him an out. "Thanks for the spot."

He pulls out his phone, leaning over the barbell to fiddle with it. "You've got two more sets before you get rid of me."

I'd rather not get rid of him *ever*, but that's an inside thought. I'm surprised he's allowed me and Hail to stay in his life as long as he has.

No one else seems to make the cut.

People on social media either recognize Liam as a musical genius or label him an egotistical asshole. They don't understand the broken boy he hides, and I don't think he wants them to.

"If I'm doing two more sets, then so are you," I say, wriggling out of my hoodie.

With Liam's presence, I don't have to worry about anyone else bothering me, and I'd rather not pass out from the heat rolling in through the cracked garage door along the side of the gym.

His eyes flick up from his phone, and my heart misfires as he takes his time looking me over.

Okay. Maybe removing the hoodie was a bad idea. I've worked hard on my body, but I'm far from perfect. I have blemishes and scars and stretch marks from growing too fast through puberty.

I'm nothing like the women Liam Beckner would have entertained on tours.

His tone is husky when he replies, "What if it's not my arm day?"

"You were doing bicep curls, tricep pulls, and shoulder presses. Of course it's your arm day." I pop up from the bench and motion to the space I've created for him.

Liam chuckles. It's barely a sound. A soft, low noise that settles between my legs. "You been watching me, Anastasia?"

"You're hard to miss," I admit.

He encroaches into my space, the heat from his massive body seeping into me. I'm taller than the average woman and carved with lean muscle, but he makes me feel small. Breakable inside and out.

Damn it, the man *does* scare me. When I think about him touching me or kissing me, my knees threaten to give out. I'm not sure I'd survive him. Only because I'd crave more than he'd ever be willing to give.

A heavy sigh escapes me. He gently bumps my shoulder with his own as he moves to the bench and lays down, his big, tattooed hands gripping the bar.

"Oh, hell no. You think I'm going to let you get off easy?" I say.

Liam raises a curious brow. Grinning, I hurry over to the weight rack, striding right through another group of gym bros to grab more steel plates. Though I feel judging gazes on me, I'm more confident with Liam in my corner. More like me than when I'm alone.

Liam watches me patiently as I load the plates onto the bar. Once I'm done, I clap my hands together. "Better."

But it's *not* better. Not when Liam handles the two-hundred seventy-five pounds beautifully, muscles shifting under inked scenes of angels and demons locked in a bloody, eternal battle on his skin. Defined abs crunch beneath the worn scrap of fabric that can't even be called a shirt.

I can see the outline of his cock beneath his sweats. There's no ignoring it. And there's no way it *couldn't* be hard right now. The size...

Good lord, he melts all the intelligent thoughts in my brain. Accepting the invite to his house was a bad idea. It feels like the foreshadowing of regret. Or inevitable heartbreak.

But the idea of spending the night by myself in my apartment is way worse.

When Liam sits up and swings his legs around so he can look at me, I stick out a hand to demand his other earbud. "If you're going to put me to shame like that, I'm going to find ways to pick apart your recording."

Smirking, Liam rises to his full height and moves closer. Nerves fire as his calloused fingers trail up my neck. My breath catches.

He wraps his hand under my jaw and eases my head to the side. I don't fight him. I don't want to. At this moment, I exist for him alone. A puppet on strings only he controls.

His mouth lowers to the shell of my ear, hot breath fanning over my skin. "I expect a full critique when I'm done making you sweat."

He places the earbud in my hand, then steps away. I fail to hide a full-body shudder.

Suddenly, I can think of a *lot* more interesting ways to get in our workout.

Listening through Atonement's final track, I fight back a grin at the rightness of the music washing over me.

Stas has an ear for this. Her suggestion to pull back on percussion during the chorus allowed the outro to hit like a brick wall of unforgiving sound. The sudden explosion of drums at the end, combined with Maria's harsh vocals, has goosebumps rising on my arms.

"Please tell me this is the one," Griff calls out, his voice sounding through the control room speakers. He's shining with sweat and panting as he braces his forearms on the top of his beanie, drumsticks clutched in his trembling hands.

I cock my head in Hail's direction, leaning forward in the other leather chair behind my digital mixer, a captivating smile on his face. He waits for Maria's last high to run its course before he confirms, "Yeah, that hits the spot."

My gaze drifts to Malek behind us. He's got one foot propped on my junior sound engineer's desk. His long, nimble fingers pluck out a muted rhythm on the bass guitar he snatched from my collection of instruments hung in the moody painted hallway. His blood-red locks are spiked out in all directions like he stuck a finger in an electrical socket.

Honestly, I wouldn't put it past him to do just that. The guy challenges death on the regular.

"The world isn't ready for this album," Malek says.

"They better be." Maria pops her head in the room, dreads swaying from a high ponytail and a slice of meat lover's pizza folded in one hand. We ordered a feast hours ago when we realized it was past dinnertime and no one was ready to leave.

I take pride in the fact that my previous bandmates trust me with their new album. They'd been in the market for a new producer and had faith I wouldn't fuck it up due to my workaholic nature and dedication to perfection.

I might have been a bit of a tyrant when I played with them.

As much shit as they've given me for leaving Atonement, they've come to understand that succeeding in music was never about fame or money for me. It was an outlet for the messy things I didn't know how to wade through as a kid.

And when Hail offered me friendship—when he gave me reason to wake up each morning—music became a way for me to give back to him.

Once his position was secured at the top of the metal world, I knew it was time to help other aspiring musicians. It's one good thing I can do. One way I can prove to myself I'm not what my parents believed I would become. I'm not the criminal teachers whispered about or the murderous goth other kids feared. I get to submerge myself in music production, something I came to love more than performing on stage.

"Aw, you didn't have to," Malek says, reaching for Maria's pizza. She yanks it away from his hand, and when he goes for it again, she takes off down the hall. Malek sets my bass on the desk and chases after her.

"Come hang that up, dickhead!" I shout.

Both of them are bickering so loud in the entry area, they don't hear me.

"Is that a yes? No? Someone? Anyone?" Griff asks in a defeated tone.

I take pity on him, hitting the button for the microphone. "You're done."

Griff pops off his headphones and drops his head back with an exhausted growl that sounds more like a dying creature than a small, normally goofy human.

"The fuck was that?" Malek reappears in the doorway with Maria hanging off his back.

I nod in Griff's direction. "Think it belongs to you."

Malek's brows furrow. He runs his thumb under the curve of his bottom lip as he takes in his bandmate. "Nope. I don't claim ownership."

Maria jumps off his back and smacks him in the arm. "Go get your man."

Panic momentarily flashes across Malek's face. He glances around the room, almost like he's gauging our reactions, before slipping into the recording room to scoop Griff up and toss him over a shoulder.

Shockingly enough, Griff doesn't try to fight him. His limbs dangle uselessly as Malek holds him.

A laugh bursts out of Hail. "I think we broke him."

I snort. "He'll be back to his annoying self in an hour."

"Oh, for sure," Hail agrees.

"Guess we're out then." Malek salutes us.

Bells above the front door ring out, signaling their departure. I assume Maria already bailed. She's not one for greetings or goodbyes. Not that I'm complaining. She lives her life like everything is constant. Like relationships won't change without effort, and people won't leave.

I have a very different perspective on that matter.

Now that it's just me and Hail in the studio, I'm about to interrogate him about his family situation, worried about the impact it's having on both him and his sister.

However, the sight of him clutching his phone in both hands as his knee bounces up and down has me taking a softer approach.

"Hey. You good?"

"Yeah." After a pause, he adds, "Would be better if Z were here, but you know..."

"He's putting in the work," I remind him.

Therapy isn't easy, and Hail's boyfriend's struggles run deep. I had hesitations about Z when Hail first dragged him into our world, only because I recognized the demons lurking in those ice-blue eyes. We were both exposed to them when Z toured with us as my guitar tech for a bit.

After some deeply reckless behavior, it was decided that Z would hang back in London and work through his trauma and addictions.

Hail nods. "He's putting in the work."

I've checked in with Z a few times, and I couldn't be more proud of him for the progress he's making. He plans on moving here as soon as he feels mentally strong enough.

"Don't feel like you need to keep me company," I tell Hail.

"Can't I be worried about *you*?"

"No," I say firmly.

He does his best to glare at me, but he's all golden retriever energy, even with the piercings and tattoos.

I glance at the clock on the wall. "About to be morning across the ocean. Get the fuck out of here."

Hail looks at his phone for the hundredth time. The fact that he hasn't jumped on a plane and flown out to see his boyfriend proves he's respecting Z's wishes. His self-control is something to be admired.

Wish I could rein myself in when it comes to filthy thoughts about his sister.

Hail hops to his feet. "I'll see you tomorrow, yeah?"

"Tomorrow."

"Thanks, Liam. Love you, man."

"Yeah, yeah."

I linger in the studio after Hail leaves, reflecting on my career with Atonement. What's it going to feel like when they're back on tour without me? How could I crave solitude so much when I was crammed in buses and bouncing between cities and yet hate it so much when I finally have it?

I think about Stasi, the only other soul I've interacted with outside of work since I moved back to this godforsaken city. I fear what might happen if she gives in to me. If I cave to my desires and claim her. What if we can't get back to what we have now?

I almost laugh at myself. What the fuck do we have now? A frayed friendship I put little effort into?

I drag a hand down the side of my face. I just need a distraction. I haven't had a single hookup since I moved home. Didn't want anyone getting ideas. Just because I set up roots somewhere doesn't mean I'm looking for something permanent.

Opening my phone, I scroll through hundreds of phone numbers.

Somehow, I end up in my messages with Stas. The last one she sent me was over a year ago. It was a picture of a starry night sky. I'd sent her one back of the Tokyo skyline after we'd played a sold out show there.

As I'm scrolling through our history, I see more photos of sunsets and stars.

Did we ever actually talk?

There's a cute video of her giggling and apologizing for a horrible view of a meteor shower she sent me from her apartment balcony.

Sighing, I shut my phone and push up from my chair. It's a little after midnight. There's the lingering feeling of dread, knowing it's going to be one of those nights where I either wake in a sweat or sleep evades me entirely.

Locking up the studio, I debate finding someone to take home and fuck into oblivion.

Maybe then I'll be able to keep my hands off my best friend's sister.

Four
Beau

L ast night was the worst performance of my life.

Between the flop of this recent album and the chords I missed on stage, I feel like I'm staring defeat in its evil face and submitting to it.

I lift and flex my right hand, glaring at it as if that will drive away the tingles running from my fingertips up to my shoulder. Already been to the ER for it.

After hours of enduring tests to make sure my episode wasn't stroke related, I'd bowed out of a CT scan, finished up the IV they'd stuck in my arm, and rushed to hop back on the tour bus.

Should I be concerned? Probably. Do I have time to worry about it when my career is literally crumbling around me? Nope.

Still, I cave to a little self-inflicted torture, pulling up old videos of Lithos on my phone. 10.3 million views on our first track title.

Like what the actual fuck?

It's hard to fathom a nobody like me—a wild dreamer brought up on a ranch in the middle of the Arizona desert—could achieve this kind of reach with music. Early mornings and late evenings spent on the back porch strumming an old classical guitar turned into an opening act with the notorious band Atonement.

Years later, we're headlining our own shows. Except we're no longer selling out venues. I've stressed about it. Smoked too much. Lost sleep over it.

I should be proud of what I've accomplished, right? So many artists don't reach this point in their journey. Yeah, we're not a household name or anything. Hard to achieve that when you play progressive rock. Most people don't understand it.

But fame has only highlighted the fact that this album is performing worse than our last album, and that one performed worse than our debut. We set the bar high, and according to fans, we haven't been able to rise to that level since.

We've been judged and deemed unworthy.

Hard not to feel like it's entirely my fault. Shit hasn't been good lately. These stupid headaches I've been experiencing keep laying me out, and the creative juices aren't flowing.

Groaning, I drop my phone onto my thigh. At least the weather is perfect here in Vancouver, if not a bit on the hot side. I'd snuck out here in a slouchy black hoodie and ripped up jeans, eager to alleviate the shit lingering in my head. I'm already rocking a red tint on my exposed knees.

That'll make for a fun tan line.

Tipping my head up, I watch a flock of birds soar across the glassy blue sky, almost hypnotic in their movements.

Must be nice to have your body listen.

I've been popping Tylenol like it's candy in a Pez dispenser, determined to make it through this tour. Definitely a mistake skipping that CT scan, but I'm afraid of what might be found. I've never been sick like this.

Or maybe I'm spinning myself up over nothing. Maybe I'm subconsciously trying to find an excuse for why I suck as a musician.

Taking another hit from my blunt, I let the smoke burn in my lungs until tears well in my eyes. My heart rate settles into a normal rhythm.

Tension melts from my body, and the pain in my forehead eases *just* enough.

The door to the balcony bangs open. I turn my head and squint at the man striding toward me, arms swinging with purpose and mouth turned down.

I'm not proud of my snicker. "Oh, wow. You look *super* angry."

Noah kicks the end of my chair with his boot, making it screech across the concrete. "Are you kidding me, Beau?"

I offer a lazy shrug. "Didn't make a joke."

Noah dives both hands into his fluff of ginger hair. "You missed the interview with Heavy Verse. You missed every single sound check this week. You fucking missed a show in Seattle, Beau. A *show*! You haven't been responding to anyone's calls or texts. You're always smoking. You've been a fucking ghost for months, man."

I don't tell him that the stage lights make my head hurt so I've been avoiding them as much as possible or that sometimes my vision gets so bad on stage, I can't find the effect pedals or that I spent the morning of that interview with Heavy Verse in a hospital bed, hooked up to an EKG machine and an IV.

"You work hard on that list of failures?" I taunt.

Fuck. I'm so high. I shouldn't be making light of this, but maybe he'll feel better if he assumes I don't care. Maybe he'll get over this faster.

Noah waves at the thick cloud of smoke that curls out from my parted lips in irritation. "*Jesus*, Beau. What's going on with you?"

I drop my sunglasses over my eyes. "Don't know what you're talking about."

A long pause stretches between us, and I wait for his lecture. Wait for him to exhaust himself like he usually does when something is bothering him. Noah's strung that way. Coiled up so tight, one day his head and limbs are going to pop off from the building energy.

I chuckle at the jack-in-the-box image playing out in my head.

"You know what?" His tone is sharper than I expect, instantly ruining my vibe. "I'm not gonna wait around for the others to break the news. Beau, we think you should take a break. I've talked with our manager and the label already. They've got someone else lined up to get us through the rest of our tour."

Air sticks in my lungs until the blunt I forgot I was holding burns down to my fingertips. Cursing, I drop it onto the ground and try to stomp it out with my shoe, but it feels like gravity has suddenly decided to crush me into my chair.

I rub my palm over my chest. *Whew. Still breathing.*

My brief internal crisis has Noah tugging his hands through his hair again. It's clear this decision has caused him a lot of grief, and *I'm* an asshole for pushing him to make it for me. I'm an asshole for making him *feel* like the asshole because I didn't have the strength to call it quits earlier.

Pushing my sunglasses up, I take in Noah's flustered form. I remember the day I met him at summer camp. He was round in his cheeks with a frizz of hair. Bullied, but never one to drop his head or stay silent. He was determined to go places. We were both so fucking determined...

A new feeling washes over me. A heaving, sickening one that starts in my stomach and seeps down into my bones.

Fuck, if it doesn't taste like fear.

I've spent most of my life chasing this dream. What happens if this is the end of it?

"You kicking me out of the band?" I ask, careful to keep my voice from cracking with emotion.

Noah swallows and then gives a little nod. "Yeah, Beau. We are."

Sunglasses go back on. *Everything's fine.* Even if the reality of this situation is suffocating me, this moment in time is just a drop of water in the ocean.

Nope, I don't want to think about the ocean while high.

"Cool," I reply.

Noah deflates, dropping his arms to his sides. "That's it? You're not gonna fight for this?"

I drum my fingers softly on my thighs, pretending to give it some thought. "Nah."

Noah hangs around long enough to have me squirming in the chair. Tears blur my eyes beneath my sunglasses, and the words bubble up in my throat to beg for my spot in the band.

They'll go so much further without me. They deserve someone capable of writing hits and actually performing.

"Thought I knew you, dude," Noah mutters.

And then he's gone. Vanished into our hotel to share the news with the others that I don't give a rat's ass about the band.

I rub a hand over my aching chest, but the hurt won't go away because it's everywhere now.

Birds continue to circle above me. Suddenly, I want to scream at them. I want my voice to carry over the mountains. I want the world to *hear* me.

Truth is, no one's listening. Learned that hard truth when a drunk driver took my mom from me years ago.

Knocking my head back against the chair, I try to rid the memory from my brain. All this accomplishes is making my head hurt worse.

What the fuck do I do now?

It'd be awkward to stay in Vancouver with the people who no longer want me. But the thought of returning to my quiet, gated property in Phoenix has me searching for another option.

One that will give me temporary relief from everything weighing me down.

FIVE
STASI

My heart skips when I see Liam's text appear on my phone as I'm rolling up my yoga mat.

Would showing up this early scream desperation? I suppose I can hide under the guise of helping him get ready for the party this evening.

A hand touches my arm. I look up to see Ryan, one of my regulars since I started teaching this class on Saturday mornings to ward off my loneliness. He has perfectly highlighted beachy hair and the whitest smile I've ever seen.

"Awesome workout today, Stasi."

"Oh, thanks." I flush with heat. "I wasn't sure if the scorpions were too much..."

"Girl, are you kidding me? My arms were barking."

With a laugh, I walk away to shove my mat into my oversized bag. Leave it to me to be awkward. I don't really know how normal conversations are supposed to go between adults. I lost the friendships I had when I changed majors in college and threw all of my time into studying. And sure, those relationships were built off alcohol and sex, but at least I had company when I needed it.

Ryan lingers, engaging in animated conversation with another person packing up their things. I never know if he's just being polite or if he actually wants to be friends. Social interactions are so confusing in your thirties.

Slipping out the door with a quick wave, I rush to my apartment for a shower before pulling up to Liam's place with a load of groceries in my trunk.

Not gonna lie, I pictured Liam in an old Victorian manor to match his gothic vibe, somewhere outside city limits on acres of private land. Not holed up in a line of identical black and white modern townhouses.

But a lot of Liam's recent decisions have shaken both me and Hail. Like the fact that he begrudgingly agreed to host an unofficial album release party for Atonement when we'd never received an invite to any of the places he's lived before.

Liam has always clung to his secrets. I assume that's due to leftover trauma from his upbringing, having witnessed the touch of evil on his body the first night we met.

I'd asked him about the marks again the next time he showed up at our house in the middle of the night, but he'd shut me down. Told me no one else could know, or he'd be taken away from us, and that was the last thing he wanted.

So I was forced to watch him put on muscle like his life depended on it. Because it did.

Reflecting back on it now, I wish I would have known to speak up. Not that my parents would have listened. They weren't fans of Liam. Teachers didn't seem to care much for him, either.

I nudge his doorbell with my elbow, one arm draped in grocery bags and my other hand clutching a tiny plant with dark green and purple leaves—a late housewarming gift. It seemed like a good idea in the store, but now I'm convinced he's going to hate it.

The door swings open to reveal Liam in all his devastating glory, waves of silky black hair tied up in a high bun. He's dressed down in a t-shirt that clings to every defined muscle in his chest and a pair of basketball shorts that show off his inked thighs and muscular calves. I blink at them a few times, not sure I've ever seen them before.

It's a crime, really.

"Stasi," Liam greets in a low voice that brings warm tingles to my body.

"Hi," I whisper.

Before I can launch into an apology about showing up early, he takes the grocery bags from my hand and saunters barefoot down the hall, disappearing around the corner.

"Okay then." I blow out a breath and step into his house with a stuttering heartbeat.

What I find inside is a little depressing—a practically empty house that smells like fresh paint and new flooring. There's a U-shaped staircase to the right, and a boxy formal room to the left, shrouded in darkness.

I'd worry Liam wasn't planning on staying if not for the fact that he opened a recording studio in Dallas.

Wandering down the hall, I take in a small living room with a gray sectional and a large TV hanging above a black marble fireplace.

Between the living area and the kitchen is a sliding glass door leading out to a surprisingly large patio with a grill. Two decorative wood-paneled walls on either side offer privacy from the neighbors.

I turn to Liam as he rifles through the grocery bags in a sleek kitchen with glass-front black cabinets.

"You eat lunch?" he asks.

"You know I came here to help you, right?"

He throws me a dark look that has my spine snapping up at attention.

"Possibly forgot to eat," I admit.

Liam opens the double doors of his fridge. His house may be empty, but he doesn't shy away from stocking up on good food. Fresh fruits, vegetables, protein shakes, and neat stacks of meat line the shelves.

I smile at the single row of Coca Cola to counter his healthy options.

Did I know Liam could cook? It's not something I expected from a man who's spent half his life traveling the world, stealing hearts on stage.

"Cheeseburger sound good?" He pulls out ground beef and a block of cheese.

My mouth waters. "God, that sounds amazing."

He nods at the plant I'm still holding. "What's that for?"

"Oh, I...got you this. Um, for the new house. Well, not so new any-more."

His movements slow as his thick brows push together.

Shit. He *does* hate it. I'd stood in the garden area of the store for fifteen minutes trying to decide where the line was between us. If he'd assume I was trying to force things on him like all the crazed fans Hail used to tell me about.

"It's okay if you don't want it." I start to walk it to the front door, prepared to leave it on the porch where I won't forget to put it in my car later.

"Anastasia." The firm tone of his voice has my body locking up. My pulse quickens, thudding in my ears.

I don't notice that he's moved behind me until he murmurs for me to turn around. I keep my head down to avoid the intensity of his gaze, but then he touches a palm to my cheek, and my eyes flick to his in surprise.

"Breathe," he murmurs.

I fill my lungs, drawing in his masculine, spicy scent.

His fingers drift to my chin, callused from nearly a lifetime of playing guitar. I don't mind the roughness one bit. In fact, I lean into it.

"I want it. But don't get upset with me when it dies under my care," he says.

"It's just a plant, Liam."

His dark eyes glint with something fierce. "Not to me."

Heat spreads through me. I do my best to ignore it, terrified of the consequences of allowing space for hope when it comes to Liam.

"Put it wherever you think is best."

He leaves me malfunctioning in the hallway, questioning if my brain hit a snag or if someone unplugged me.

By the time I remember how to be human again, Liam's already moved outside to start up the grill.

I place the little plant on the windowsill above the sink, where it should get enough sunlight to stay happy. Then I wander out onto the patio with him, perching on the railing.

"How's the studio?" I ask nervously.

A delicious sizzle comes from the grill as Liam flips the burgers. "Busier than expected. I'm considering bringing in more help when Hail goes back on tour."

Sadness washes over me. I know this is the reality of my twin's successful career, but I miss him when he's gone for months at a time.

At least Liam won't be going with this time.

He closes the grill and strides over to me, leaning against the railing. "How's the new job?"

I smile. "Good. Really good. I love my patients."

"Yeah?"

"Yeah." I nod, tucking my hands under my thighs as I kick out my feet. "There's this one older lady named Iris. She's an absolute fireball. No one else knows how to deal with her, but I won her over with football talk. It'll be bittersweet when I get her up and walking again."

Liam assesses me with that emotionless mask of his.

"What?" I flush.

"I'm proud of you."

My chest tightens as surprising heat builds behind my eyes. I wasn't aware I needed to hear those words of approval. My own parents hadn't shown up at my graduation. My dad was too busy giving corporate presentations, and my mom went to get a pedicure.

But Liam was there, propped up against the back wall. He'd snuck out before I'd had a chance to thank him.

Liam returns to the grill. "Want to grab us some plates?"

Grateful for the distraction from my emotions, I jump down from the railing and browse through his cabinets. Most of them are empty, and my worry about Liam heightens.

Did I miss something? Does he regret retiring? Is he planning on returning to the stage?

It's hard to glimpse anything under that fortified armor he clings to. I'm not sure I've seen the true Liam since that first night he appeared outside our house, clothes torn and eyes haunted.

I pull out plates as Liam walks in with the cooked burgers on a tray. He stacks up ingredients on toasted brioche buns, topping them with a homemade sauce.

"Sit," he orders, setting one of the finished plates on the kitchen island.

If I wasn't so worn out from work and the gym, I'd sass him a bit. Probably for the best I keep my mouth shut. I wouldn't put it past him to force my ass into a chair, and I'm not sure I can handle that dominant side of Liam right now.

I sit on one of the island stools as he slides a can of strawberry lemon Poppi across the counter. My *favorite*. He's effortlessly smooth like that, remembering the small details when you're convinced he doesn't give a shit about you.

I've seen him turn on the charm. I had to bear witness to those mind-melting grins he flashed at everyone else in school and on stage.

Liam pays attention, even if he acts indifferent most of the time.

"Family shit?" he asks.

My head jerks up to him. "What?"

Dark eyes hold me. I lower mine to the untouched burger in front of me. "No...that's not it. Well, maybe a part of it. My parents are lying about trying to mend things with Hail. I can't figure out why, other than the fact that they know we're a packaged deal. I just...I didn't think they cared about keeping me around, you know? But since I have a 'doctorate' now..."

Liam moves over to me and lifts his hand to brush his knuckles along my cheek. "However you choose to handle them, you're not going to lose Hail. Or me."

Speechless, I burn up on the inside as he sits down beside me, one knee resting against my thigh. His basketball shorts ride up to show off thick quads that make my throat tighten.

I pick up my burger and take a bite. My eyelids shudder as flavor blooms on my tongue. "So good, Liam."

His lack of response has me glancing over. *Did I do something wrong?*

My pulse spikes at the heat reflected in his eyes. I shouldn't get any ideas about what's happening here. I *can't*. He doesn't date. Not that I necessarily *want* a relationship right now. I'm not sure what I want. I guess to be inside his head? To stay in his life?

We eat in comfortable silence. Funny, Hail used to fill that space with endless chatter or music.

Just as I've had the thought, an explosion of heavy music comes from Liam's phone. He grabs it off the counter. Whatever name pops up on the screen has him frowning.

"The fuck..." he mutters, rising to his feet. "Be right back."

I do my best to ignore the discomfort in my chest as he slips out the patio door. I don't want to think about who could be calling him. He's probably got hundreds of numbers saved in his phone.

When Liam returns, there's tension in his jaw. "I've got a situation to deal with. You good to hang out?"

My heart sinks, but I nod. "If you're okay with me being here."

He pauses for a moment before replying, "More than you know, Stas."

Snatching up his keys, he strides out the garage door.

I have a lot of connections in the music industry.

Most of them were necessary business relationships with powerful figures who could influence the trajectory of Atonement's career.

There were plenty of others, though. One-night stands. A few repeat hook-ups with people I knew wouldn't expect more from me. People who understood my *preferences*.

I wasn't expecting to hear from Beau Whitaker ever again. Somehow, thinking his name the other day at the gym must have manifested him back into my life.

For the third time since I hopped in my Pantera, I confirm it's actually his name on my phone. That it was his voice I heard on the other end, heavy with sadness foreign to the troublemaking, sexy musician I once knew.

Fuck my need to fix things. I was having a perfectly good day with Stas. I don't like leaving her when it's been ages since we've hung out like that. Just the two of us.

But I also can't leave Beau stranded at the airport.

Pressing the gas pedal down to the floorboard, I weave through traffic. Several middle fingers point in my direction.

Welcome back to Texas.

In record time, I park at the airport and head to the baggage claim area for the incoming flight from Vancouver.

Sensing curious eyes on me, I amp up my "fuck off" energy to keep them away. I might look murderous on the outside, but on the inside, I'm more than a little anxious about this reunion.

If I were certain Beau had someone else to pick him up, I wouldn't have offered. But he's flying into Dallas without his band when the last time I checked he lived in Phoenix.

Something's definitely wrong.

A mob of tired-looking people floods down the hall toward the baggage area. I tense up, not sure what emotion will surge through me when I see him. Regret? Worry? Excitement?

Will I even recognize him?

That concern is put to rest *real* quick when I hone in on a tall man who looks like sex clad in artfully torn up lounge clothes. He's got a tattered army green backpack slung over his shoulder and bulky headphones over his shag of dark brown hair with a deliberate streak of white through it.

Deep blue eyes glitter back at me, and I'm drawn to him like a black hole.

I thought I'd escaped him. But here I am. Sucked right back in.

His pace slows. His brows furrow, almost like he's having regrets about calling me, just like I'm regretting showing up.

As he takes those final steps toward me, he slides his headphones down to his neck. "You came."

I look him over, noting the addition of a gold hoop through his nostril and a slight sunburn to his cheeks. My cock gives a twitch, reminding me how much I like the way he looks. How much I liked being inside him.

"Luggage?"

He fusses with his hair. "Don't have any."

I assume that means he's not staying long. The tightness in my chest doesn't ease, though. Have I ever seen him travel without a guitar? Beau's the kind of guy you lose at a party because he's found some sort of instrument to play with in a back room.

Irritated by the looks we're drawing, I start walking toward the exit. It's rare that anyone asks for my autograph. Not many fans have the balls to approach me, and I'd like to keep it that way. People can appreciate my music without needing to know who the fuck I am.

I don't bother checking to make sure Beau's following. I can *feel* him behind me. His very existence demands attention. His dimpled smile earned a horde of followers on social media. I admit I sometimes scroll through his profile in brief moments of weakness.

Hot air engulfs us as soon as we step outside, and Beau moans. "*Fuck, that feels good.*"

Stride faltering, I glance back in time to see him close his eyes and tip his head up toward the sun. Locks of hair slide away from his face, revealing a patch of vitiligo at the hinge in his jaw he likes to hide. He has more spots under his arms and behind his knees. Another on his stomach I enjoyed kissing because it made him quiver.

Forcing myself to keep walking, I hit the unlock button on my car and pop the trunk for him. Then I open the passenger door and wait.

He holds my gaze as he approaches, those gem blue eyes more guarded than I remember. Like the world's shown him its teeth.

Or like he doesn't fully trust me.

"So. Thanks for this," he says, ducking into my car and saving me from having to find an appropriate response.

I almost ignored your call.

I hadn't planned on ever seeing you again.

You shouldn't be here.

You still take up space in my mind.

Clenching my teeth, I climb into the driver's seat and start up my car.

"Care to explain what you're doing here?" I ask.

Beau mulls this over. "Only if you tell me why you retired."

Sighing, I gun it out of the airport parking lot. I don't know what else I expected from him. Beau's never been afraid of speaking his mind. He'd ask personal questions without hesitation and push buttons until he got reactions. Usually, this resulted in me punishing him like the brat he is.

"I'm not retired," I say, merging onto the highway. "I opened a recording studio."

When I glance over at him, a soft smile appears on his face. "I approve of your decision then."

I snort. "Thanks for the sign off."

"Hey, you were a huge inspiration to other musicians."

"Musicians like you?" I cock a brow.

The corner of his mouth lifts higher, teasing me with one of those dimples. "You don't care for fanboys, remember?"

"You're not a fanboy. You're trouble."

This earns me a chuckle. "Glad we reestablished that."

"Where are you staying?"

The words are out of my mouth before I can register what the fuck I'm doing.

"Some hotel called the Sandman? Name sounded fun. Enter Sandman. Get it?"

I grip the wheel tighter. He showed up here in the middle of a tour without his band or instrument just to stay in a hotel?

Yeah, I need to pinpoint his fucking problem. Then I can patch him up and send him on his way. Beau doesn't belong in Dallas. He belongs out in the world, sharing his talent.

"How long you in town?" I ask.

He's silent for a beat, and my pulse speeds up, thinking we're finally getting somewhere with this conversation.

"Not really sure," he admits quietly.

I throw my car into park at a stoplight so I can glare at him. "Beau."

"It's all good. No worries."

Frustration curls in my chest. As many times as we hooked up, I never got to the bottom of him. He's an ocean that hasn't been fully explored. Maybe I didn't try hard enough. Maybe that's why I kept taking his calls, enticed by the enigma he is.

Blue eyes meet mine. "Green light. Or you can keep staring at me if you want."

Gripping the wheel tighter, I blurt out, "I have a spare room. Stay with me."

He runs his hands over his thighs, visibly wearing through the worn material of his black joggers. "Nah, I'm good."

"Why did you call then, Beau?" I demand, ignoring the wailing horns of trucks as they swerve around me.

He cranes his neck to glance out the passenger window like he's suddenly found something fascinating in the night sky. "Don't know."

An uncomfortable tightness wraps around my lungs. I reach out to take his jaw in my hand, bringing his face back to me. "Cancel the hotel reservation."

I glimpse the first shimmer of life in his eyes since he stepped off that plane. "Make me."

As his teeth catch his bottom lip, I pop it free with my thumb. Then I dig out my phone and search for the hotel number. Putting the phone on speaker, I request a cancelation from the customer service member who answers. "What's the name on the reservation, sir?"

"Beau Whitaker," I reply.

Keys clack in the background, and Beau squirms in the seat. "I'm sorry. I'm not finding anything under that name. Do you have a confirmation number?"

I raise my brows at Beau.

"Must not have hit the booking button," he mumbles.

Hanging up the phone, I shift into gear. "You're staying with me."

He doesn't respond, so I take the exit toward my townhouse.

I don't understand why he would lie about where he was staying. Where did he plan to go? Am I self-centered in my thinking that he actually came to see me?

A storm of unwanted emotions rage in my chest. Anger. Frustration. Concern over having both Beau and Stas under my roof when my self-control is already flagging like I've run a marathon.

At least I've only fucked one of them.

Jesus.

Beau throws me a curious look when I pull into my double garage. "Nice place."

I don't entertain him with an answer as I get out of my car and stalk through the interior door.

"Stasi?" I call out.

"I'm here."

I feel the burn of Beau's eyes on the back of my head.

"I'm not sleeping with her," I say, quiet enough for Beau's ears only.

"Did I hear a 'yet' at the end of that sentence?" Beau teases.

I clench my jaw. We're not done with our discussion about what he's doing here, but my interrogation will have to wait until I can use more *elaborate* tactics to get him to talk.

Rounding the hall into the kitchen, I spot Stas behind a line-up of baking ingredients. She's in the middle of fixing her hair, head bowed as she gathers the layers into a hand.

When she straightens back up, I can't keep my gaze from dipping to the cropped black tank top she's stripped down to, clinging to her fit body.

"Got hot. I didn't want to mess with your thermostat," she explains.

Her gaze darts to Beau, and her lips part. I look back at Beau, surprised to find he's just as captivated by what he sees.

"Holy fuck," he utters, his backpack dropping to the floor.

I'm tempted to wrap my hand around the back of his neck and steer him right the fuck out of my house. Last thing Stas needs is to be drooled over by both of us. Does she get any peace in her life? Does she want it or would she rather a little chaos?

"This is why you left me on read, huh?" Beau chuckles.

His words spear through the defective organ in my chest. I didn't realize he cared. Was he pretending to be apathetic every time I left him after a hookup? Never once did he bat those long lashes at me or show signs of wanting more.

Did I take advantage of that? Did I...hurt him?

Beau drags a hand through his hair, his eyes stuck on the beautiful woman standing before us.

Yeah, she's a lot. Perfection on a bad day. Life-changing on a good one. How the fuck she's still single... it's got to be by choice.

But when I think about it, I can't recall a time she's ever mentioned dating someone. I know she messed around in college. It used to drive Hail crazy to be labeled the only black sheep in his family when he was paying his bills with music and Stas was flunking classes and partying. He couldn't see that they were both seeking attention in their own unique way.

Beau moves over to her and holds out a hand. "Hey. I'm Beau."

"Stasi," she replies, flushing.

He cracks a full dimpled smile, and I *know* it's game over. She's about to be sucked into his event horizon just like everyone else. "Pretty name. So, did Liam work his sorcery on you too?"

Seven
Stasi

My head snaps to Liam, eager for answers on the mysterious man he brought home.

Is this the 'situation' he was referring to? And if so, what exactly *is* the situation?

I'm not one to pry. But *boy*, am I curious. I mean, I had a suspicion Liam was attracted to more than just women. His flirtations showed no preference back in high school.

But I didn't hear of any rumors circulating about his sexuality during his time with Atonement. Other than Hail commenting on Liam's insatiable appetite in the bedroom, he's managed to keep his personal life mostly out of the media.

Then again, I'm learning people can shock you at any turn. I hadn't expected my twin to date a man...

Liam grabs Beau's backpack off the floor and saunters by me, stopping momentarily to tuck a missed lock of hair behind my ear. "Ignore him. He's just a stray."

Hot blood pumps through my veins. Why does he get to have this effect on me? This intense, rapid melting of my insides?

I've thought about sex with Liam. A *lot*. More than I'm willing to admit. It's a secret I'm prepared to take to my grave because I know for a fact it'll never happen.

Unable to stop myself from watching Liam stride away—a powerful, dangerous mass of muscle and confidence—a twinge of jealousy hits me. Is Beau here to stay? How long have they known each other? How come Hail and I are just now getting to see Liam's house, and this cute stranger waltzes in out of nowhere with that heart-stopping smile and gets to hang out?

Awareness of curious eyes on me has me looking back at the stranger. I forget my jealousy as my heart trips up.

Okay, so he's *really* cute.

He's not as tall as Liam, but I still have to tilt my head up to meet his gaze. And his energy is so different from Liam's intensity. A lighter, more buoyant thing that has anticipation, or maybe excitement, thrumming under my skin.

I get stuck on his hands. The prominent veins snaking up under the sleeves of his white hoodie. The long fingers and tan skin. Would they be rough like Liam's or soft as they glide over my skin?

Okay. I'm *beyond* starved for touch.

Beau rocks up on his toes, breaking me from my daze. "So how do you know Liam?"

"Oh, um. My brother's in Atonement."

"Oh, *shit*. You're Hail Koval's sister, aren't you? Yeah, I can't unsee it now."

With a playful roll of my eyes, I reply, "Nothing I love more than being compared to my brother."

His soft, melodic laugh flutters around in my chest. "Well, for what it's worth, I find both of you distracting."

He gives me a coy little wink, and warmth floods my face. All I can manage in response is a brainless "oh".

Does that mean Beau's bi? I don't know that I should make assumptions. I find women attractive, but I've never been with one outside of a hazy, alcohol-induced threesome in college. An appreciation for someone doesn't necessarily mean you want to connect with them romantically or sexually.

My brain whirs into overdrive, taunting me with visuals of Liam dragging his inked hands through Beau's hair and ordering him to his knees, dark eyes burning like hellfire as blue eyes glitter up in worship. I imagine Beau pressing his mouth to the bloody angel above Liam's knee and Liam tightening his grip on Beau's hair enough to make the muscles pop in his arm.

Alert. I've stepped too close to the sun. My body ignites, and my heart hammers in my chest, threatening to punch free from its cage.

Why did I come over so early? Now I feel like I'm interrupting something. A third wheel—a label I'm acutely and painfully familiar with as I grew up an outsider to Hail and Liam's bromance.

"Sorry in advance. I tend to say whatever pops into my head," Beau comments.

Flustered, I shake my head. "No, it's fine."

"You baking for an army?"

"Ah, yeah. An army of hungry musicians. They requested a home-cooked meal, craft beers, and time with friends tonight."

"Sounds about right for a band in their thirties." He assesses my progress in the kitchen. "Need help?"

I consider him with wide eyes. "Don't you like... have plans or something?"

"Plans with you, yeah." His smile trips up my pulse as he tugs off his hoodie, revealing more of those delicious veins that make my knees weak.

"Have you ever made chocolate chip cookies?"

"Nope, but I'm good at taking instruction." He beams.

I'm beginning to think this spark of something exhilarating is a constant feeling when Beau's near. I envy charismatic people like him. He's the type to win over a room with little effort.

Beau slots in next to me at the kitchen island. "Alright. Boss me around, sweetheart."

Blushing, I reach into his space to grab two sticks of softened butter. "Okay. This goes in the bowl first. Then one cup of both of your sugars."

He watches me rearrange ingredients in order of how he needs to incorporate them. Then I go on the hunt for more bowls to start on another dessert. He keeps his gaze on me the entire time. "What all are you planning to make?"

"Cookies. Triple fudge brownies. Possibly peanut butter bars..."

"Sweet tooth?" Beau teases, eyes shining.

God, he's a shock to the system this close up. A piece of art you appreciate the more you study it. His lips might be the prettiest I've ever seen on a guy, and his eyes are pools of deep blue that beckon me in.

"Huh?"

His head drops as he chuckles. "I asked if you have a sweet tooth. Or maybe the band does?"

Nodding absentmindedly, I begin tossing ingredients into my own bowl. "Mostly my brother. If I ate sweets like him, I'd lose all my progress in the gym."

"Highly doubt that." His gaze runs down my body in appreciation, and I'm engulfed in flames. I'm glad I stripped down to my tank top.

Beau starts chaotically mixing ingredients. R.I.P. to Liam's clean kitchen.

"Are you close with your brother?" he asks.

"Ah, yeah... I don't get to see him much, though."

He nods in understanding. "Touring's hard on everyone involved. Not just the band."

"Is that how you met Liam? On tour, I mean." I hand him the carton of eggs, fighting to keep from appearing too eager for information.

"Yeah. I opened for him and your bro, shit, like seven years ago?"

My head jerks up to him. "Are you serious? What band?"

I sift through memories, trying to place him at the few shows I attended before school swallowed me whole. Most of Atonement's new releases came to me through Spotify or YouTube when they dropped. Hell, I would have lost track of Hail had he not called frequently to update me on what city he was in.

I think I would have remembered Beau.

"I played guitar for Lithos," Beau answers. "We only did one tour with Atonement, but sometimes we'd end up at the same festivals or in nearby cities. What's next?"

"Um." My nose scrunches as I refocus on our task. "You can fold in the chocolate chips."

Beau dumps in the whole bag and starts mixing with his left hand, spilling chocolate chips all over the counter. I bite down on a laugh.

"This is sort of relaxing," he comments, peeking over at me with a grin. He pauses mixing, one hand lifting to my face. I'm stunned as he gently brushes his thumb over my cheek. "Got some batter there."

When he licks the chocolate off his thumb, my body temperature spikes to dangerous levels.

Where the hell did this guy come from?

Beau's soft laughter has my eyes growing wide. "Oh, shit. Did I say that out loud?"

"Liam never mentioned me?"

"Sorry, maybe I just forgot..."

"I'm teasing. Wasn't anything serious between us anyway."

My lips part in shock. So they *were* together.

Thankfully, Beau's no longer looking at me because I'm gaping at him. My chest tightens as I glimpse the pain he's trying to hide, betraying his carefree words.

I don't believe Liam would ever intentionally hurt someone, but isn't this wounded, beautiful man next to me proof that he's entirely capable of causing internal damage?

It was supposed to be a low-key cookout.

Naturally, the entire local metal community found out. Cars flood the streets outside the rows of uniform townhouses, heavy music blares from Liam's open patio door, and people spill out onto the green space to smoke and lounge around a community fire pit.

I'd bet the neighbors are all terrified of Liam, considering the cops haven't been called. It's early in the night, though. There's still time for handcuffs.

I'm sitting on the patio railing under a glow of string lights, nursing a sweating bottle of beer.

It's been ages since I've had a drink. The desire is always there to let go, but tonight I have a better distraction from the monologue of self-deprecating thoughts in my head.

I seek out Liam, bathed in the ethereal orange glow of the fire. He's standing beside Hail in a half-circle of musicians and crew members from Atonement, away from the crowded house. His inked, ringed fingers hold a Coke while everyone else drinks beer or liquor.

It's strange…why would he bring Beau here if he's just going to ignore him? He'd left us alone for hours this afternoon, eventually drifting back into the kitchen just in time for the party.

Of course, he was wearing another pathetic scrap of material for a shirt, fitted black jeans, and thin chain necklaces.

It doesn't matter that Liam looks like a sex god, or he's an incredibly talented musician, or a successful businessman. He won me over long ago with his kindness. Liam's a protector at his core.

A *provider*.

Sipping at my beer, I turn my attention toward the house where Beau's engaged in conversation with the chaos duo—Malek and Griff.

"…ocean is *infinitely* more terrifying than space. Think of all the unknown monsters lurking below your feet…" Griff rattles off.

"…chances of getting rescued are way greater in the ocean than in *literal* fucking space…" Malek argues.

I'd think Beau needed rescuing, but judging from his dimpled grin, he seems to be enjoying himself.

Settling into a buzz, I touch my fingertips to my cheeks. They still ache from how much he made me smile earlier.

After we'd finished baking, I hadn't been mentally prepared for him to reappear from his shower in a backwards hat, a crisp white t-shirt that clung to his chest and arms, artfully ripped up jeans, and a pair of worn leather boots.

My open-mouthed gaping earned a few laughs from him as I contemplated how an edgy rock artist could transform into a country boy so effortlessly.

So, I'm *definitely* attracted to both versions of Beau.

Over the course of the night, that little stripe of white hair has snuck out over the snaps of his hat. I kind of want to curl it around my finger.

Socially awkward Stasi wins out though, and I force my gaze up to the sky. It's a velvety blue tonight. Not a star in sight, which makes me a little sad.

Lonely, too.

I shouldn't feel this way when I'm surrounded by people. I have to remember, everyone here has some sort of connection tying them to music. I'm not being left out. I just have different interests.

I don't regret my choice to pursue a career in the medical field. I love what I do. I love witnessing the progress my patients make after experiencing life-altering injuries or suffering at the vicious hands of disorders or neurodegenerative diseases.

But I hate the winding path I took to get here. I hate that I lost years of my life that I could have spent building relationships like these or treating more patients had I buckled down in my early twenties instead of spiraling out the moment I was free from my parents.

I'm going to hate it when Hail's back on tour, and then Liam and I don't have a reason to interact outside the gym. We'll go months without talking again. *Years* even.

Our childhood friendship was always doomed to unravel.

My hand tightens around my beer. Maybe I *should* get drunk tonight. Hail would give me a ride home. I'd fall asleep without thinking about the quiet or the darkness of my apartment.

"Cheers, chica." Maria clacks her beer bottle against mine. She's got her eyelids shaded a sparkly black and her lips painted a bold red few people can pull off.

For all her bravado on stage, she's a bigger sweetheart than my twin brother. Hail was more than happy to let her step in for him on lead vocals. It gave him the opportunity to focus more on side projects with his boyfriend.

Whom I have yet to meet in real life.

"You gonna come hang?" Maria asks, waving toward the fire.

Despite my hunger for conversation, I'm not really sure how to mesh with the others.

"I'm okay right here, but thanks." I smile.

I watch Maria's petite form cross the grass, hips and dreadlocks swishing.

More drinking it is.

Too soon, my bottle's empty. Balancing it on the railing, I twist my hair back up into a bun to keep it from sticking to my neck. Then I leap down to my feet and sneak into the kitchen for another drink.

Knowing I'm gonna regret it in the morning, I fill a red solo cup with whatever blue concoction Malek brought in a sealed pitcher.

I'm about to head back to my roost when Beau appears, a half-eaten chocolate chip cookie in hand.

"Sweetheart, these are criminal," he says around a mouthful.

I laugh. "Well, you get to take most of the credit."

"Nope. All you." The other half of the cookie disappears in one bite, his eyes never leaving me. "What are you drinking?"

I sniff at the liquid in my cup and wince as the scent burns the inside of my nose. Testing a small sip, I shudder at the potency of alcohol steamrolling through me. "Oh, god. I'm not sure it's safe for consumption."

He reaches for the fridge handle. "Bottle of water is the safer bet then."

I expect him to wander back to his previous conversation, but he leans against the counter beside me, elbow and thigh lined up against mine, bringing tingles of awareness to my skin.

A little confused by his actions, I glance up in time to catch his Adam's apple bobbing as he drains his water in a couple gulps.

I get the sense that Beau doesn't hold back in life, but I could be making assumptions. I've only known him for a couple of hours.

Which is why I'm questioning how he can wreak such havoc on me. I don't normally have this kind of reaction to others. I was convinced I was wired wrong. Even in my exploratory years in college, I never felt a rush of nerves or experienced an attraction like this.

Not with anyone but Liam.

Beau leans closer to peek into my cup. "Fuck. That smells horrible."

"Oh, it tastes horrible. Like fruity household chemicals."

"How do you know what that tastes like?"

He's smiling so big, I don't have to give him more than a playful eye roll to get him to laugh.

Our heads pop up in unison as the back door slides all the way open to let in a massive body of muscle and ink.

My heart forgets what it's supposed to do. It was hot outside, but now it's hot in the house, too. Or is that the toxic sludge burning through my DNA?

Liam prowls over to us, crowding Beau as he opens the fridge and grabs another Coke. Unperturbed, Beau swings those deep blue eyes back to me. I have to commend him for his bravery.

"So, do you play any instruments?" Beau asks.

And now two men are staring at me expectantly. Swallowing, I shake my head. "No talent for it."

"She's a neurologic physical therapist," Liam answers.

Beau's brows raise. "No shit?"

Heat rushes to my cheeks. "Ah, yeah. The title feels a bit much…"

Pride was as absent as my parents when I walked across that final graduation stage. Koval kids don't earn attention by failing half a dozen college classes and graduating late.

"Fuck that. Don't downplay your accomplishments." Beau's tone is surprisingly firm, earning a look of approval from Liam before he strides out the back door, leaving me to blink up at Beau in awe.

"See something you like, sweetheart?"

I purse my lips, and his eyes drop to them with a glint of lust. My heartbeat pulses low in my core.

Oh, this is *definitely* a crush.

"You've got something to say. Don't hold it in."

Buzzing from Malek's drink, I give in. "Seriously. Where did you come from?"

With a slow smile, he shrugs. "Middle of nowhere."

I narrow my eyes at him, but he's unfazed, so I pop his hat off and rest it on my head. He quickly runs a hand through his poof of frizzy, dark brown hair. "Don't look. It's unruly. Unnatural. An eldritch horror."

As I burst into a fit of giggles, his arms lazily encircle my waist. I rest my cheek on his chest, enjoying the solid beat of his heart.

"You're real fucking cute, Stasi. Liam's lucky to have you."

"Oh, we're not...we haven't..."

Beau eases back to look at me. "But you want to."

My stomach swoops. "God, could you imagine?"

His gem blue eyes light up. "Mmm, I can. And I am. You know, we could get his attention."

He must be casting some kind of spell on me because the word slips out before I have time to think. "How?"

Beau offers me his hand. "Play along."

A hard thud comes from the organ in my chest. Slipping my hand into his, I let him guide me past the back door. I could be imagining dark eyes watching us, but I don't allow myself to look as Beau leads me down the hallway and up the stairs.

"You think someone stole all of his stuff?" I joke.

Earning laughs from Beau is becoming my newest addiction.

"I think he's got serious commitment issues, but you probably know that already."

My brows furrow as he pulls me through the only open door on the second floor.

It looks like Liam hired the same designer for the room as he did for his studio. The vibes are minimalist, with earthy tones and wood honeycomb soundproofing on one wall above an antique desk and record player. Two small leather couches face each other, one of which is occupied by people I don't recognize.

We sit down on the other couch, and someone holds out a fist to bump against Beau's. "Hey, what's up, man? Haven't seen you in a minute."

As they fall into conversation, my nerves creep out like spiders. *What am I still doing here?*

Just as I'm about to push up to my feet, a strong presence makes itself known. I look toward the doorway to see Liam walking into the room.

When he drops into the small space on the couch on my other side, I fall into the dip his body creates. Heartbeat skipping, I do my best to wiggle out of his personal space, but he stops me with a heavy hand on my bare thigh.

"Relax. I won't bite."

A breathy, flustered laugh slips out of me. Liam cocks a brow. "Sorry, you've just got that whole vampire lord thing going on."

"A vampire lord, hmm?" Those sharp teeth come out to play, sinking into one side of his bottom lip to hold back a grin.

I want to tell him not to rob me of it. I've spent half a lifetime looking at this man. *Dreaming* of him. Searching for someone who could live up to him because I was convinced he would never look back at me.

Liam's thumb moves over my skin in a teasing pattern. "These are a sad excuse for shorts."

Indulging, I let my gaze run down the thick column of his neck to the wide cut out where his sleeve should be. "Well, you're not really wearing a shirt, so I won't accept judgement from you."

His rumbly laugh zips through me like a hot sizzle of electricity. I grin. *I* did that. I made him laugh. I could probably count on one hand how many times I've heard that wonderful sound from him.

Beau leans back fully on the couch. I'm not sure when his buddy vanished from the room, but now the three of us are alone, snugly fit together.

Swallowing, I fight the urge to move from between these two men. Should I excuse myself for the night? I hadn't planned on staying late, anyway.

But then Beau leans closer, his warm breath fanning against my neck. "Should we keep playing, sweetheart?"

I shiver, lured back under his spell. I'm not sure what game we're playing. All I know is I can't find the desire to say no.

Beau's eyes glitter with mischief I'm all too familiar with as he whispers something in Stas's ear. I wait for a twist of jealousy, but even after listening to them flirt all afternoon, I'm overcome by a surge of undeniable lust. As much as I don't like to admit it, both of them have me in a fucking chokehold.

Would I mind seeing them *together*?

My cock jerks in response. No, I don't think I fucking would.

"You playing games with her, trouble?" I ask darkly.

Beau grins. "Nah. Stas and I are just friends, right?"

My jaw clenches at the way her expression sinks just a fraction. Unnoticeable to most, but I pay attention to everything she does.

Honestly, it's a little exhausting.

To my surprise, Beau nudges her chin toward him with a knuckle. "But sometimes friends have fun together, don't they?"

Her throat bobs. She's hanging on his every word. Is she even breathing?

Fuck. My dick likes this too much. My brain does too as it conjures up visions of them, lips locked and perfect bodies moving seductively against each other.

Beau's an unselfish lover, singularly focused on making his partner feel good. Years ago, I didn't want that. I was too messed up in the head, and he was too fresh in his career to think about anything outside of music. At least, that's what I had decided for him.

But I want that for Stas. I want her to feel good. I want her firmly out of her head.

Beau could do that for her.

Then again, do I want him messing around with her when I haven't gotten to the bottom of why he came to Dallas?

Ever since he finished baking with Stasi, he's successfully kept himself surrounded by people to avoid a difficult conversation with me.

Whatever it is that pushed him here, I sense I'm not going to like it.

By the time I untangle from my thoughts, Stas has climbed onto his lap. My blood runs hot. I take in the way their bodies are fitted together, her hands on his chest, and his palms coasting from her waist down to tighten around her thighs.

Beau's voice is drenched in sex when he says, "You know, sometimes friends kiss."

Her lashes flutter as her painted fingernails curl into the front of his t-shirt.

"Do they?" Her voice is a whisper.

I watch Beau's fingers creep up to the hem of her shirt, sneaking under it to wrap around the sexy curve of her hips. He inches his mouth closer to hers. "So soft."

And then he kisses her.

I clench my hands over my tensed thighs. I'm rock hard. Fixated on what's unfolding before me. Wrapped around their fingers as they melt into lust with panted breaths and hungry touches. It's sexual chemistry igniting right in front of me, pure and addicting.

There's a flash of a wicked smile from Beau before he slides his tongue along her full bottom lip. His next kisses are slower. Deeper. Absolutely *filthy*.

Stasi sinks into him. And when her hands drift up to cradle his face?

She touches him with a tenderness I could never give anyone. It's one of the reasons I never replied to him. Why I've left her in charge of whatever is developing between us.

Beau lets out a little growl as he pulls away, almost like he can't handle the distance he's creating between them. He gives her lip one more nip, reminding me more of the heated way we used to fuck. When I'd drag him into a hotel room to rip off his clothes and thrust deep into his ass.

"Aren't you friends with Liam, too?" Beau asks.

Stas and I lock gazes. Her blown pupils and flushed cheeks have me aching to palm my cock.

Yeah, I want to kiss her. I want to do a lot of things with her.

Seeing her perched on Beau's lap wearing his hat shouldn't do things to me, but I've always enjoyed watching. The anticipation of claiming my partners *after* they think they've had enough is almost more fun than the act itself.

Almost.

If Stasi had picked anyone else to mess around with tonight, I would have been out that door already. Would have told myself to move the fuck on. I'm not her keeper.

Stasi bats those thick lashes at me, waiting for an answer. I hate that hesitation. Does she honestly believe I don't want her? Or is she concerned about my nature? It's reason enough to hold back. If I were ever capable of love, it was beaten out of me by the man who helped bring me into this world.

So this can't be *my* choice. I don't want to take control like I normally do. Not when my brain is firing off warnings to push her away. To protect her.

Stasi draws in a deep breath, and then she cautiously moves onto my lap like I'm some deadly creature that could snap at any sudden movement.

I keep my hands off her for as long as it takes her to rest fully on my thighs.

And then my pathetic self-control snaps.

I wrap my hands around her warm thighs, squeezing them and pulling her body closer. Her hands jerk to my shoulders, and I give her a moment to settle into this.

Usually, I don't give my partners a chance to touch me. I don't enjoy it. But as she begins tracing the ink designs on my neck almost in reverie, I find I don't mind it. Could be just because it's her. Could be my therapy finally fucking paying off.

Has she been holding back, too? Has she craved me just as much as I crave her?

I slide my fingers into her tiny back pockets and drag her against my hard, jean-clad length. The friction is enough to draw a little gasp from her parted lips.

What other noises could I get her to make? Would she beg? Cry? Scream?

Too fucking far, Liam. Calm down.

Stas blinks those big brown eyes at me and whispers, "Are we friends, Liam?"

No. *Fuck* that. I don't want to be friends with her. I want to fucking *own* her.

Everything I've bottled up for this woman comes spilling out. Gliding my palm up her spine, I wrap it around her hair and tug until her neck is exposed to me. I press a lingering kiss to her warm skin. Her citrus scent has my mouth watering to take a bite. To mark her.

Nails sink into my biceps as I drag my flattened tongue up the column of her neck, pausing at the hollow behind her ear. Slowly, I kiss and nip my way to her mouth.

I'm barely containing my desire to flip her over and show her just how thoroughly I would wreck her.

Hovering over her lips, I murmur, "Don't think I can ever be your friend, angel."

Then I crush my mouth to hers, devouring the sweet, surprised sound she makes. Cupping her thick ass with both hands, I'm practically thrumming with the need to take *more*.

Movement has us breaking apart. I look over to see Beau pushing up from the couch. It dawns on me what he'd been scheming all along. Fucker played me. Lured me up here and manipulated me to get with Stas.

I'd say I'm not upset about it, but I don't like that sad look on his face.

Before I can speak, Stasi reaches out to grab Beau's forearm. He glances down at where she's holding him, brows furrowing. Then he looks at me in question.

Is he asking me for permission? *Fuck.* I'm not sure I can get any harder. It's almost painful at this point.

Gripping Stasi's jaw, I turn her head to face me. "Is this what you want? Both of us?"

She swallows, and I wait for her to summon up her confidence. I've waited years for this. I can wait longer if she's not ready to blur lines.

"Please," she replies breathlessly.

I let out a growl of approval before hauling her into my arms. "Let's go finish what you started, trouble."

one of my belt loops and shoves me against the wall. He pins me there with his giant hands, and I'm drawn back into memories of him. How he used to toss me around and take control of me.

"Liam..." I whisper.

Surprisingly light fingers brush my forearm. I realize it's Stasi touching me. Glancing in her direction, I blink a few times to adjust to the darkness. Once I'm able to appreciate those beautiful, warm brown eyes, my heart sinks at the fear swimming in them.

Fuck. I started this. I can't leave her now, can I? No, that would be irresponsible.

It seems we're both doomed to be shattered by this man.

"I'm here, sweetheart," I tell her.

She stretches up onto her toes to bring her mouth close to mine. "Good. Thought we were playing."

My cock strains to break free from my tight jeans. "*Baby.* Don't tell me you're secretly naughty?"

She kisses me in confirmation, and I'm flooded with molten desire. I slip a hand beneath her shirt, resting my palm on her lower back to secure her to my side. We explore with lips and soft rolls of our tongues. I'm eager to learn what she likes. What makes her toes curl and her body arch into me.

All the while, lust-filled, dark eyes burn into us. I wriggle against Liam's hold, desperate to get my other arm around Stasi, but this only triggers him to grab my jaw and turn my head to claim me with a hard kiss.

I fucking love it.

I've been so lost lately, it's a relief to let Liam run the show. I want him to have his way with me. I want to be overpowered and wrung out by this inked up man with terrifying energy. I want to forget about the heavy burden of life.

Liam slides his other hand up my neck and threads his fingers into my hair. He grips me tight enough to earn a moan from me as our tongues meet and battle for dominance.

I rock my hips forward, stiff cock throbbing for friction. For him. For *anything* at this point. The solid press of his answering erection has me easing a hand between our bodies to run it along his considerable length.

"You gonna let me play with this tonight?" I ask.

Liam sinks his teeth into my neck. "If you behave."

Stasi's been too quiet, so I reach for her hand and guide it to the button on Liam's pants. If she wants to play, then we're gonna fucking play.

"Trouble," Liam whispers, kissing the hinge of my jaw.

Easing away from me, his attention shifts to Stasi. I could get off on the way he looks at her. I want someone to look at me like that. Like the universe starts and ends with me. Like I'm the reason for the stars in the sky and the tides in the ocean.

No one's going to put up with my bullshit, though. No one's going to hang around. Liam didn't the first time. Not like things will be different now.

Liam crowds Stasi against the wall. I bet her heart is racing as fast as mine.

"You're in control, angel," he says huskily.

A smile creeps onto my face when she slips a hand into his opened pants. Her head drops to my shoulder. "Oh, god."

Liam's teeth flash as he nuzzles against her neck. Without looking, he reaches over to flick open the button on my jeans. I tip my head back against the wall, overwhelmed with the anticipation of him touching me, skin-on-skin.

I'm faintly aware of voices downstairs, but I don't care enough to stop what's happening in clear view should someone walk up those stairs.

What's a party without a bit of cock?

Liam dives a hand into my boxers and wraps it around my dick. The sensation of his warm, rough fingers combined with his cold rings has me shuddering. When he nudges the piercing beneath my crown, I hiss in pleasure.

"The fuck is this?" Liam circles a rough finger around the ball of jewelry.

"Apadravya," I mumble, lost in the sensation of him toying with me. I shove his hand lower, and he gives my shaft a firm squeeze.

"What am I going to do with both of you?" Liam muses.

"Destroy us, I hope," I whisper.

He removes his hand from me to shove open the door beside me. "Bedroom. Now."

Stasi looks stunned, so I take her hand in mine and tug her close to steal another kiss. "We're completely fucked, sweetheart."

"Completely your fault," she murmurs.

"Mmm, giving you most of the credit on this one."

I usher her inside the bedroom with my hands on her hips. Pretty sure my dick's in charge of making decisions for the rest of the night. So much for sitting fireside and smoking myself into sleep. Now I'm chasing the adrenaline of this wild night.

We bump into Liam's massive bed. I remove my hat from her head, and we exchange nervous smiles. Then I toss her onto the black comforter like I mean it.

Crawling after her, I fit my body between her legs and brace my arms on either side of her head. I press gentle kisses to her lips. Her neck. Her collarbones. Everywhere I can reach.

When I roll my hips against her, she lets out a little whimper that shoots right to my dick. I pause to take in her pretty face, illuminated by the streetlamp bleeding through the blinds.

"Can I touch you?" I ask.

"*Please*. But I want to touch you, too."

"Fuck yes." I move down her body to nip at the curve of her breast through her shirt. "Anywhere. Everywhere."

Gliding my hands under her shirt, I press them flat against her lower back. She's warm and smooth and *strong*.

Stasi rests her hands on my shoulders, pushing me upright so she can pull my shirt over my head. A note of worry strikes me that I'm not fit enough to hang with these two. I'm not one to stick to a workout routine. I have squishy parts.

She doesn't seem to mind, her brown eyes widening in what I can only hope is admiration as she twists the lock of my bleached white hair around a finger.

"Wanted to do this all night," she whispers. Then she drags her hands down my pecs and soft stomach, her fingers teasing along the little trail of hair disappearing beneath my boxers.

I feel unhinged as I tug out her hair tie, unleashing waves of blonde hair before I kiss her back down onto the bed.

Soon, we sync up the movement of our hips, finding a rhythm to give us both glorious friction, only pausing when we hear the solid thud of Liam's footsteps as he approaches.

Daring a glance, my pulse leaps at the silhouette of Liam joining us in the bedroom. We both tense up when he strips his shirt from his lethal body. I have a brief thought of putting my shirt back on. His physique isn't fucking normal, and he hasn't even pulled out his dick yet.

How did I survive him?

I brush a thumb over Stasi's cheek. "Sorry, Stas. I might be drooling."

"S'okay. I think my soul left my body."

I glance down at her, grinning when I find that she's admiring Liam, too.

My heartbeat hammers in my chest when I hear him stride closer. He touches a knuckle to my spine, and I hold my breath as he drags it up each node.

If that isn't enough of a sensory fuck, his other arm comes around me, that hand grazing down my bare torso to grip my boxer-clad cock and make me groan.

In a quick movement, Liam flips me onto my back next to Stasi. He climbs over us, big knees slotting between our legs, and ripped arms caging us in.

He lowers his mouth to Stasi first, worshiping her with deep kisses that have me squirming impatiently. I feel like I'm being edged just watching the two of them.

By the time Liam moves over to me and sucks one of my pebbled nipples into his mouth, I bow off the mattress with a groan. He kisses his way up to my mouth, repositioning his leg so he has room to push down my jeans. I frantically kick them off my ankles.

Liam rumbles in approval when he rubs his palm over the damp spot on my boxers. He teases me with hard strokes as his tongue slides over mine.

"I want you naked, Beau," he orders. "Back against my headboard."

The instant he rises to his knees, I'm scrambling to obey. My cock bobs free as I peel off my boxers and toss them onto the floor. Then I leap to the headboard, causing it to rattle against the wall.

In this new position, I'm able to witness Liam in all of his glory as he moves himself fully over Stasi and licks into her mouth. My fingers curl into my palms. I'm aching to reacquaint myself with his exquisite tattoos, but I also know how he gets about being touched like that.

"So perfect, angel," Liam praises, working his way down to the sliver of exposed abdomen where her cropped shirt ends.

My blood burns hotter at the way she comes to life beneath him. I close a hand around my cock and flick the silver piercing speared through it.

With bated breath, I watch his hands spread over her stomach and inch her shirt up and up. Over her full breasts, nearly visible through her lace bralette. He drags his flat tongue along the fabric, and the little whimper she releases has my hips moving.

"Hand off that pretty cock, Beau," Liam says darkly.

The desire to come almost wins out, but I behave and drop my hand. I'm left to suffer as Liam strips off Stasi's tiny shorts.

Where Liam is a broad expanse of black ink and hard edges, she's all smooth, creamy skin and toned lines.

"On his lap, Anastasia. Facing me," Liam says.

Golden waves tumble over her bare shoulders as she crawls to me. She's an absolute vision. My hands reach for her, pulling her onto my thighs.

"I'm dreaming," I mutter, staring at her peachy ass resting right over my cock.

Liam prowls toward us. He kisses Stasi with enough force to push her back against my chest. We're touching nearly everywhere now, but it's not enough. I want to be inside her. *Need* it.

Liam nudges my legs wide, which spreads Stasi's legs, too.

"Hold her tight, Beau," Liam instructs.

Stasi's fingernails press into my skin as I wrap her up, one arm secured under her breasts and the other banded over her waist. She's breathing hard even before Liam begins his torture, kissing and nipping his way down her mostly naked body.

"Hey, come here," I say softly.

Stasi lifts her head enough to meet me in a quick kiss. I don't want to pull away, but I'm too enticed by the idea of watching Liam put on a show when he finally settles between her legs.

He hooks a finger around her thong and tugs it to the side. Lowering his head, he runs his tongue up her center. Immediately, I struggle to keep her still as she whimpers.

"Beau." Dark eyes flick up at me at the same time that he swirls his tongue around her clit. "*Hold. Her.*"

I tighten my arms. "You gotta be good for him. Can you do that, sweetheart?"

She's nodding and writhing and moaning all at once. My arms are going to hurt tomorrow. *Everything's* going to hurt tomorrow because I don't think Liam's going to bottom. He never has before. At least, not for me.

But maybe I'm jumping to conclusions. Maybe he doesn't want to do that with me anymore.

Liam's tongue slips lower to lick at my balls, and I groan. I'm not even ashamed of my leaking cock, now wonderfully slick between Stasi's cheeks.

He amps up his focus on her, licking and sucking until she tenses in my arms.

"Let go, baby," I murmur, cupping one of her breasts.

She shatters with the most beautiful sounds of pleasure, and I can't help my hips from rocking against her.

Liam works his way back up her body, bringing his mouth close to mine. I lick my lips, ready to taste her.

"You're going to fuck her properly," Liam tells me slowly. "If you make her come, you get my cock. If she's left wanting, you go to bed with sore balls tonight, understood?"

My pulse skips. This can't be real life. I'm going to wake up on a tour bus, wracked by pain from another annoying migraine.

For Liam Beckner, though, this is just another night.

I'm not sure why he's not going to claim Stasi. It's clear he wants her. She's right *here*, blissed out in my arms, desperate for him.

Knowing I have my work cut out to bring her to orgasm again, I kiss her neck. "You okay with that, sweetheart?"

"Please."

Yeah, so leaving tomorrow is going to be harder than I thought.

Liam hoists Stasi off my lap, lowering her onto her back. I see the strain of his muscles. His thick cock is practically bursting out of his jeans, eager to sink deep inside her. Right where they both want it.

As he nuzzles her neck, I hear him murmur, "Not tonight, angel."

Pushing up to his knees, Liam grabs me around the calf and drags me over to them. I curse as he manhandles me onto my knees between them. He gives my cock a stroke from root to tip and wiggles my piercing.

"Ah, *fuck*. Liam."

He tugs at it gently. "I like this little piece of metal. It feels good, doesn't it? Will it feel good for her, too?"

"Should. If it doesn't, you can tell me. Okay, Stasi?"

She's still all melty boned from coming, but she manages a little nod. "I want it."

Sex with Liam is a marathon. Next time she'll be prepared. Well, *if* there's a next time with him.

"Strip her," Liam commands.

I ease her upper body off the bed enough to push the lace bralette over her head. She lifts her hips for me so I can slip her thong off her legs.

Laid bare before me, I have to take a breath to calm myself.

A hand grips my hair and yanks my head back. Liam kisses me at the same time he rolls a condom on my hard length.

"Show us what you've got, bad boy," he murmurs, giving my head a little shove.

"You play dirty," I complain. Then I look down at Stasi. "Are you sure about this?"

I don't want to ruin this for them when it's evident something has been building between them. I don't ever want to be the cause of anyone's pain.

Stasi rolls up, abs flexing, to cup my face in her hands. She places a tender kiss on my bottom lip. "I'm sure."

Well, *shit*. I cave like she already owns me.

Holding those big brown eyes with mine, I kiss her flat on the bed. Then I grab her thighs and lift her ass to rest it on my thighs as I line up my cock with her pussy. Soon, I'm pushing balls deep into the most gorgeous girl I've ever met.

My head falls back onto Liam's shoulder. "*Fuck*. Sweetheart. You feel so good."

I wasn't expecting things to progress this far. I was just looking for an escape from life. I'm surprised Liam even took my call.

And now...*shit. Don't blow. Don't blow.*

I brush a hand down her stomach, slipping it between her legs to seek out that little bundle of nerves. Circling my thumb over her clit, I give it a pinch, well-aware from her breathy moans that the ball on the top of my crown is rubbing just right on the inside.

I keep my hips moving while I reach my free hand back to touch Liam's thigh. I trace the inseam of his pants up to his straining erection. It must be painful. Hell, I'm edging on pain, just trying to keep myself from coming before Stasi does.

I don't want this to be over, and that thought troubles me.

Liam's deep growl snaps me back into the moment. "Take it out, Beau."

I fumble to unzip his jeans in such an awkward position, but soon enough I have his boxers shoved down below his heavy balls. I sigh in relief when his cock is in my hand. "This thing should be illegal."

Liam runs his calloused fingers down my ribs, causing my hips to stutter. His hands drop to my ass. He spends some time there to palm and squeeze my flesh. Every few thrusts, he physically pushes me into Stasi harder.

"Do you like fucking her, Beau? You like filling her pretty cunt with your cock?"

"Fuckkk yesss."

I peer down at Stasi splayed out, her lips red and swollen from abuse, her brown eyes alight with pleasure. It's too much. I have to slow my pace. I'm shaking as Liam's hands coast over me and play with my nipples.

"Give it to me. *Fuck*, I need it, Liam."

Never thought I'd beg for cock in my ass again. I'm usually the one doing the fucking. Not with him, of course. But I'm too caught up in this to care.

Liam tortures me by withdrawing his touch entirely. I bite down on a growl, my frustration quickly turning into hot lust as he moves his fingers to Stasi's mouth.

"Suck, Anastasia. Get them wet for Beau."

Eyes sparking, she wraps her full lips around them and sucks them deep into her mouth. I curse, imagining my cock there instead.

Liam returns soaked fingers to my ass and circles them around my hole. When the tip of one finger begins to test the muscle there, I tense up. "Liam..."

He pauses. "Do you want me to stop?"

I squeeze my eyes shut, taking a second to breathe. "No. It's just... I haven't done this since..."

Since you.

I don't have to say the words. Liam brings a hand to my jaw and turns my head to kiss the corner of my mouth. "I'll be gentle. If it's too much, we can stop."

I shake my head. "No. I don't want to stop."

The click of a bottle sounds before Liam slides a lubed finger inside of me. Slowly, he strokes it in and out.

"Sorry, sweetheart," I whisper, realizing I've just been hovering over her and not moving.

She runs her fingers down my chest. "It's okay."

My chest tightens uncomfortably. This is too much already. I'm in over my head. How did I allow myself to get into this situation?

Liam continues to finger me as his other hand drifts down to where Stasi and I are connected. Stasi whimpers, hands clenching the sheets as Liam rolls her clit between his fingers while he presses on that spot that's lighting me up.

He chuckles. "So needy. Both of you."

"*Fuck*. I need to come. Don't want to come until you're inside me," I utter.

Liam pushes on my shoulder blades, bending me over Stasi to expose more of my ass. It's a vulnerable position, so I distract myself by kissing over her smooth, perfect skin.

"Should I make him feel good, Anastasia? Has he earned it?" Liam asks.

"Yes," she whispers, wiggling beneath me.

Grateful she's taking pity on me, I bury my cock deep inside her once more.

The tear of a condom wrapper has my heartbeat skipping. Liam rests his hands above my ass. I hold my breath.

And then starts to breach me.

"Shit." Even with Liam going slow, the stretch burns. I bite down on my lip and breathe through it.

He pushes deeper and deeper. So deep, I'm not likely to forget where he's been inside me anytime soon

When the burn finally recedes, all that remains is mind-numbing pleasure. Liam begins to thrust into me.

"You're not human. Not human. *Fuck*. Fucking heaven between your legs and with your cock in me. Don't stop."

A low laugh sneaks out of Liam. "Still so vocal."

I've never been one to contain my thoughts or feelings. I was blessed to have two affectionate parents who valued my words. But sometimes I wonder if I shouldn't develop a filter.

"*Ungh*. Jesus...fuck...B-bad thing or—" Another moan escapes me when Liam slams the rest of the way in.

Stasi was right. I'm dead. I don't exist anymore. He's pounding the soul from my body. Pushing aside vital things to carve his mark into me.

Liam slides his cock out to the tip and drives back in. "So good, Beau. Now fuck yourself on my cock as you worship our girl."

Stasi looks between me and Liam like she can't quite believe this is happening.

"Still okay?" I ask, needing confirmation that we're not hurting her. That she's good with me in the middle when she could have *him*. My brain tells me I shouldn't be here, but her hands slide up my arms and loop around my neck, drawing me down to her awaiting mouth.

Her little whimpers mingle with my groans as I keep fucking her. My cock throbs, my ass filled to the brim with Liam's massive cock every time I rock back. His hands run over me, alternating between stroking along my sides and gripping my ass to pull me back against him.

"Beau," Stasi whimpers, eyelashes fluttering and back arching. She's close.

"I know. I got you, sweetheart."

As I grind against her harder, she matches the movement of my hips. Her breath catches. Her muscles constrict. And then she slams her eyes shut as she throws her head back with a cry. I lean down to suck on a perky nipple while she comes undone.

Liam doesn't hesitate. He shoves his massive cock so fucking deep in my ass, it forces me to push farther into Stasi.

After we've wrung out the last of her orgasm, Liam switches to shorter, targeted thrusts to pinpoint that sensitive spot inside of me. I tease him by bearing down, and he smacks my ass before slamming into me.

I'm barely holding on by the time he pulls me up into his arms. Is he splitting me in two? Will I die from this orgasm? Will anything ever top this night?

With a curse and a full-body shudder, I come. Pulse after aching pulse spills into the condom. It's never-ending as Liam pounds through my release. He shows me no mercy, reminding me that the word gentle isn't in his vocabulary. I should have known better.

Liam follows me over the edge, coming with a growl. His thrusts never seem to end, pushing me to the edge of sensitivity. My twisted brain wants to know what it would feel like to have him fill me with his warm cum, no condom in the way.

Completely at odds with his aggressive fucking, Liam plants a kiss between my shoulder blades while he eases out of my body.

Well, that's new.

Without his support, I collapse next to Stasi on the bed. Her fingers press to my skin, feeling for a heartbeat. "Still alive."

My smile is weak as my heavy eyelids shut. "Check me again in a few hours, okay?"

He groans, popping an eye open. Then he smiles. "Wasn't a dream, huh?"

No. Not a dream. More like a nightmare. Now things are going to be awkward. Messy. Painful.

I suppose if Liam goes back to ignoring my existence, it'll be like last night never happened. Liam and I didn't really *do* much.

Though he definitely watched me and Beau.

Fanning my cheeks, I remember I'm still very much naked. Another sweep of the bedroom, and I spot my clothes folded on the counter in the comically large bathroom. I dive for them, shaking my underwear and bra free. My clothes smell like laundry detergent, not sweat or the nuclear waste I regretfully consumed last night.

Liam must have washed my clothes. Tiny splinters wedge into my heart.

Tossing grace aside, I fumble to pull on my clothes. When I slip out of the bathroom, Beau's propped himself up in bed. His hair is a fluffed up mess, and the sheet is tangled around his bare legs. I wish I could etch the sleepy, relaxed vision of him into my memory.

He frowns. "You okay, sweetheart?"

The question sends me into a mental spiral. *Oh my god.* Did I really have a threesome with Liam and someone I literally just met yesterday? How do I even process this?

Normally, a one-night stand results in me waking up in an unfamiliar empty bed with a sinking feeling in my gut. It didn't matter who I slept with, I never woke up feeling good.

Dropping into a squat, I press the heels of my palms into my eyes.

"Stasi?" Beau repeats, his tone laced with concern.

"I might be freaking out a little," I admit.

"Fuck." He wastes no time jumping out of bed. "Don't do that. I got you."

At some point during the night, he'd slipped back into his boxers, and I'm thankful for that. I'd probably combust at the sight of him rushing toward me naked.

There's no denying I'm attracted to Beau. He's a heady contradiction of edgy and soft. Of mischief and sweetness.

He picks me up off the floor, arms wrapping around me tightly. I cling to him as he rocks me side-to-side. I could probably map him out on paper with how much I touched him last night. Artfully sculpted arms. Beautiful patches of vitiligo. A softer torso, perfectly comfortable to rest my hands and head on.

The man has an ass, too.

I press my ear to his heart and focus on the steady beat. He's warm and real and wonderful.

"Tell you what. Why don't I figure out breakfast while you take a hot shower?" He leans back to look me over. "Sound like a plan?"

He was all sinful smiles in the night, but in the daylight, I notice a hint of something sad lurking in the depths of his blue eyes. Did he drink too much last night, or is he having regrets about what we did? Is Liam? My heart sinks as I glance around and don't see any sign of him.

Beau guides me back into the bathroom. There's a giant porcelain soaker tub that calls to me, and a glass-enclosed shower with a strip of mosaic tile the shade of crystal blue glaciers.

I catch our reflections in the mirror. God, we look disheveled, with swollen lips, flushed skin, and messy hair.

"Where the hell is all his stuff? Can you confirm he's human?" Beau asks, rifling through the closet.

A soft laugh bubbles out of me. It seems it's gonna be a morning of roller coaster emotions. My brain can never let me have more than a few hours of calm.

"No, I don't think I can," I reply.

Beau kneels down to look through the wooden vanity. He raises a fluffy white towel like a victory flag and sets it on the counter. "I'll leave you to it as long as you promise not to have an existential crisis on your own. That's a group activity."

Part of me is tempted to ask him to stay, but then I'm not entirely sure I won't have a complete meltdown, and he didn't sign up for that shit. I'm surprised he's even doing this much for me. We barely know each other.

"Stasi?" Brows furrowing, he lifts a hand to my cheek.

I give him a nod. "Yeah. Thank you."

After pinching my chin, he pecks a kiss to my forehead, and my heart swoops down into my stomach.

So, I definitely didn't imagine this crush.

But what do I *do* with it? I don't even know where Beau came from or why he's here. He could be trying to win over Liam, and I'm getting in the way.

Would I prefer being kicked to the curb now? Or do I want to hang around long enough for the inevitable, crushing rejection?

Patting my hands to my cheeks, I mutter, "Get it together, Stas."

Undressing, I ease into the steamy shower and wait for the tension in my muscles to dissolve.

Things will be okay. It's Sunday. I have the entire day to recuperate and watch football. I'll resume my normal schedule on Monday.

And things with Liam... they won't change.

Everything is *okay*.

Browsing through his expensive products, I use all of them to wash the sex off my body. I smell like glorious man spice when I get out of the shower and redress.

As I head downstairs, I notice that the house is dreadfully quiet. It reminds me of nights when Hail and I would stay up late waiting for Liam to arrive.

Seems I'm destined to wait on him forever.

Deciding I shouldn't linger, I toe on my flats at the front door. Footsteps thud on the stairs, and I hesitate with my hand on the doorknob.

Beau appears, wet locks curling over his forehead. The black shirt and sweats he put on look like they're a size or two too big for him. Did he raid Liam's closet? Would Liam be upset?

My nose scrunches. "I should probably leave."

"Or you could stay. I ordered food. Thought we could use a good meal after last night's activities." He waggles his brows, and I can't help but smile.

He moves to pull me into his arms, a place I'm beginning to like more than I should. "Hey, sweetheart?"

"Hmm?"

"Thank you for last night."

I shut my eyes and squeeze him tighter. Without Beau, I'm not sure I ever would have found the courage to make a move on Liam.

Without Beau, I would have woken up alone.

Somehow, I find myself watching football in Liam's townhouse with the pretty musician he brought home, and we both had sex with.

It's not my worst decision.

Beau nestles beside me on the sectional, a piece of bacon in his hand. He doesn't seem to think twice about physical contact, which I don't mind.

"You're gonna have to explain the game to me," he says, biting through half the bacon in one go.

I smirk. "Not into sports?"

"No TV at my place. No TV growing up either," Beau says with a shrug. "So what's the goal? To score baskets?"

My eyes nearly bug out of my head. When Beau laughs, I push out a breath of relief. "I thought you were serious."

He leans forward to snatch another strip of bacon from our spread of styrofoam boxes and paper cups on the coffee table. I survey the mess with a prickle of guilt. "Liam's going to be annoyed."

Beau flashes me one of those dimple-popping smiles. "Mission accomplished then. My time here is done."

He's teasing, but a frown pulls at my mouth. I don't like the idea of Beau disappearing.

"Are you not planning on staying long?" I ask.

Beau doesn't meet my eyes. "I shouldn't…"

The desire is there to ask him to stick around. But this isn't my house to offer up, and I don't have the extra space in my cramped apartment.

I drop my head to his shoulder. "I don't think I've ever met anyone like you."

"Uh oh. Is that a good thing?"

"You're just…special."

He drops a kiss on the top of my head. Does he hand out affection to everyone? Why don't I like that thought? I've known him less than a day, and I'm already being greedy when it comes to him.

Beau slides a hand around my thigh, pulling me snug against him. "Is this okay? Sorry, I'm not good with personal space."

I rest my hand on his forearm, stroking my fingers along his thick veins. "It's okay. I like it."

We end up running commentary throughout the entire game. Anytime the Cowboys make a touchdown, Beau cheers with me, lifting me off the couch and spinning me around. It's romcom movie worthy. I'm trying not to think much about it. Those little butterflies fluttering around in my chest need to chill out.

I expect him to leave after the game, but he drags me onto his lap and rests his face in the crook of my neck. "So...you wanna tell me what's going on with you and Liam?"

My fingers trace the outline of a lighter patch of skin on the inside of his bicep. "Nothing? We've known each other since we were kids."

Beau gives me space to continue. It reminds me of how Liam would always encourage me to say more. I still question my voice sometimes, but I'm miles away from where I was growing up.

"We spent a lot of years not really talking. He was touring with Atonement. And I...had my hands full with school. Then you happened."

I feel him smile against my skin. "Just needed a troublemaker to shake things up, huh?"

Reflecting back on his little manipulation game last night has me smiling, too. "You are trouble, aren't you?"

He kisses the tip of my nose, riling up those foolish butterflies in my chest even more.

"He'll come around. He's different than I remember," Beau says softly.

I hum in response, not wanting to sign off on hope. "Can I ask how you two...um..."

Beau chuckles. "Hooked up? I don't even know how it happened. I caught him looking the very first show we played together. He wasn't shy about it. I wasn't aware he was into guys, but I leaned into it anyway, not thinking anything would come of it. A few cities later, we were making out in the back of a venue. I was in his hotel room a few hours later. Somehow, I managed to earn a couple of repeats over the course of our tour."

"Do you regret it?" I ask.

He drops his head back on the couch with a heavy breath. "I don't think anyone regrets Liam. I think they hurt when they realize they aren't gonna be the one to change him."

I swallow, eyes dropping to my lap. "Yeah."

After a few seconds, I ask, "Where will you go when you leave?"

"Home, probably. Phoenix." He shrugs.

"No touring?"

Beau's smile is weak. "Nah."

I trace my fingertips along the veins in his arms. "What kind of music does Lithos play?"

"Progressive stuff. But I'll let you in on a secret."

Heart skipping, my eyes dart up to meet his. "Okay."

"Soulful indie shit is my *jam.*"

My brows lift high. Maybe it's because I haven't heard him perform, but his edgy vibes scream heavy music. I try to picture him on a stool with an acoustic guitar, but the image won't fully materialize in my mind.

"See, I knew I'd get that reaction. I was raised on country music. Artists who pour their hearts into stories. Songs are short. Why shouldn't we make each word count?"

"Yeah. Wow. Sorry, I may have judged you on your appearance."

"I'm a bit of a conundrum."

"What a nice conundrum you are."

His answering grin spreads warmth through me. "Stasi. Can I kiss you again?"

I should say no. He just told me he plans on leaving. But I can't erase how last night made me feel. I can't help wishing we could have another night like it, all three of us together.

That's *wrong*, isn't it?

Before my brain can fully process and shut down the idea of seeing two people, I'm nodding.

And when Beau touches his lips to mine, I forget what I was worried about.

I don't want to admit to him that I can't go home. Not when there are two people snuggled up in my bed—a place that's off-limits for everyone but me. Not until I decide what to do about them.

My brain teases me with visions of my night with Stas and Beau like erotic strips of film. Whimpers and moans. Soft, warm skin and firm muscles contracting. Rich bourbon and dusky blue eyes. Both of them were so eager for my instruction. For my *praise*.

Fuck. It was hot. I won't deny that.

As much as I want to let it happen again, I'm on edge, waiting for something from the shadows to come swallow me whole for crossing lines and taking what doesn't belong to me.

What I don't deserve.

Something about being told you're a waste of space as a kid really fucks with your ability to form healthy relationships as an adult.

Which is why I can't let anyone gamble on me. Stas is at the start of a new chapter in her life. And Beau...

Well, I'm not sure what's going on with him, but I refuse to kick him out until I slaughter whatever it is that chased him into my unreliable arms.

Unfortunately, it's like any other night when I come home late from work. Quiet. Dark. Unsettlingly so.

I've decided I hate it.

Unease stirs in me when I don't find Beau on a bar stool or sprawled on my sectional.

Did he leave? Was one good fuck all he needed to get back out there and conquer the world? Or was I just a stepping stone on the way to connect with someone else in Dallas?

I think about him with Stas. How he made her laugh with such abandon, head tipped back, long hair spilling down her back, and brown eyes lit up with joy I haven't seen from her in years.

Was it jealousy that drove me to follow them up to my music room last night? I'm not sure *what* I was thinking. Only that I didn't want to miss whatever was playing out between them.

No, I'm not jealous. I'm selfish. I'm hella overprotective, too. I'd do anything for my twins. Chalk that up to being raised in a dangerous house where I witnessed just how horrible humans could be. How easily they can tear a chasm inside you when they refuse to give you the most basic of necessities.

Like fucking love.

I don't want Stas or Beau to ever experience that kind of pain.

Cutting through the formal dining room, I take the stairs by twos. When I don't find Beau in the music room, my head turns to the spare bedroom with the door closed.

I approach cautiously, ear straining for some sort of confirmation that he didn't leave without saying goodbye.

Then again, he doesn't owe me shit.

What if he's in there with Stas? What if the two of them want to pursue something without me?

Soft plucking of nylon strings comes from behind the door. I listen for a few moments, stunned in place by the emotional melody Beau's playing. It splits me open. Makes me bleed. Makes me question why he's here and not out on tour playing with Lithos.

I crack the door, peeking in at him resting against the headboard in bed, one of my guitars held against his bare chest. His left fingers move fluidly over the strings, but he keeps pausing to shake out his right hand in frustration.

Did he injure it?

Concern spreads through me. The last thing I should do is close myself in a bedroom with him.

"Liam?" he asks hesitantly.

I sigh, the discomfort in my chest growing. "Yeah. We should talk."

The bed creaks, and he pads over to fully open the door. I can't help my eyes from running down his chest. He's wearing a pair of my gray sweatpants, and they're barely clinging to his hips.

Clenching my jaw, I fist my hands at my sides to keep from putting them on his body.

Beau gives me a knowing little grin. "Or we could skip the talking."

I have a brief moment of weakness where I think about leaning down to capture his mouth. Of pushing him back until he collapses on the bed, pinning him down, and spending hours driving him to the brink of pleasure.

When I don't give in for once, the spark in his blue eyes fades. He runs a hand through his still-damp hair and walks over to the bed to plop down on the edge.

It's then I realize there are no lights on in his room, just the faint glow of the streetlamp through the half-closed blinds.

"Why are you playing in the dark?"

"Had a headache," he mumbles.

I stride into the connected bathroom to retrieve medicine from the cabinet above the sink. I pull out two Tylenol, grab the bottle of water from the nightstand, and hold both out for him.

He looks up at me defensively. "You know, I didn't come here for this."

It takes a glare to get him to accept my offerings. After swallowing the medicine, he rolls out flat on his back.

"What *did* you come here for, Beau?" I ask firmly.

He leaves me waiting in anticipation, so I position myself over him on the bed. He sucks in a breath and holds it as fear glints in his eyes. I want to strangle it. I want to take on all his problems and free him from his troubles.

I touch my fingers to his neck, right over his thudding pulse. "If you don't tell me, I'll find someone more willing to talk. I have your band manager's number in my phone."

He swallows. "You fuck him, too?"

A growl threatens to rip from me, but he mumbles a soft "kidding" before my anger can lash out.

Curling my hand around his neck, I bring my mouth to his ear. "You better start talking, or I'm going to fuck *you* until your ass is raw."

He tips his head up to expose more of his neck. "Joke's on you. I choose the ass fucking."

"*Beau.*"

"Yeah. Yeah." He shuts his eyes. "I'm done, okay? I got kicked out."

"Kicked out," I repeat, blinking down at him.

"Out of the band. They were tired of my shit."

My brows furrow. "Who's they? What shit?"

If it's drugs or alcohol, I can't be involved. Doesn't mean I won't point Beau toward resources, but after walking in on the corpse of my father after years of his drunken abuse, I can't go there ever again.

"Everyone. I couldn't perform," Beau replies, striving to keep his tone light.

I remember watching him from the side stage the first time Lithos opened for us and thinking he had a permanent place in the music industry. That his career would soar. It was part of the reason I stopped responding to his texts. I knew he was going places. He didn't need me to fuck up his focus.

And now he's here, laid out in my bed, a place I never imagined I'd find him, doing his best to keep secrets that are obviously impacting his mental health.

"What changed?" I ask.

He winces, and I feel his right hand flex against my thigh. "Everything."

Eager to free him from this invisible pain, I brush my fingers through his hair. Then I lean down to kiss the corner of his mouth.

"Liam." His hands touch lightly against my sides, slowly working their way to spread over my back.

"What do you need?"

I've never been this gentle with him, but tonight is different. He's obviously hurting. Still clinging to secrets, too.

"Less talking. More touching."

His desperate words trigger me into action. I reach back to grab his wrists and plant them on the bed above his head. When I seal our hips together, I drag my lips over his neck.

Beau gasps my name as I kiss my way down his body, shoving his hands away when he tries to touch me again.

"Sorry. Forgot you don't like that. You can tie me up like you used to."

Hovering over the ridge of his cock in his sweats, I lift my head to take in his lust-filled expression. I'm tempted to fetch my rope, but the thought of removing myself from him right now doesn't please me. Especially when I think about how long he's been sitting in the dark all alone.

"Hands to yourself or I stop." I tug his pants down and run my tongue from base to tip of his hard cock. His head drops on a moan, and I catch his fingers curling into his palms.

If this is what he needs, who am I to deny him pleasure? Maybe after an orgasm, he'll be more willing to open up to me.

Every time he tenses up like he's about to come, I pull away. I smirk as he whines for my mouth to return to his skin. "Fuck, Liam. I need it."

"Then lay there and take it."

He nods frantically and keeps himself still. I suck him harder, savoring the salty taste of precum he's leaking. I focus on rolling my tongue over his crown and nudging his piercing.

When I take him all the way down my throat and hold him there, he hisses and bucks his hips. "*Fuck*. Liam."

Warm cum spurts into my mouth, seeping down my throat. I swallow it all, draining him until he's clawing at me from the sensitivity, pleading for me to stop.

When I pop off, he collapses into a heap. I push off the bed and adjust my cock in my pants.

"Damn it. That wasn't supposed to happen that fast," he pants.

After a few labored breaths, he slips onto the floor in front of me. Perched on his knees, he lifts those deep blue eyes to mine. "Can I suck you off?"

I run a hand through his hair. Using my other hand to unzip my pants, I grip him at the roots and guide his parted lips to my cock.

"Open. Tongue out," I command.

He obeys beautifully, sticking his tongue out for me. I slap my cock down on it before gliding it back and forth on the slick, warm surface, reveling in the feel of him. When I push deep into his throat, he gags but doesn't fight me.

"Come on. You know how to suck dick. Remind me what that mouth can do. Show me what I've been missing."

His eyes narrow at the challenge, and I grin as he wraps his hands around my thighs. Though my teeth clench at his hold on me, I return the favor by gripping his hair even tighter.

He can take it. He took so much from me before, all without complaint.

I slam into him, and he receives me with little moans and whines around my cock. I bring my other hand around the back of his neck.

"Ready for this load?" I murmur.

His fingers dig into my flesh, and he hums around me. The vibrations have sparks building at the base of my spine. I rock into him a few more times and then hold his head to the base of my shaft as I come with a growl.

When I release him, he slumps down to the floor and runs the back of his hand across his bright red, spit-slicked lips.

Tucking myself away, I drop into a squat and take his jaw in my hand, planting a kiss to his mouth.

His eyelashes flutter. "I missed this."

Gazing into his solemn eyes, something constricts around my lungs and chokes my air supply.

I help Beau to his feet, my brain searching for a proper response to his admission. This is where I tell him I'm different now. That I made a mistake ghosting him. That I missed him, too.

Leaning in to kiss him one more time, I stride out of the bedroom without speaking another word.

Twenty-five minutes later, I'm standing in the parking lot outside Ascension Records.

The image online only shows the front entrance, but there's a stunning mural painted on the side wall facing the street. It must be the same artist who did Liam's tattoos. The imagery and style are identical—hooded figures wielding scythes and swords, winged and clawed demons, and elegant angels tangled up in a flurry of blood and feathers.

I snicker. Does the man realize how loyal he is? Hell, here I am, seven years after we had our fling, and he's taken me back in with little complaint.

Popping a cigarette from the fresh pack I picked up when the Uber driver had to get gas, I light it up. The woman had apologized profusely for being so absentminded. It was obvious she was having a bad day, so I tipped her extra.

I'm not sure if Liam's waiting for me. Not that I worry about following his orders much when misbehaving results in more attention from him. I just want the nicotine to hit me before I walk in there.

It's a bad mental health day. I spent too much time huddled under the blankets of Liam's spare bed this morning playing a fucked up game of "what if" in my brain. What if I never write a hit again? What if these weird, stroke-like symptoms get worse? What if I sold my house and stayed in Dallas?

What if I asked Stasi on a date?

Damn it, everything feels heavy today. I'm tired. I stayed up late watching Lithos clips on social media. Between my poor attitude and my replacement's stellar performance in Toronto last night, I doubt I'll be getting a callback.

It's for the best. Even if I feel like my strings have been severed and I'm drifting into the void.

I glance down at my right hand. It feels normal today—no tingles—but there's a slight pressure in my skull threatening to turn into a brutal headache later. I should have bought a bottle of medicine from the gas station.

Stubbing out my cigarette, I push out one last breath tinged with smoke. I'm not sure what Liam thinks he'll get by summoning me here, but I'll humor him temporarily. Maybe long enough to prod him about why the hell he's not dating Stasi.

As I waltz through the front door, bells jingle above me. I'm greeted by two friendly faces behind the front desk. A taller man with short, tight curls and brown skin, and a peppy girl with a beehive of ginger hair atop her head. She bounces over to me.

"I'm guessing you're Beau. I'm Emma, one of Liam's sound engineers. And that's Walter. Hail already left for the day. He likes to FaceTime his boyfriend before lights out across the Atlantic, if you know what I mean." Emma exaggerates a wink.

I chuckle. Her bubbly personality is contagious.

"Hey, man," Walter greets with a nod. "How's it goin'? Badass work with Lithos. That first album? Top shelf."

"Yeah. Thanks," I reply, pushing down my disappointment.

Is anyone talking about the new album? Do I care at this point? Or would I rather bury it in the past and not let my failures further take root?

"Yeah, you're perfect for the temp gig." Emma nods.

Brows lifting, my gaze cuts to Liam as he steps out of his office. *What the hell did he tell them?*

"Hey, bossman. Since Beau's here, does that mean I finally get a break?" Emma asks.

Liam doesn't look away from me. "You always get breaks, Emma."

"Yeah, but I feel guilty taking one and leaving you with loads of work."

"Get out of here. You too, Walter. It's after five."

Emma and Walter collect their belongings and drift out the door, lost in enthusiastic chatter about new artists they're working with.

When the studio falls quiet, I soak in the interior. The walls are part dark green paint, part exposed brick, warmed by soft golden lighting. There are instruments everywhere, some displayed as artwork, others propped up with cords connected to amps. Liam's got a grand piano. Not sure I've seen anything sexier in my life.

Okay, maybe the two people I had sex with recently.

Something stirs in my chest, urging me to sit down on the plush bench and touch my fingers to the ivory keys. Maybe play a few chords...

"I didn't agree to this," I mutter.

"And yet you're here. I have one more artist coming in tonight who needs help."

I let out a quiet chuckle. "Ah. So you just want me for my musical talent."

Liam's dark eyes slide down my body. "Might as well use you while you're bumming it at my house."

Delighted by this flirty exchange, I walk right up to him. He's got a couple inches on me and a lot more mass, but I've never been scared of him hurting me. At least, not without consent.

"You gonna pay me?"

Liam licks his lips. "Oh, I'll pay you."

"In sexual favors?"

Is this what I was hoping for when I reached out to him? Someone to reignite a spark inside me I haven't felt in years? Someone to remind me I'm alive? Or was I hoping some of his talent would rub off on me?

He flashes a wicked grin. "And you used to call me the deviant?"

"Oh, you are. But our freak matches."

He brings his mouth closer to mine, his breath warm against my lips. "You accept my paychecks, and sex is on the table."

My pulse leaps. I know he's just teasing, but it's the most commitment I've ever gotten out of him.

Cocking my head to the side, I ask, "And what about Stasi?"

His expression twists. "What about her?"

Maybe I'm hoping I can push his buttons enough to send me away because I obviously don't have the strength to do it myself.

"Why aren't you with her?" I ask.

Liam eases back on a long breath. "You know why."

"Because you don't date. Yeah, I know. But have you ever tried?"

His eyes darken as he contemplates this. "I grew up without a reference to what a healthy relationship looks like, Beau. I'm not about to subject anyone to my deficiencies."

Deficiencies. What a horrible word.

I bring our bodies together, my hands resting between us on his abs. He tenses and gently pushes me away, but not before giving my arms a squeeze in silent apology.

I want to keep testing him, but it's clear something from his childhood still has its claws in him. If only he could see what I see in him. How deeply he cares for others, even if he doesn't vocalize it.

"Would you be upset if I hung out with her?"

He moves over to the chair behind his mixer and sits down. "Why would I?"

"Wouldn't you be jealous?"

"No," he says simply.

Liar. He chased us upstairs that night of the party.

Tilting my head to the side, I ask, "So I can date her?"

His eyes flash with murderous intent, and my heartbeat skips. "You fuck her up, and I'll disown you."

I hold his intense gaze as long as I can before dropping my head. "I'm just fucking with you. We both know I'm not here to stay."

Thankfully, the bells above the door jingle before Liam can poke more at my wounds.

The last artist on his schedule is a talented female folk singer by the name of Nora Woods. I don't mention that I have a few of her songs on my daily playlist. Just like I don't admit how much fun I have working with her, strumming out heartfelt chords and harmonizing with her vocals.

Nora's been battling writer's block. The fact that Liam was willing to give her studio time to work through her mental barriers further proves he's got a bleeding heart in that big, sexy chest.

In the gaps between recordings, I feel his eyes on me. I can almost hear him taunting me. *See, I can play games, too.*

And I fell right into his trap.

I allowed him to lure me here and ease me back into playing when I told myself I was done. I'd even shipped my guitars to my dad in Phoenix, unable to stomach the idea of touching them after my swift kick in the ass from Lithos.

But it's nice to perform without the pressure or expectations that come with fans and bandmates. Here, I'm able to create something wholly new. Something outside the realm of gallops and tremolo picking and power chords.

There's no disconnect between my brain and my right hand, either.

Nora claps her hands together. "That voice! Handsome, you've got some soul in you!"

Grinning, I lift my head to Liam standing behind the recording window. He gives a nod of approval.

"I aim to please," I reply.

By the time Nora makes her exit, I'm still buzzing with energy. I continue lazily plucking at the strings of Liam's guitar, no purpose behind what I'm doing. I'm driven solely by the need to let this living, breathing thing out of me.

I've always had a deep-rooted love for writing music, but for the last couple of years it's felt more like a chore. More like I'm writing for listeners than I am for myself.

Liam strides in and sinks a hand into my hair.

"Time to leave?" I ask, digging my phone out of my pocket to check the time. "*Damn*. How is it midnight already?"

"Are you ready to leave, Beau?"

It feels like a weighted question.

Swallowing, I shake my head. "No."

His hand falls away from me as he gives me another little satisfied nod. "Then keep playing. Spare bedroom's yours for as long as you need it."

He drops a set of keys on a nearby table, and then he's gone.

Who is this man? Is the real Liam tied up somewhere in a closet?

Maybe I should hang around a few more days.

Maybe I should ask for Stasi's number, too.

I crouch down beside her. It's a relief on my achy legs. I'm on my feet most of my shift, constantly using my own muscles to help patients work to regain mobility.

"Did you take my advice and find yourself a hot man last weekend?" Iris asks.

Heat floods my cheeks, and she waggles her patchy silver brows. "You did, didn't you?"

She's been harping me since day one to go out and "paint the town".

I roll my eyes, holding out a hand to her. "More walking."

"Thought we were friends, doc," she mumbles.

I assist her with the first few steps to get her balance and stride.

It's not like we haven't had open chats before. She's the only patient I've shared personal details with. If I don't talk with her like this, she's less inclined to participate in her exercises, and then I'd feel responsible for her lack of improvement.

Even though Iris has told me countless times that she doesn't give a shit about her rehabilitation, I'm not sure I believe her. I think she's scared of hope. Scared of the possibility of not being able to live on her own anymore.

I don't blame her. I'm scared of hope, too.

Glancing around the hall to assure no one can hear us, I whisper, "This stays between you and me."

Her light blue eyes sparkle with delight. "Spill the tea. I'm living vicariously through you, beautiful girl."

I blush again. What is it about receiving a compliment from a woman that holds such power? It's like some higher form of magic.

I shake my head and push down my nerves. "Okay. So there is a guy—"

"Hot? Muscled? Rich?" She rattles off, pausing her steps.

"Keep walking. All three. More. All the things."

Kind. Loyal. Considerate…

"Wonderful. Keep talking," Iris encourages.

My stomach flips as I sift through words to find the right ones. Would she judge me for what I share? Others would. Others have in the past.

Worse, if Iris doesn't like what I share, she might mention it to my boss, and I can't risk losing this job when bills need to be paid.

"Focus, doc," Iris snaps.

"Yeah. Okay. Well…there's another guy. And we all sort of…"

Iris sucks in an audible breath. "*No.* You overachiever."

My shoulders collapse on an exhale. I drop my gaze to the patterned linoleum. "Do you see my problem?"

She balks. "Problem? Honey, there is no problem. Unless the orgasms were lacking."

"Iris!" A laugh punches out of me.

One of the doctors peeks out of us from another patient's room. I wince and wave a hand in apology.

Iris leans in closer. "Well, do you get to keep them?"

I sigh. It's been a struggle to keep my emotions bottled up. I haven't heard from Liam since the weekend. I spent last night pacing my apartment, wondering if I should text him and worried Beau hopped on a flight to Phoenix, never to be seen again.

"No one keeps Liam. *Ever.* And the other guy is only in town temporarily, I think."

Why am I telling her all of this?

Because she might be the closest thing I have to a friend outside of my brother, which is pretty pathetic, considering I've lived in Texas my entire life.

Iris pats my arm. "Do you want to keep them?"

The question catches me off guard. I hadn't given much space for those thoughts. At the end of the day, it doesn't matter.

But the idea of carrying on alone has my heart sinking. I'm sick of quiet nights in my apartment. Sick of counting down the days until my brother comes home so I can have some company. Soon enough, he'll have his boyfriend here with him, and then I'll have to find someone else to bother.

"I think I do. Yeah."

"Then listen to me, you little whippersnapper," Iris says firmly.

"Whippersnapper?" I echo, frowning.

"Life is meant to be lived. Not feared. You need to speak up. Tell them what you want. Be brave. Make demands."

I push out a long breath, sinking further into my internal despair. "You make it sound so easy."

"As easy as you make these exercises sound. Now take me back to my chair. I'm done walking until you start talking to these men of yours."

A call vibrates my phone on the nightstand.

It's *late.* Way past the appropriate time to call someone. I've been lying in bed for over two hours, stuck in my head, churning on thoughts of Liam and Beau and weighing the consequences of severing relationships with my parents and how that might trickle down into the bond I'm starting to rebuild with Max, my older brother.

Shooting upright, I bobble my phone as I snatch it off my nightstand, panicked that my twin needs me.

But it's not Hail's name lit up on my phone.

"Hello," I answer breathlessly.

"Hey," Liam replies in a husky tone. "Why aren't you asleep?"

I fall back onto my bed and stare up at the ceiling. "How do you know I wasn't asleep? Maybe your 2 A.M. call woke me."

"You answered on the first ring, Anastasia. Don't get smart with me."

A smile creeps onto my face. "Next time I'll let you go to voicemail."

His laugh is a hit of dopamine I didn't realize I needed. *Sorry, Iris. You're no longer the highlight of my day.*

Although, it is technically a new day...

We fall into a comfortable silence, and I mull over Iris's words. I'm tempted to lay out what I want. Him in any form he can offer. Beau, too. But that's not something people do in their thirties, right? College was different. You're expected to experiment there.

And what if Liam called to end things?

Anxiously, I wait for him to speak.

"Can I come see you?" he finally asks.

My heart skips. I don't mean to hesitate. It's just, this is the last thing I'm expecting from him.

When I find my words, they come out twinged with sadness. "Please."

"Be there in fifteen. Keep your door locked until then."

He hangs up before I can ask him how he knows where I live. He must have gotten the address from Hail.

Leaping out of bed, I quickly brush my teeth and finger comb my tangle of hair. I refuse to let myself hope, but maybe Beau's right.

Maybe Liam *has* changed.

Why did I wait this long?

My stride falters when her big brown eyes land on me. She's got her long, thick waves unbound, and she's wearing a crop-top and black yoga pants.

Fucking yoga pants.

"Stasi." I wait for the normal crushing pressure on my lungs that usually makes me want to run away. When it doesn't come, I stride forward and pull her against me. I bury my face in the warm crook of her neck and ask the question I've been afraid of since I ditched her in my bed. "You okay?"

Her fingers glide up my back, spreading over my shoulder blades. "I am now."

Dipping down to grip her thighs, I lift her up into my arms. She wraps her legs around me. Her hands come to rest over my heavily beating heart.

An apology sticks like a barb in my throat. Our night together was incredible, but I can't reassure her of anything. I can't pin down my own fucking nature. I'm afraid of promising something and then going back on my word. Afraid of risking her heart in some fucked up experiment to see if I can do this when I'm not even convinced I'm worthy of love.

She touches her palms to my cheeks like I'm something precious. Unable to hold myself back any longer, I surge forward and capture her mouth with mine.

What begins as a desperate kiss quickly transforms into a wild lashing of tongues. I don't even pretend to be in control of myself tonight. I'm too tangled up in my lust for the woman clutched in my arms.

I want to give her more. I do. I really fucking do.

"Stas." I feather kisses over her mouth. "I *need* you."

She nods and whispers, "Always need you."

Drawing back, I gaze into her eyes as my heart pounds hard enough to break ribs.

How could she be so reckless with her heart?

She guides me out of my thoughts, reaching up to undo my hair. Her little smile as it tumbles down has me leaning in to nip at her bottom lip.

These glimpses of her naughtiness absolutely wreck me. As her confidence grows, I can only imagine how dangerous she'll become. How she'll put both me and Beau on our knees.

Maybe I won't ruin her.

Maybe she'll be *our* downfall. Because in my head, we're doomed to come together again.

Stas wiggles out of my arms and drops to her feet. Clutching my hand, she leads me through her apartment. I frown at the boxes piled in the dark corners, wondering if I should offer to help her unpack.

That concern vanishes when she pulls me into her bedroom. Tugging her against me, I run inked fingers through her silky hair, taking a moment to admire her. "You are so fucking perfect, angel."

She shakes her head, her little nose scrunching. "I have no wings. No halo. I'm stuck down here on the ground, looking up at you on a pedestal."

I blink at her in shock as she eases her hands up my shirt to rest over my abs. They quiver beneath her warm touch. A little rumble of approval slips from me.

We trade off stripping pieces of clothing from each other's bodies. When she gets me down to my boxers, her eyes flash with panic as she slowly removes them.

I grip her chin between inked fingers, bringing her eyes back to mine. "What do you need?"

Her eyes shine with determination. "You. I don't want you to hold back."

Growling, I move her hand to wrap it around my cock. "Do you feel what you do to me when you say shit like that?"

"I'm not afraid of you, Liam."

I force her body back until her legs hit the bed. She collapses onto it. I lean down to kiss her hard, coaxing my way into her mouth with my tongue. Her fingers claw at me, eager to drag me on top of her.

"You don't know what you're asking for," I warn.

"I do, Liam. *Please.*"

She thinks she can handle me. I can't help but want to give her a taste. Wrapping my hand around her neck, I position her body sideways along the edge of the bed. It's a heady vision, seeing her mouth level with my cock. She's at my mercy, and I'm drowning in a sea of fixation.

"You think you want me unhinged, Anastasia?" I brush my thumb under the curve of her lip.

Wide-eyed, her throat bobs as she nods. I hadn't planned on actually testing her, but she seems to enjoy being handled this way, so I dive a hand into her hair and drag her closer. "Good. Open for me."

My blood thunders in my veins when her lips part. She quickly wets them with her tongue before sneaking a lick at my crown. I groan, tightening my fingers in her hair. I shouldn't love stepping over this boundary, but I get off on breaking the rules. So yeah, I'm gonna let my best friend's sister blow me if that's what she wants to do.

"Easy," I murmur, slowly feeding her my cock. Her chest rises and falls in rapid succession as I let her get comfortable with my crown. She bobs there in a lazy rhythm, sucking me hard enough to have my knees threatening to buckle.

"*Fuck.* You're so good at being bad for me."

I ease deeper into her mouth, relishing in the way she's running her tongue over me. When I hit the back of her throat, tears form in her eyes. I swipe a rogue one away.

As much as I want to stay buried in her warm, wet mouth, I pull out a few inches so she can catch her breath. I'm not tame when it comes to sexual activities, and the idea of finding her limits has me nearly spilling prematurely.

"Do you want me to touch you?" I ask huskily.

She whimpers on my soaked length. I trace my free hand down her curves and rest it between her legs to cup her sex, smirking at the way her body tightens in anticipation.

Dragging my cock out of her mouth, I bend down until we're breathing the same air. I take her jaw in my other hand, and lick up one of her tears. Then I sink a finger deep into her slick, hot pussy. Her eyes shudder closed, more tears rolling down her cheeks.

I move my mouth to her ear, basking in the way she's trembling all over. "Want you to deep throat me one day. Would you do that for me? Want to feel the tip of my cock right here." I tap my thumb against her throat.

She whimpers on a nod.

"Perfect girl." I push another finger inside of her and hold it there until she grips my forearm and tries to make my hand move. "Uh uh. I'm not done playing with you."

She gasps as I curl both fingers slightly, running them along her inner wall as my thumb traces circles over her clit.

As I straighten back up, she leans forward to swallow my cock again. I hadn't planned on finishing this way, but who am I to deny anything this woman wants?

Anything except commitment.

I let her suck me for a little while longer. When I finally pull my cock free from her swollen, spit-soaked lips, she looks up at me in a haze, waiting for my next instructions.

I'm done *taking* tonight. That's not what she needs. That's not why I came here.

Carefully, I reposition her in the middle of the bed. Bracing my weight over her, I kiss her tenderly, thumbs brushing over her damp cheeks. I keep it to just hands and lips for as long as she can withstand it.

"Do you need me to tell you again how much I want you?" she asks, those big brown eyes weaponized against me.

I kiss her over and over again. Her lips. Her cheeks. Her neck. "So fucking precious. If I had a heart, you would be holding it in your hands."

A little wrinkle forms between her brows. I kiss it away, not wanting to give her space to argue with me. I let Beau get inside my head, and look where that got me. Calling up my best friend's sister, determined to make love to her.

"Condom?" I ask.

"Birth control."

I drop my head to her collarbone on a long exhale. "I get tested frequently. Haven't been with anyone but you and Beau since I've been home. Stas, if you want this—"

Her hands touch my sides. "I do. I trust you."

With slow movements, I push into her tight body until I'm fully settled. We begin to move in synchrony, matching gentle thrusts. I can't bring myself to break away from kissing her. I swallow up her little moans and gasps, hungry for more, as my hands explore her body.

Of all the shit I've experimented with when it comes to sex, this right here was always my hard limit. It's an entirely new experience. I should have known it would be good with her.

Muscles tighten around me, and she lets out a breathy moan as she comes. I cling to her as I come undone right after.

We stay like that for some time, molded together, covered in a sheen of sweat and panting. I've never let anyone hold me like this. Barely let anyone touch me.

The cool kiss of a tear against my cheek has me lifting my head to look at her. "Stas."

"Who are you and what have you done with Liam?" she asks in a broken tone.

That damaged organ in my chest swells, putting terrifying pressure on my lungs. "I don't know. I don't know what I'm doing." I nuzzle my head against her neck. "You can't trust me not to hurt you."

She brushes fingers along the back of my neck. "Hurt happens. Whether we choose to inflict it or not."

I squeeze her tighter as I let some of my worries slip past my armor. "I used to swing back. Did I ever tell you that?"

Her fingers pause on my skin. "Liam..."

"I'm wired for violence, Stasi."

She's silent for a beat. "Your dad did horrible things to you."

I'm not having any of her excuses. That's not my goal.

"I hurt a kid, too. In elementary school. Remember Gavin? Gave him a concussion and a scar."

"He bullied you relentlessly. I saw him wrap his hands around your throat and try to choke you."

I lift my head up to meet her eyes and share the warning I came here to give, hoping she refuses to listen to it. "I'm no good at these things.

Labels terrify me. This isn't something I've ever wanted, and I can't say for sure that it ever will be."

Her fingers stroke from my temple down to my jaw. I've never given anyone as much control as I'm giving her now. Never had two people flip my world upside-down like the two of them did in one evening.

"This is enough," she murmurs. "Half or a whole, you are enough for me."

Her words are a serrated knife to the chest. This isn't fucking fair. She deserves more than that. She deserves more than me.

Pushing through the discomfort in my chest, I kiss her again. I kiss the tears that sneak out of her eyes. I kiss her cheeks and her chin. The world could be burning around us, and I wouldn't be able to stop kissing her.

When a frown pulls her lips down, I ask, "What's wrong?"

Her hands slip away from me. "What about Beau?"

Silent for a few moments, I study her expression, wanting to know exactly what she's thinking.

But I came here to offer up honesty. I don't want to put an end to whatever is developing with Beau, which further proves how much of an asshole I am. I'm already messing this up before we've even started.

"I don't think I can push him away. Not right now," I admit.

She swallows. "What if I tell you I don't want you to do that?"

My heart gives an extra thud. "Yeah?"

"Yeah," she whispers, her gaze dropping to where her finger has started tracing a tattoo on my forearm. "Liam, I think I like him. Is it wrong to have feelings for two people at once?"

I hate that she's constantly fighting that voice in her head seeking to make her feel less, but neither of us is ignorant of the cost Hail paid when he fell in love with a man. Unconventional has no place in her family.

"Wrong by whose standards, angel?" I challenge.

She pushes out her lips. I lean in to sink my teeth into the bottom one and then kiss away the pain. "The only thing to consider is how *you* feel about spending time with both of us."

I watch her process my words as I run my fingers over her hair.

"I feel good with both of you." A smile forms on her full lips, stopping my pulse. There's that little glimpse of rebellion that has me hooked on her. "It feels like I'm breaking rules."

Grinning, I kiss her mouth. "Good. Go ahead and keep breaking them."

"I've learned to read you."

My gut churns at the idea of my thoughts and emotions laid bare to this man. But I think Liam needs the control. I think he's been afraid of feeling too much his entire life.

Do I credit Beau for his recent shift in behavior? Or has he been working up to this for a while? Beau mentioned Liam had changed. Can we have faith that this is a permanent thing?

Submerging myself under the spray of water, I'm surprised smoke doesn't come out of my ears with the rate my brain is spinning.

Liam waits for me to step out of the water with soapy hands. Delicately, he slicks up my wet skin. I don't know how he could ever believe he would truly hurt anyone. So he fought back in self-defense against his dad. The man abused him. And Gavin was a notorious bully.

After Liam guides me back under the water, I return the favor and lather him in soap. He watches me silently as I wash every hard ridge of his body.

God, no one should be allowed to look like him. He's a curse designed to leave us mortals in ruin. The death he brings isn't swift. It's a slow onset of pain starting in the heart. Eventually, it consumes you.

As if he can sense my inner turmoil, Liam emerges from the spray of water and flattens me against the tile wall. He brings his mouth to mine, kissing me until I'm no longer stuck on thoughts of him crushing hearts or vanishing like smoke.

Then he shuts off the water and gently towels me off, brushing light kisses all over my skin. He leaves me momentarily to grab a t-shirt and shorts from my closet, helping me slip into them.

Embarrassingly enough, my stomach growls with a vengeance.

Liam gives a low laugh. "You got anything to cook?"

"I might be horrible about grocery shopping. I do have some leftovers, though."

We heat up the massive quesadillas I ordered for lunch and didn't finish, accompanied by chips and salsa.

There's something intimate about eating with another person at home. The pauses between conversation leave space for lingering stares and overwhelming emotions. Desire and happiness, tinged with a bit of fear that I may not get to have moments like these with him again.

"You know, cardboard boxes are not decorations." Liam nods at the tower of boxes stacked precariously in the corner of my small living room. I meant to tuck those in a closet. I'm afraid if I fully unpack I'll never make it out of here.

"I'm not gonna take advice from a man whose house is practically vacant." I scoop salsa onto a tortilla chip and pop it into my mouth.

How easily I can transform from bedroom Stasi that wants Liam to use her as he sees fit, to old t-shirt wearing Stasi crunching on a mouthful of food.

Liam cocks a brow at me. "Don't make me spank you."

Heat rushes to my cheeks, the possibilities already flooding my brain. Liam sprawling me over his muscled thighs. Liam tying me up naked in his bed. Liam covering my ass with those big hands and spreading me open.

I scoop an even bigger pile of salsa onto my next chip. "So, what other kinky stuff are you into?"

He nearly spits out his drink on a cough. "The fuck has gotten into you?"

A sly grin eases onto my face. "You."

His deep laugh has my spirit taking flight. He's experienced so much in his life, touring the world and bedding whomever he desires. It's nice to catch him by surprise.

"Beau, too," I add, unable to forget the beautiful musician who snuggled me on Liam's couch the other day.

Once Liam regains his composure, he leans over to kiss my cheek. "He's corrupting you."

As if summoned, my phone buzzes with a new message from an unknown number.

"I sent him your contact info," Liam says nonchalantly, tossing a chip into his mouth.

My heart swoops as I open the message. A laugh breezes out of me. "Oh my god, look at him."

I angle my phone to show off the selfie. Beau's shirtless in bed, an arm curled under his head. His eyelids are hooded with sleep, but his dimples are tireless.

Miss you, sweetheart.

It's a strange feeling to share a picture of a man I'm crushing on with the man that just ravished me in bed.

Liam snorts and says, "Shameless flirt."

As I roll my eyes, he catches my chin in a hand and gently turns me toward him. The sudden click of my phone camera when he kisses me has me lurching back. I swipe at my stolen phone, but Liam's already sent the picture to Beau with a message.

She's busy.

Despite my nerves over whatever we're doing, I can't help my smile. "You are such a tease."

He chuckles. Then he gathers up our trash while I try to wrap my head around seeing two men at the same time. I can't completely erase the feeling that I'm doing something wrong. As much as I want to be brave and say fuck it to anyone who cares to judge, I'm still working on developing my backbone. Words have done nothing but cut me down since I first understood them. It's hard to shake that, even as an adult.

I know my parents wouldn't understand this. And while they're not on my good list right now with the way they're treating my twin, it's hard to say I'm ready to completely sever ties.

Then there's the matter of Hail. Would he be okay with me sleeping with his best friend? Or would he try to warn me away from Liam?

Sunlight peeks through the back windows, and I groan. I'm gonna need a large coffee to survive the workday on such little sleep.

Liam hangs out until I'm ready to walk out the door. Surprisingly, he hauls me against him and kisses me one more time. "Come by the studio tomorrow?"

"I have to teach a yoga class in the morning."

"Sounds like you've got all afternoon to spend with me."

And now I'm smiling again. My phone buzzes in my back pocket, breaking the tender moment. Liam rumbles with a low laugh. "He's good for you, Stas."

Fisting his shirt in my hand, I use it to pull myself up and peck a kiss to his stubbled cheek. "You are, too. Even if you don't believe it."

Shaking my head, I return to my mat at the front of the class. I catch Beau stretching in the mirrors, and I already know he's going to be a distraction. I can't just kick him out of class, though.

It hits me that somehow Beau knew where I taught yoga. I don't think I've ever told Liam. I didn't tell Liam where I live either.

This reeks of twin meddling.

Scooping up my phone, I fire off a text to Hail. *Have you been dishing about my life to Liam?*

His response is quick, which means he's clutching his phone in hopes that Z reaches out. *Yeah, he's been asking about you. He needs a friend. I'm about to be on tour again.*

The word *friend* has my pulse spiking.

Do friends do filthy things with each other?

Yeah. I'm not about to ask my brother that.

By some miracle, class goes without a hitch. I manage to keep my voice level and my eyes mostly off Beau as he bends and twists with a surprising amount of flexibility.

As people trickle out, Beau ends up in a conversation with Ryan. Can he go anywhere without making friends?

When Beau finally goes to put his equipment up, Ryan wanders over. "Another great class, Stasi. *So* who's the boy toy?"

Hot blood rushes to my cheeks. "Um. He's... a friend."

"Oh, honey. He doesn't look at you like you're a *friend*."

Beau decides it's a good time to interrupt with an arm around my waist. "Nothing friendly about what I want to do with you."

"Oh my god. I knew it." Ryan breaks into a wide grin. "You two should come to brunch with the gang this morning."

"Yeah. Love to," Beau replies immediately, patting his stomach.

I throw him a look that earns me an expression of pure mischief.

"Great! We meet at Sunny's at eleven. See you there." Ryan waves and struts from the room.

My frown must indicate I need some sort of talking to because Beau holds up his hands in submission.

"Hey. He told me he's been trying to invite you to brunch for weeks. He said you just put your head down and rush out of here like the place is haunted. It made me a little sad. And I'm severely hungry. Bad decision hungry."

I rub at my brows. "I don't know what to think about this right now."

Beau brings me into his arms. "Then don't think. Let's just go have fun and fill up on mimosas."

His words melt the tension in my body.

"Fine." I sigh. "We can have breakfast."

He drops a kiss to my temple. "Mind if I hop in your car? Ubered here."

"Hijacking my class, bumming rides, forcing me to make friends..." I rant off, unable to stop my smile.

Beau scoops me up in his arms again, and I giggle. "Don't forget coaxing you into a threesome."

"Oh, yes. I'd nearly forgotten about that."

"Maybe we need to refresh your memory."

I break out of his hold with a breathy laugh. "We are *not* going to make it to brunch with your new best friend if you keep doing that."

"Hmm. Mimosas or sex. Hard decision."

Smiling, I hold out my hand to him. "I'll make it for you. Come on, trouble."

It's a perfectly acceptable day. The sun is out, but not quite angry. We're shaded beneath a giant teal umbrella on the side patio of a trendy breakfast joint.

Beau keeps my hand in his under the metal table as Ryan introduces his husband and two women from my yoga class with their significant others. Apparently, it's tradition to come here after I bend them into weird shapes.

Normally, I fade into the background in a crowd, but Ryan keeps the conversation flowing. I had no idea he worked in the medical field as a nurse. Penny, another regular from my class, introduces her wife as a sonogram tech. I'm deep into a conversation with her about our baby nieces when a towering figure walks through the side door.

My heart drops.

Again, I have to question if this is a mirage brought on by the Texas heat or if I'm stuck in some sort of strange dream. That can't be Liam walking toward us, sunglasses on and black tee fitted to his muscled form, right? I haven't seen him out in the real world for anything but music and workouts.

A tidal wave of nerves crashes over me. What will the group think about my two "friends?" I wish I could say I don't care about outside opinions on my life choices, but unfortunately, my confidence has been eroded by the suffocating pressure of a strict upbringing and bad friend-ships.

"Hope you don't mind. I invited him," Beau leans over to whisper.

I don't speak as Liam drags out the empty chair on my other side. A table of captivated eyes watches as he pushes up his sunglasses and sits down.

Those curious gazes soon turn to me when Liam rests his arm along the back of my chair.

Seeming to realize I'm floundering for words, Ryan comes to my rescue. "Dear god, Stasi. I think you just became my new favorite person."

Laughter breaks loose, and then introductions happen again for Liam's sake. He's perfectly polite, if not quieter than me. We're both exercising muscles we don't normally use, all thanks to the smiling man on my left.

After dining on pancake flights and fresh-pressed juice for two hours, Ryan checks his watch and complains about weekend chores that need to get done. The other couples soon drift off as well to start their days.

I glance at Liam. "Are we doing this?"

There's a calm determination in his eyes. "If that's what you want. I'm willing to try."

Swallowing, I look over at Beau, but he doesn't seem to be paying attention. He's slouched in the chair, eyes closed and head tilted back like a lizard baking in the heat.

A soft laugh breaks free from me. "You really are a Phoenix boy."

"Born and raised, baby."

I have a thought to ask if he misses it. Time at home is precious when your career is in music.

Shouldn't he be out touring?

Beau's head tilts my way. "Hey, pretty girl."

Shoving down my sadness, I force a weak smile. "Hi, Beau."

"You come here often?"

"Nope. This weirdo dragged me here and cleaned my plate."

Beau jerks upright, his expression twisting. "*Shit*. I'm sorry. I thought you said you were done. We can order you more food—"

"I'm teasing, Beau. I offered you my last pancake."

Blowing out a breath, he drops his forehead to the table. "And here I thought I'd fucked it all up."

Liam chuckles. Pushing up from his chair, he says, "Gotta get back to work. You're coming to the studio, Stas."

My smile grows at his demand. "Yeah."

I expect Beau to hop in Liam's car as we walk to the parking lot, but for some reason, he climbs into my passenger seat instead.

What would it take to convince him to stay? Is that fair to ask when I've witnessed firsthand how much Hail and Liam fought for their musical careers?

Burying those thoughts, I hold out my phone with Spotify pulled up. "Put on your band. I wanna hear you play."

It's all good. I can sleep for a week straight when I get home. Right now, I don't want to miss anything during my short stay in paradise.

Not only do I get the pleasure of watching Liam Beckner work, I get to hang with Stasi, too. She's currently nestled in one of the leather studio chairs, blonde hair pulled up in a bun, and something she called manga propped open on her lap.

I'm straddling the piano bench, left hand tapping out a melody on the keys while I watch Liam chat with one of his artists.

There's no question he's a workaholic. *This is my way of giving back. I know how it feels to be passed over when you're trying to get your footing in the music industry.*

I almost swooned at his excuse for working six—sometimes seven—day weeks. Pretty sure my heart hasn't found a normal rhythm the entire time we've spent in the studio together as I've witnessed him respectfully push artists to reach their highest potential.

Wish Lithos had him to produce our last album.

Nope. I'm not going to give space to thoughts like that today.

Wandering out of the recording room, I grab a guitar off the wall and plop down in the chair next to Stasi. She peeks up at me from her book. Her cute smile fills me with joy. I smile back, strumming out a few light chords to match the way she makes me feel.

One minute, I'm messing around, and the next I'm singing a melody to go with the notes I'm stringing together. I'm not sure how long I play, but when I reacquaint myself with my surroundings, two pairs of shocked eyes are locked on me.

"Louder, Beau," Liam orders.

My pulse quickens. I've had plenty of face-offs with my nerves, having played on big stages, but something about this intimate setting with the attention of a highly talented musician and a girl I'm hot for has me getting hung up on my failing album and absent creativity.

I'm not about to be a martyr and admit any of that, so I return the guitar to the hook on the wall. "I was just messing around."

Dark eyes stalk me all the way out the front door as I fish out a cigarette with shaky hands. Leaning against the brick exterior, I light one up and suck in lungfuls of smoke to get that nicotine hit faster.

The door opens, and I brace for Liam's appearance. It's Stasi who graces me with her presence. She rests beside me on the wall, loose tendrils of blonde hair whipping around her face in the hot breeze.

Sighing, I pop my snapback off and fit it to her head.

"There," I say, grinning.

She doesn't smile back. "Beau, are you okay?"

Tipping my head back against the bricks, I squint in the harsh sunlight. "Had a moment. I'm better now."

After a pause, she says, "Liam mentioned you're not in Lithos anymore."

"Couldn't take the pressure, I guess."

"Do you think Liam could help? He's got connections..."

I take another hit from my cigarette and blow out the smoke. "I appreciate it, sweetheart, but I'm not looking for solutions to a problem. I'll figure my own shit out."

When she doesn't respond, I glance over at her. She's got her nose scrunched up in a troubled expression, and that doesn't sit right with me. Dropping my cigarette, I stomp it out and pull her against my chest. I hold her for a while.

"You smell like an ashtray," she mumbles in complaint.

"Sorry. I'll quit."

"I should head home. I've got babysitting duty for my niece tonight."

I drop a kiss to her forehead and walk her to her car. "Text me if you can, okay?"

"No promises. Felicity's already a handful. A chaos baby born from the most anal retentive people I know."

Chuckling, I steal one more kiss from her. She goes to hand me my hat, but I stop her. "Keep it. I like knowing you have something of mine."

As soon as she pulls out of the parking lot, my mood plummets. It's like my sunshine has been stolen away, and I've been plunged into a cold, starless night.

I glance back at the studio, knowing I should finish my shift. But I can't bring myself to head back inside, so I call up an Uber instead.

I think I need a long nap.

Liam hasn't come home yet.

I've been laid out in his bed for hours, full starfish pose, with my finger hovered over the button to call him.

Am I being too needy? Is he mad that I bailed out earlier? Wouldn't it be a good thing to have him push me away?

I don't realize I've hit call until he speaks my name like a prayer.

My pulse leaps. "So you *do* have my number saved in your phone."

Staggered grunts and heavy breaths come over the line. At first, my stupid brain assumes I've caught him at the wrong time. Normal people wouldn't answer the phone during sex, but Liam's not normal.

"Sorry." The clang of something heavy sounds. "At the gym."

Air rushes out of my lungs in relief. "I didn't mean to interrupt—"

"Don't you fucking hang up. Talk to me. What's wrong? Why'd you leave today?"

I wriggle deeper under his blankets, further messing them up. I have no intention of fixing them. I want him to know I was here. Want him to think of me when he finally crawls into his bed tonight.

"You know, for someone who claims he's not good at this relationship shit, you're doing a pretty good job," I say.

"Give me time to fail."

"Nope. Wrong answer."

His breath hitches—a sign he's working through another set of reps.

"Arm or leg day?"

"Legs." He grunts. "Worst day of the week."

"Mmm, I disagree. Those thighs are unholy. Feel free to send me a pic."

"Shameless flirt on the phone, too. Your little selfies have been distracting."

I've enjoyed sending them any chance I get since Liam gave me Stasi's number and I created a group chat between us.

"Yeah? Stasi said she likes them. Guess I'll send her more and leave you out since you never reply to them."

His voice drops to a threatening murmur. "You stop sending them to me, and I'll make sure you don't get off the next time we're in bed together."

Smiling, I close my eyes. "Stasi seems open to this."

"Yeah."

I don't know if I expected him to tell me otherwise, but when he doesn't, I ask, "We're playing to her comfort level, aren't we?"

"I'm not sure how else to do this," he admits.

After a few beats of silence, I do my best to lighten the mood. I chat with him about musicians we've been working with in the studio. He shocks me by offering his Porsche for me to drive so I don't have to sleep at the studio or rely on Uber to get around. I don't tell him it's not safe for me to drive. Not with the way my vision sometimes warbles and blurs with these persistent migraines.

Instead, I ask him for his best Atonement tour stories. He tells me his wildest experiences always involved his bassist and drummer. He tells me about Hail and how he fell hard for the pretty, broken singer from Visage in a smoky London bar.

Running my hands over the soft fabric of his comforter, I ask, "Did you ever hook up with any of them?"

"I don't hook up with people I work with."

"You're working with me."

He pauses. "You're the only one I've broken that rule for."

"Yeah?" A goofy smile takes over my face. "Maybe I *am* trouble."

Another grunt. "You have no idea."

I rub my socked feet together under his sheets. "Are you partial to solo workouts, or could I come with you to the gym next time? Does Stasi work out with you?"

"Solo. But I'm trying this new thing where I don't shut people out. Fair warning, I won't go easy on you. And you *cannot* interrupt Stas, no matter what she's wearing."

The visuals his words summon up go straight to my groin. I've been rocking a semi since he picked up the phone and rumbled my name. Now that I'm thinking about Stasi in tight shorts and sports bras, I'm aching to get off.

I slip a hand beneath my sweats and give my shaft a slow pump. "Warning heard and ignored."

He lets out a laugh, and then his voice drops low. "Are you touching yourself, Beau?"

This conversation has effectively turned my entire night around. "Would you like that?"

"Hold on."

He cuts the call, leaving me frowning with my hand around my cock. Seconds later, a FaceTime call pops up.

"Oh, hell yeah." I grin, sliding a finger across the screen to answer it.

My mouth waters at the image of him in the empty locker room, dressed in a sleeveless tank and gray sweatpants. His tattooed skin glistens with sweat, and his hair is piled on top of his head.

I'm so done for. I'm in over my head for sure. Obviously, the only reason I came to Dallas was to torture myself.

"Do you ever *not* look good?"

Liam smirks as he drags his shirt off his body, revealing each set of rigid ab muscles and those defined pecs I want to run my tongue over.

"You too, trouble. Shirt off," Liam demands.

"Shit, is that what we're doing? What if someone walks in on you?"

Liam's smile turns wicked. "Let them watch."

"You don't have any limits, do you?"

I scramble to pull off my shirt as he stares at me with his usual intensity. My face in the tiny little square box next to this sex god is laughable.

"Very few. Don't care to be touched. I want to be in charge. It's how I stay safe. Shorts off, Beau."

I hesitate, my mouth parting at what he just shared. He doesn't let me dig into the piece of him he just exposed.

"Are you in my bed?" he asks.

I wet my lips as I shove a hand back into my pants. "Yeah. Problem?"

Liam draws his sweatpants down those thick thighs, exposing tight black boxers that barely contain his massive erection. Anyone walking in on that thing would fall to their knees and beg to worship it. I don't give a shit if they think they're straight.

I prop my phone up on his nightstand, kick away the comforter and sheets, and strip off my pants.

Liam rumbles in approval. "Fist your cock for me, Beau."

Tipping my head back, I squeeze my shaft. I make a show of running my hand up and down my length, eager to please him. The fact that someone could walk in on him has me worked up even more.

"Look at that beautiful cock. Drawer in my nightstand has lube. Slick yourself up."

My voice comes out strained and raspy. "Want to see your dick first."

"Cute how you think you're in charge."

How can he both terrify me and turn me on at the same time?

I fumble for the bottle of lube in the drawer. My eyelids shudder at the tight, slick sensation when I wrap my lubed up hand around my cock. I stroke myself slowly. Tightly. Turned on by the obscene sounds I'm creating while sprawled out in his bed.

"Play with that piercing, Beau."

I do, imagining Liam tugging on it with his teeth and sucking it into his mouth. So glad I left it in. I hadn't planned to. It was a drunken decision egged on by Noah and my bandmates early into our career when maturity wasn't a word we knew the definition of.

"*Fuck*. That feels good," I utter.

Liam picks up his phone and walks into a shower stall. Heat floods my groin as he sets the phone on the bench across from the showerhead, giving me a full view of his naked body.

"Why aren't you home right now?" I whine.

"Because I can't keep a body like this if I skip gym days. Keep stroking yourself, Beau."

"Fuck yeah. You got it."

I watch water slither down his gorgeous body as my orgasm begins to build. It's a scene I could appreciate forever, especially when he lathers up his own cock and runs a big hand along his length.

"Want that in my body again soon," I beg.

"You'll have to earn it. Use your other hand. Play with your balls."

Groaning, I do just that. It's a struggle to keep my focus on my own pleasure when I'm glued to the screen, watching Liam jerk himself.

"Want to suck you so fucking bad. Want you to fuck me hard like you used to." I ramble.

"Finger yourself, Beau. Now." Liam's tone takes on a growl. He's starting to come apart at the seams.

Working two fingers inside my hole, I imagine they belong to him. That he's pressing me down on his bed right now, spreading me open. That his dark eyes are searing into mine as he gives me orders up close and personal.

"Come for me, Beau," Liam says roughly.

"*Liam.*" I let out another groan and arch off the bed as my release shoots up to my chest. As I ride the waves of pleasure, Liam's growls from his own orgasm fill my ears.

Panting, I grab my t-shirt and use it to wipe away some of my sweat and cum.

Liam falls into his shower routine. I continue watching silently, admiring the way his long black hair molds to his chiseled body under the water.

There's no way I can ignore my feelings for this man. Not when they're growing at an exponential rate.

"We should go on a date," I blurt out. "All three of us."

Liam pauses. With a blank expression, he glances at me through the phone, and I brace for rejection. "When?"

It's my turn to hesitate. Did I hear him right? Did Liam Beckner just agree to a *date*?

"Tomorrow?" I ask, suddenly nervous. "Aren't Sundays the only day you allow for fun?"

He's silent, and my heart sinks. "Never mind. It was a stupid request."

"No. We can try it."

Slowly, my smile finds its way back to me. "I need you to really commit, Liam."

"Bossy after you come, aren't you?"

"If I say yes, are you going to deprive me of orgasms? 'Cause then it's a no."

I'm not sure I've ever glimpsed a gentle smile from Liam, but here it is to warm my bones.

Fuck. This is already starting to get heavy. I know I can't stay here. I'm the type to fall headfirst into love. I'm affectionate and clingy and too fucking much.

But that doesn't mean I don't want to learn all the things that would make them smile.

"Get some sleep," Liam says. "I'll be home soon."

When the line clicks, I find I'm in a much better mood as I make myself comfortable under his sheets.

Carding my fingers through his hair, I realize I didn't have any nightmares last night. I also didn't wake up covered in sweat or trapped in my closet, where I'm sometimes driven by the ghost of steel-toed boots on the stairs.

Is this what I've been missing out on?

Would I have been ready for this seven years ago if I'd known how it would feel with him? Or would I have hurt him, regardless?

How would it feel to let him touch me? Hold me? Comfort me?

I reflect on how Stasi touched me in her apartment. The tenderness in her movements. The *care*. I've rarely accepted that kind of affection. I didn't even know it existed until I witnessed other kids at school receive it. Hugs and kisses from their parents when they came to school events. "I love you's" at drop-off.

I was allowed to exist to provide for my deadbeat dad, forced to become an adult too early. Even when he'd overdosed and I'd been placed with a foster family until I turned eighteen, I didn't let my guard down. I *couldn't*.

But now...

Something's still missing. Another pretty human in my bed with blonde waves and pouty lips.

Sitting up, I reach for my phone to check my messages. "What the fuck?"

Beau jolts upright, wide-eyed. "What?"

Was he pretending to be asleep?

"It's after eleven."

"Oh." He blows out a breath. "Is that all?"

I'm working up a glare when he suddenly leaps out of bed.

"What the fuck?" I repeat.

He rushes into my bathroom and starts up the shower. "You agreed to a date. We have to meet Stasi somewhere by one. It'll take an hour and a half to get there, so get that sexy ass up."

Suppose he thinks he has permission to trespass everywhere in my house now since he crashed in my bed. Wonder if he found my collection of toys...

He'd definitely be asking to use them if he had.

Sighing, I roll out of bed and join him in the shower.

Eyes wide, he backs against the tile. "What are you doing in here?"

"My bathroom," I remind him, cocking a brow.

"Yeah. Sorry. Trying not to get distracted." His eyes drag down my naked body, counting my abs and tracing the V leading down to my half-hard cock. "Nope. Not sorry at all."

"Keep looking at me like that and we're gonna be *real* late."

Beau fumbles out of the shower, and I chuckle as I scrub shampoo over my scalp. I sneak looks at him as he tugs on a fitted black t-shirt and cargo pants.

He looks *good*.

I kind of want to tie him up and keep him forever.

"Keep on the route. Keep pace with the group. No stragglers. And last rule...everyone have fun!" Jacob, our cameo-clad UTV tour guide, smacks his hands together, dismissing us to our assigned mud-coated off-road vehicles.

I see Beau mouthing a *thank you* at the young guy and instantly bristle. Leaning closer, I murmur, "You know him?"

Beau glances at me with a smirk. "You jealous?"

Grimacing, I'm surprised to find that I *am* indeed jealous of the way the guide is looking over at Beau. And yet, I don't feel anything but a rush of excitement when Stas and Beau look at each other like that.

"Does he think he's gonna get your number or some shit?" I ask defensively.

"*Jacob* was kind enough to sneak us into this time slot when they're booked up for weeks," Beau explains.

I cross my arms over my chest. "Well, *Jacob* can fuck straight off with those flirty little looks."

Beau's smile inches close to where I know those dimples exist. Next time they make an appearance, I'm gonna sink my teeth into them. I don't care if we're in public.

The crunch of boots on gravel has us both turning our heads. My anger immediately dissolves, incinerated by a snap of electricity as Stasi jogs toward us with three pairs of goggles in her hand. She's wearing a dark tank top, frayed shorts, and hiking boots. Beau's snapback is pulled low on her head, her long braid fed through the back. The whole get up reminds me of Tomb Raider.

I'm fucking here for it.

"See? Dates aren't so bad, are they?" Beau says quietly.

I find myself giving a single nod, unable to tear my gaze away from her.

"What else do you think we could get her to dress in?"

"I'd rather not think about that right now," I mutter, already uncomfortably tight in the jeans.

Stas holds out a pair of black goggles for me. She's so light on her feet today. Did Beau know she likes a bit of danger? Did he know she'd show up in that outfit?

If this is all it takes to make her smile, maybe I can make an exception to my no dates rule.

Hooking an arm around her waist, I tug her against me. That pretty smile of hers has me weak in the knees. *She* makes me weak. There's not a touch of make-up on her face today, and it makes me crave waking up next to her in my bed, snuggled between me and Beau.

An odd fluttering spreads through my chest as she stretches up on her toes and kisses me. I wasn't sure how the two of them would feel about public displays of affection with our current arrangement. I don't give a shit about outside opinions, but I've watched Stas struggle with judgment her entire life, so I was prepared to hold off.

Sliding a hand up her spine to cup her nape, I kiss her long enough for her to let out a breathy laugh.

After we break apart, she tugs my bandana up over my mouth and nose. Then she gives me a curious look. "I cover most of your face and you still make my heart race."

I have to nudge her over to Beau to keep myself from attacking her and getting kicked out for inappropriate behavior.

Wouldn't be the worst thing to happen. People expect that shit from a rockstar.

"Ready to get dirty?" Beau asks with an impish grin.

Faster than he can react, Stas grabs the keys from his hand and books it toward our off-road vehicle. If I wasn't already tangled up in this woman, she'd win me over the second she hops into the driver's seat and starts up the engine like she was raised out here in the wild, not in the wealthy suburbs.

She *is* a little wild.

I bring my hand down on Beau's shoulder, striding past his stunned form. "Better buckle up, trouble."

Engines rumble in response to our own aggressive-sounding UTV. I cram my giant body into the back seat—the best spot for viewing those sexy legs about to work the pedals.

Stas maneuvers us into the line of creeping vehicles headed for a thicket of trees. When we approach the first rocky hill, she breaks into a grin and tugs her own bandana over her mouth and nose.

Then it's our turn to hit the gas.

She tears up the steep hill like she owns it. I chuckle as Beau's hand snaps to the roll cage bar. Stas tightens her grip on the wheel in determination, battling to stay in the deep tread marks like instructed.

Why can't she go through life like this? Full fucking force. No concerns over what anyone thinks. No worrying about pleasing anyone.

I know the answer. In all the ways I was broken physically, she and Hail were torn apart mentally. Hail bounced back quicker. He had music. He had fame.

He had me to hold him up.

Anastasia drowned for a while longer. She was silent about it. Didn't flail or scream for help. She continued to support Hail with pep talks as he pursued his dream. Pep talks she should have been giving herself.

Stasi slings us over hills and through mud puddles with reckless abandon. Hidden beneath my bandana, I'm grinning so hard my cheeks ache as we get tossed and bounced around. I'd let her drive us off a cliff with that smile plastered on my face. She can be my angel of death.

It takes Beau some time to relax in the passenger seat. When we're back on flat terrain, he glances at me, face splattered with mud, and gives me a thumbs up.

We reach a checkpoint—a collection of smooth rocks overlooking the lush treetops—and the crew gives everyone time to take pictures and switch drivers. I make no move to climb out of the backseat.

"Need a sec. Still hard," I tell Beau when he wanders over.

His gaze drops to my crotch. "Want me to help with that?"

"Oh, you're gonna help me later. Once we wash these dirt tans off, I'm going to fuck you without mercy, Beau."

That wipes the smirk off his face.

Between the glint of desire in his blue eyes and Stas stretching her arms overhead nearby, showing off those hard-earned abs, I'm fighting to calm down.

Beau hustles toward her, drawing her into his arms. "Should we take a pic together, sweetheart? Liam can't come out to play right now on account of his *massive* boner."

Stas glances at me with wide eyes. And then she tips her head back to let out a laugh.

I gain a newfound appreciation for Beau.

It's hard to ignore the heavy dose of regret I have for going silent on him years ago. I want him to be able to trust me with his heart this time.

When Beau walks over to Jacob with his phone held out to ask for a picture, that bubble of jealousy returns. I leap out of the UTV and storm over to them. Forget hiding my dick. Let Jacob see what he's competing with.

We gather on the edge of the hill, Stasi squeezed between me and Beau. I sense the eyes of the other drivers on us. I do my best to shield Stasi. If anyone thinks it's wise to comment on our wandering hands and heated looks, they're gonna receive an earful from me. No one makes my twins feel bad. That protection extends to Beau, too.

Jacob snaps our picture. Even with the death glares I'm handing out, he chats Beau up for a few minutes while I walk with Stasi back to the UTV, keys in hand.

Beau claims he doesn't feel like driving, but I bet he's scared to look like a fool after Stas handled the UTV like a pro.

As we slide into the front seats, Stasi peeks over at me. "Thank you for coming. Beau had asked me what you might like to do."

I cock a brow. "You two been talking?"

A rosy tint highlights her cheeks. "He's quite chatty. Except when y'all are in the studio. Then he sneaks pictures of the two of you to send to me."

I snort. No surprise there. The man takes more selfies than anyone I know.

"How's he doing? In the studio, I mean..." Stasi asks softly.

I give the question some thought, sifting through our workdays together to make sure I haven't missed any odd behavior. It shouldn't come as a surprise how easily Beau's woven himself into the studio family. He's quick to win people over.

"He seems happy there," I say quietly.

"I wasn't expecting his voice to sound so..." she shakes her head, at a loss for words.

"He was hiding in the background when he played with Lithos."

"If he released something on his own, it would do so well, don't you think?"

I nod. "Record labels would be lined up to sign him."

She drops her head and picks at her nails. "Figures I'd end up falling for two talented musicians. At least you're home now."

My heart thuds off beat, almost painfully.

Thankfully, Beau returns to us before I have to come up with a response I'm not ready to give. As he hops in the back, I turn to ask, "Sure you don't want to drive?"

"And let Stasi show me up? No thanks."

I keep a slow pace with the group down the hill, but as soon as we're back on the winding dirt roads, I gun it like I'm trying to outrun the apocalypse. Stasi's carefree laughter has my smile returning.

As much fun as I've had today, though, I'm ready to take both of them home. My desire for them has shifted from want to undeniable *need*, and not just in the bedroom.

I'm not sure where this path leads for us. I'm not convinced I'm the right piece to their puzzle. But the thought of stepping aside now feels like clawing open that hole in my chest I'd stupidly thought I'd healed with meaningless hook-ups.

Once we're parked at the entrance, I shed my protective gear.

"Oh my god." Stas laughs, stretching up to swipe her fingers over my cheeks. "You've got mud everywhere."

I plant a kiss on her lips, mixing our dirt and sweat. Then I stalk after Beau and push him up against the UTV to kiss him hard.

"Take it you had a good time," he says against my mouth.

"Mmm. Jacob watching?" I murmur, kissing him again.

Beau shoves at my chest. "You're so bad."

Grinning, I smear mud on his neck. "Let's go home so I can get you dirty all over again."

I rest my chin on her shoulder after successfully removing both of her boots. "Not out loud. But I sense it from people."

My longest relationship was with a ranch hand when I was eighteen. A pretty, freckled guy hired to help my dad for a summer.

It ended just about as fast as it started. I was out and proud. He wasn't. Without thinking, I'd snuck a kiss from him while we were picking up supplies at the local farm supply store. He'd blown up about how I have no respect for boundaries.

Not sure much has changed, to be honest.

Still, it hurt being dumped and left there for my dad to pick up. *Hey, it's your bi son messing up again. Sorry about running off your help.*

My dad didn't even chew me out. After he picked my sorry ass up, he swung us through the drive-thru of an ice cream place and got us both Reese's peanut butter shakes.

Now that my life has slowed down, I kind of miss the ranch. The endless stretch of wild land surrounding a generational home. The itch of tall grass brushing my skin. The scent of wildflowers and earth. The buzzing songs of crickets and June bugs.

Or maybe I just miss the calm. I never took time to slow down after my mom passed away. Just kept churning out music and hopping between stages.

Brushing my lips over Stasi's skin, I picture her sitting on the tailgate of my old rusted truck I'd left on the property, those long legs dangling and those brown eyes a melty caramel in the Arizona sun.

Stasi catches me off guard as she shifts on my lap to cradle my cheek in her hand. "Don't ever feel like you need to hold back with me."

I turn my head slightly to kiss her palm. "Liam warned me you were too fucking sweet."

She lets out a huffy laugh. "Liam thinks you're corrupting me."

As if on cue, the man himself comes stalking around the side of the house, caked in mud and hauling grocery bags.

A laugh punches out of me. "They let you walk in like that?"

Eyeing me darkly, Liam turns his key in the back lock. "No one's going to tell me no."

I chuckle, nodding. "Yeah, that tracks."

He *is* one intimidating motherfucker.

"Told you the spare key was under the mat," Liam mutters, kicking off his shoes and sliding the door open.

A rumble of thunder cuts off my response. We all turn to look at the ominous wall of dark clouds headed our way, lightning spider webbing through them.

"So much for grilling steaks tonight," Liam says, dipping into the house.

Seconds after, fat raindrops smack onto the patio. I haul Stasi upright as cold rain pelts us. We're both soaked before I can push her inside the house.

Grinning, I step back from the door into the onslaught of rain.

"What are you doing?" Stasi asks, eyes wide.

I keep moving backwards until my bare feet touch the wet grass. Tipping my face up to the angry sky, arms spreading out wide, I let the rain cleanse the dirt and sweat from my skin.

My smile grows when soft lips press to my jaw. I lower my head and blink at the beautiful woman standing with me amidst a storm, little snakes of rain slithering down her cheeks and dripping from the loose tendrils of her hair.

I welcome her into my arms. Soon, I have her skipping and dancing across the grass with me like we're unburdened kids in the summertime. No worries over lost jobs or unrequited love.

We're just *living*.

She spins with her tongue hanging out to catch the heavy droplets. I'm not sure I believe in perfect moments, but this has to be as close as it gets—a reminder that while life can be cruel, beauty still exists beneath the surface. A current you can't see. You only feel it when you wade a little deeper.

I feel the tug of it now, bringing my gaze to the back door where Liam stands, arms crossed and muscles flexed. I'm not sure how long he's been watching us, but simply observing the fun isn't gonna cut it.

I jog over to him. "You are *not* too cool for this."

"This isn't a thing. People don't play in the rain," he replies.

"Were you never a child?"

His jaw tenses. "I didn't get that luxury."

And just like that, joy is stripped from me.

"Jesus, Liam." I step right in front of him. "I'm sorry."

"It's in the past. Buried six feet under."

Holding his hard gaze, I wait for him to give me more. When he doesn't, I slowly bring a hand to his forearm. "Do you trust me?"

He pushes out a deep breath. "Honestly? Instinct tells me I shouldn't."

"Well, fuck. That kind of stings." I pout.

Liam molds his warm body against my wet one. His big hands take my face, and then he kisses me. His tongue glides over my bottom lip, caressing mine when I part for him.

I'm left light-headed when he draws back, staring up into tender eyes that don't match the aloof metal head from my memories.

"I trust you, Beau."

"Then get your ass out there in the rain."

He doesn't move, so I yank on his arm. "*Jesus*. What are you made of? Sweetheart, I need that sexy strength of yours."

Stasi bounds over and latches on to his other arm. Liam smirks down at us in challenge. My grip slips first, and as I stumble back, Liam takes the opportunity to haul Stasi up in his arms. He spreads those inked hands over her thighs and walks her out into the grass, holding her captive under the downpour. She drops her head back on a laugh, and Liam kisses between her breasts.

Longing burrows through me. Do they know how perfect they are for each other? How she moves, and he shifts with her, almost like their souls are tied together? How she exhales, and he breathes in her air, starved of her essence?

Does he know he's in love with her?

Does he even know what love *is*?

Heat prickles behind my eyes. It hurts to think Liam didn't have a happy childhood. To add to that pain, I've already done the worst thing possible and let myself hope that this thing between us will continue.

I'd say I didn't come here for this, but it's a lie. I knew I would fall for Liam again. I'm not sure I ever fell *out* of love with him.

And now Stasi's etched her mark into my heart right next to his.

I shove these thoughts aside, choosing to focus on the two people standing in the rain, mouths locked in a passionate kiss.

"Ah, hell." I rub a fist over my heart. I don't want to be sad right now. I don't want to think about going home. I want to be present and live in the moment.

Suddenly, I'm grabbed by the shirt and dragged into the grass. Before I can protest, Liam claims my mouth. I cling to his soaked shirt for dear life, only letting up when our kiss unexpectedly turns into something softer.

Light fingers dance along my cheek in addition to Liam's callused ones, brushing my outgrown hair behind my ear. Smiling, I close my eyes and lean into Stasi's touch.

As soon as Liam's sure I'm stable on my feet, he releases me. I wrap Stasi up in my arms and give her all the tender kisses Liam gave to me.

"Want you both," she whispers.

Blood rushes straight to my groin. I glance over at Liam. "Can't say no to that."

A muscle in his jaw twitches. "Inside. *Now*."

I crack a smile. "I get to taste her first."

I steal Stasi away toward the house, giddy for his wrath. He can come try to take her from me.

And he does. Within *seconds*.

Hands slam me into the kitchen wall, and a hot mouth meets mine. Eager to match his energy, I curl my fingers in his belt and pull him flush against me as I roll my tongue against his own.

Shoving up the wet material of my shirt, he draws back momentarily to pull it over my head and smack it down on the floor. I hiss as he runs the pad of a rough thumb over one of my hard nipples.

"Anastasia, come here," he rumbles.

Stasi moves between us, melty brown eyes blinking up at me from under thick lashes.

I lick my lips, gaze dropping to her parted mouth, still wet from the rain.

"Strip him," Liam commands.

My smile returns as she brings a hand to the zipper of my jeans. "Go ahead, sweetheart. I'm all yours."

I'm practically high off the anticipation of a repeat between the three of us. Who would have thought this would be my life? Forget touring.

This right here is better than any adrenaline rush I've experienced on stage.

Stasi lowers to her knees to peel off my pants and boxers. My chest rises and falls with labored breaths at the sight of her staring up at me, those pretty lips so close to my cock.

And then she's stolen away, ensnared by inked arms and placed on the edge of the kitchen island. I'd cry out in sexual frustration if not for this new desire to watch Liam get her out of those wet clothes.

I shove locks of hair out of my eyes, not wanting to miss a single interaction between them—the consideration he gives her and the gentleness she returns.

Can you fall in love with the way two people love each other?

Drawn to them, and maybe a little desperate for punishment, I fit my body to Liam's backside. Carefully, I touch my hands to his sides to start. When he doesn't yell at me or push me away, I brush my lips along his neck.

Liam rumbles in approval, so I work my hands up the front of his shirt, coasting them over his rigid abs and pecs. I fully expect him to turn around and shove me to my knees, but Stasi seems to be enough of a distraction to curb any discomfort he may have from letting me have my way with him.

Would he let me fuck him one day? I don't need it, but I've spent a good amount of time fantasizing about it.

Heart thudding faster, I drop a hand to unbuckle his belt as his big hands glide up Stasi's body to remove her shirt. My mouth waters at the sight of another lacy bralette. I bite down on the muscle between Liam's neck and shoulder.

Liam runs his mouth over Stasi's goose bumped skin, and my cock throbs against his ass. I flick open the button on his pants, swiping a thumb along the hot, smooth skin exposed there.

"Beau," Liam says in a low tone.

Is this where his line is now? I can hold him and touch him when he has clothes on, but when he's naked, he wants to be in full control?

I sigh, resting my forehead against his wet shoulder. "Just wanted to touch you a little."

A tense pause follows. "Then quit fucking around and touch me already."

Fuck. I dive a hand into his boxers and grip his cock. "This thing is perfection."

He rocks his hips slightly, so I squeeze him hard like he would do to me. Jerking him a couple times nice and slow, I lower my hand to cup his heavy balls. Then I massage them, suddenly wishing I could be on my knees for him, sucking them into my mouth.

Stasi and I work together to remove the rest of Liam's clothes. Shockingly, he even lifts his arms in the air for her.

I've seen him naked probably half a dozen times, but never in the daytime like this. It's a religious experience. My eyes follow the intricate swirls of black and gray on his skin, no spot of other color to be found. There's no question his tattoos cost him a fortune.

Brushing my palms over the designs, I notice something off. Scars hidden in the artificial lines. I run a finger along one of them, and Liam tenses. My stomach churns. I count three more. Make that six...

Dark eyes bore into me as Liam turns. He slips an arm around my waist and heaves me up onto the kitchen counter next to Stasi.

Does she know about his scars? Does she know what happened to him? I mean, I have a hypothesis, and I really don't fucking like it. Liam's the strongest person I know, inside and out.

If someone managed to hurt him...

I can understand why he might struggle with connections now.

Fighting back enraged tears, I let my head fall to the side with a deep breath. Stasi looks like a goddess sprawled out next to me, warm brown eyes staring back at me and locks of hair clinging to her flushed skin.

"So gorgeous," I murmur.

Her fingertips touch my cheek, stroking lightly over my dimples.

A groan rips free from me as Liam unexpectedly sucks my cock into his mouth.

"Fuck. Fuck me. Fucking fuck me," I spit out, gripping the edge of the counter while he works me over with brutal suction.

Stasi shimmies closer to kiss my bottom lip. "Foul mouth."

The instant Liam pops off, I seize my chance to roll on top of her. I notch my cock against her hot, slick center. "Already so wet for us. Let's see what kind of noises we can get you to make, sweetheart."

With a groan of disappointment, I'm grabbed by the hips and dragged off the counter.

"Upstairs," Liam says firmly. "I want both of you on your hands and knees in my bed."

Lust tumbles through me, and I glance at Stasi. Grinning, we lock hands and race for the stairs.

I play with fire all the way to his bed, stealing kisses and sinful touches from her.

By the time Liam joins us in his room, we're both grinding against each other in his bed, lip-locked and whining for release.

I spot his glorious, naked backside slipping into his closet, and my pulse quickens when he returns with two small, black silicone plugs.

"Oh, fuck," I utter.

Stasi's eyes blow wide as she notices the toys he's holding.

"You tell me if anything I do is too much. I only want to make you feel good," he says.

He waits for a nod before those scary eyes dart to me in question. I nod so hard it brings a pain to my skull.

"Hell yeah, I want to be stuffed."

Liam grins and crawls onto the bed with us, those big thigh muscles at work.

"Flip over, trouble. I'm gonna plug you first. Then you're gonna watch me make Stasi come before I fuck all the thoughts from your pretty head."

My heart stutters. I'm not sure if Liam's an angel or the devil. Either way, he's taking something precious from me tonight.

Shifting on my knees to get some friction between my legs, I watch Liam move his fingers in and out of Beau in a tortuously slow rhythm.

Liam reaches for one of the silicone plugs, coating it with lube. I hold my breath while he makes it disappear inside Beau.

"*Fuck*. So full," Beau groans, dropping his hips to the bed to grind against it.

Liam grabs handfuls of Beau's ass and lifts him back onto his knees, leaving red imprints on his skin. "Those curses are gonna turn into you begging for my cock soon enough, trouble."

Dark, ravenous eyes slide to me next. A shudder wracks me as Liam prowls closer.

Where Liam was rough with Beau, he gently eases me down onto my hands and knees with a palm in the middle of my shoulders. He trails his fingers down each bump of my spine as he wedges a knee between my legs to spread them.

Naked and exposed, I have a thought to feel embarrassed, but then I look at Beau in the same vulnerable position and fall into a place of desire and nothing else.

All hard muscle and hot skin, Liam covers me with his body. He runs his mouth up my neck, halting at the hollow behind my ear. "Look at you, angel. So perfect for us. Gonna train you to take both of our cocks."

Heat floods me from head to toe.

"Jesus," Beau mumbles.

Liam guides my head to the side, pressing a kiss to the corner of my mouth. While I'm distracted, he touches a finger to a place I've never been touched before. He taps me there, then circles around and around to massage me. Whimpering, I slump down onto the bed.

"Oh, no. We haven't even started yet." Liam hauls me back onto my hands and knees. His finger returns to my hole, testing the muscle there.

"More, Liam." I want to prove I can handle whatever he throws at me. I want every side of him.

Liam nips at my jaw. "An angel who wants to be bad, hmm?"

I can't focus on words when he keeps smoothing his finger over my rim. He runs his tongue and teeth along my neck as he starts to push that finger, now slicked with lube, inside me.

"Relax," he murmurs. "I won't hurt you. Let me inside."

Shutting my eyes, I give myself over to Liam fully. At first, when he pushes into the tightness of my body, I'm not sure about the sensation. It's...strange, but the more he stretches me, pressing hot kisses to my neck and shoulders, the more I succumb to pleasure.

"You're doing so good. You can take another."

"Please," I beg.

A second finger enters me. I practice a deep breath and let him work me open. I'm not sure how anything else will fit. But soon the slow movement of his fingers has me rocking backward, eager for more.

"*Liam.*"

His teeth nip at my earlobe. "I'm going to plug you. Then you're going to ride my cock. Understood?"

All I can do is nod. Words don't exist anymore. Time and logic and thought don't either. Nothing but pleasure gifted by this devastatingly hot, considerate man.

Liam carefully presses the cold plug inside me. I gasp as my muscles suck the toy into place. He kisses my spine, and then his body heat is gone, replaced with the chill of the air circulating the room.

When I sit up, I have to hold still for a few moments to get used to the sensation in my ass. I watch Liam walking over to an oversized black leather chair by the windows.

Is that piece of furniture new, too? Or was I not paying much attention the first night we spent in his room?

Liam sits down, a dark king on a throne. Moonlight bleeds through the cracks in the blinds, highlighting his sculpted, tattooed body. His thick legs are spread wide, giving a perfect view of his proud cock.

My mouth waters.

"Come here. Both of you," Liam orders.

His sultry tone is a siren call we can't ignore. Beau and I crawl out of bed to kneel at his legs. I'm not sure why I do it. I don't think I would kneel for anyone else.

A toxic voice bubbles up in my head, seeking to make me feel wrong for what I'm doing. Dirty for doing these kinds of things with two men.

Liam leans down to capture my chin with his calloused hand. "Enough."

My negative thoughts wither, crawling back into their dark holes.

"You're safe with me, Anastasia."

I nod, relieved that he knows my mind so well and can easily take control of it.

He takes control of Beau, too, sliding a hand into his hair and tilting his head slightly to the side. Beau's practically boneless, desperate to be reshaped in the likeness Liam desires most.

"You will kneel here and watch me bury every inch of my cock into her pretty cunt. You will *not* touch yourself."

"Fuck." Beau wriggles, then winces from what I assume must be the plug hitting weird. Or hitting *right*. Precum glistens along the slit of his cock, and I have the urge to lean down and lick it up.

"Climb up here, angel," Liam says sternly.

Gritting my teeth at the odd pleasure of the plug as I move, I situate myself on his lap. My knees settle on either side of his solid thighs, and I rest my hands on his stone-like pecs, spreading my fingers over his skin.

A nervous smile plays on my lips. "You're like a furnace."

The simple touch of his thumb tracing the curve of my bottom lip lights me up. Any second now and I'll detonate. Shatter and rain down to the ground like a firework.

His hand wraps around my jaw, turning me enough to bring his mouth to my ear.

"*Sit*," he commands.

With a sharp inhale, I lower myself onto him. It's a tight fit with the addition of the plug, but he grabs my hips and helps guide me down until I'm fully seated on his cock.

I drop my forehead to his shoulder. "*Ungh*. Liam. It's too much."

"You can handle it. You're taking me so well. You're going to take both of us so well one day soon."

His husky, slightly wrecked voice has a moan slipping from my parted lips. Beau groans in response. I can only imagine the view he's getting from his spot on the floor behind me.

"Stas. Look at me."

My heart dips into my stomach as I straighten up and gaze into his near-black eyes. The amount of emotion swirling in them tonight has my pulse spiking.

Don't give into hope. Don't give into hope.

Does he know his armor is slipping? Should I tell him and save us all the gutting pain when this comes toppling down around us?

Because when he looks at me like this, I *feel* loved.

He gives so much to others through his actions. Adapts to whatever they need within his capabilities.

Has anyone ever told him that they love him in return? That he is worthy and desired and so fucking *good*?

Two little furrows appear between his brows. I don't want to lose him at this moment, so I start to move my hips. Liam's hands grip my ass, squeezing and spreading me so Beau can witness the way our bodies are coming together. It makes my skin burn even hotter.

"*Fuck*. This is torture," Beau murmurs. "Can I please touch my dick?"

"Touch it and all you're getting is your hand tonight," Liam warns.

Between Beau's whispered curses, Liam's thick cock dragging against my walls, and the plug pressing on more nerves than I was aware of, I'm done for. Hot sensation builds at my core, curling my toes and tensing my muscles.

I slow my pace to keep from coming, but Liam isn't having it. He regains control, slamming his hips up to strike deep and hard.

I've never been loud during sex, but Liam's literally *destroying* me. His hand slides up my side to wrap around my neck, just under my jaw. With a gentle press of his thumb, he parts my lips.

"More of that. I want to hear you. Don't hold it in."

With his encouragement, I let go. I let him fuck the shame and the fear right out of me.

And then I'm detonating. Shattering. My vision goes black. I become nothing more than raw pleasure.

When I come to, Liam's cradling me against his chest, the plug already removed from my body. He sweeps a hand over my face to brush locks of damp hair away. "You okay?"

My smile is lazy. "I don't think I can move."

I tip my head up to assess him, worried lines were crossed, and he's about to snap up barriers. Instead, he graces me with a smile that wrinkles the corners of his eyes and shows off more of his white teeth than I've ever seen before. It's everything.

He's everything.

Liam tucks me into his bed. Then returns to Beau, still plugged on the floor. I pity him for having to wait so long, but I think I'm beginning to understand their dynamic in the bedroom.

Liam hauls Beau upright and bends him over the bed. "What do you need, trouble?"

Beau's breathing is labored under Liam's forceful touch, his eyes clouded over by something concerning. It makes my hands fist the sheets tighter.

Beau doesn't have to say a word, though. Liam already *knows*. He moves Beau onto his back, looking down at him in that same overwhelming, vulnerable way he looked at me. Like he needs us to see the emotion in his eyes because the words won't come out.

I swallow as Liam positions himself over Beau, pushing one of his legs up. His other hand slowly drags the plug free from his ass.

Immediately, Liam replaces it with his cock, still glistening from my arousal. Beau claws at him for more, and it makes my chest ache.

Liam's given us more than I ever could have expected. But that doesn't mean he's ready to commit to anything beyond this. Invisible wounds don't miraculously heal, and I'm not arrogant enough to believe that we're going to be the ones to make them disappear.

And yet here we are, offering up our hearts anyway.

I just wish Beau would hang around long enough so we can pick up each other's broken pieces when Liam decides he's done with us.

Beau sucks in a breath as his muscles coil up. Seconds after, he comes all over his stomach and chest. It's the most intense thing I've ever seen, heightened by the sight of Liam losing control as his hips slam hard and hold flush against Beau while he spills inside of him.

Liam kisses Beau's chest before pulling out. "Gonna run a shower for us."

Beau and I are left in a post-orgasm state in the bedroom. He manages to roll over, a hand reaching to stroke my cheek.

"Hey, sweetheart."

"Hi, Beau," I whisper.

I get caught up in him, pain expanding in my chest at the thought of him disappearing one day. Is it normal to feel this much this soon for someone?

Can we sustain this?

Tears stick my lashes together. Even if Liam wins out over his demons, it wouldn't be the only hurdle we face. There will be people who don't understand us. Who criticize this part of me. This rebellious, carefree woman I've been burying for decades to garner attention and win approval because I had so little of it growing up.

"Stasi?" Beau asks, a note of worry in his tone.

"Sorry." I blink back the heat in my eyes. "I'm happy, I swear. I'm so happy when I'm with both of you."

He kisses my temple as he runs his fingers up and down my back. "I'm happy when you're happy, baby."

Liam returns to the bedroom and freezes at the sight of us entwined. Something indistinguishable flickers in his expression. He quickly hides it away.

He strides over to sink his hands into our hair. "You're both a mess. Come on. Let's get you cleaned up."

Grabbing my phone, I slip inside and open the messages from an unknown number sexting me. I debate calling them to cuss them out for ruining the night.

But I only have myself to blame for this.

Scrolling through hundreds of messages in my phone, I wait for any of the names to register. I don't recognize ninety percent of them. They never mattered to me as long as they agreed to give me temporary relief from the shit I didn't want to feel at the time.

I block the number before wandering back onto the patio with made up plates for the two of them.

"I'll delete them. All of them," I say.

Beau glares back at me, and I feel the weight of his pain. Almost as if he's questioning if I would have deleted him, too, had he not shown up here. I doubt it will make him feel better to know he'll always have a place in my phone.

I have to imagine I've tread on more than my fair share of feelings in one lifetime. I've *hurt* people.

I'm hurting the two of them now, even if they don't want to admit it.

"I didn't ask you to do that," Stas replies softly.

"I'm choosing to. I don't expect exclusivity from either of you. Lord knows I haven't earned it. But that's what I'm offering. I haven't been with anyone else since I came home, and I won't be with anyone else for as long as we're doing this together."

Wide eyes hold me. I can't say I'm not afraid, but my fear means nothing in the face of their happiness.

"No one else," Stasi agrees.

Beau doesn't answer. I know his trust won't be so easily earned.

Moving over to Stas, I lean down to kiss her on the cheek.

"Only you," I promise.

Then I move to Beau, dropping to a knee to press a lingering kiss to his jaw that makes him hum and melt just a little.

"Can we eat now, or are you going to carry on with sappy declarations?" he mumbles.

I knock the baseball hat off his head, unleashing his fluff of hair and a string of complaints.

As they both tear into the food, the vice-like tension around my lungs eases. I'm not good with words or showing affection or generally being a kind human, but at least I can cook them some comfort food. The rest will have to come with practice.

Beau holds firm to his guard throughout our meal, every now and then assessing me with a stern look. Part of me hopes he's becoming protective of Stasi. If that's the case, maybe he won't leave. Maybe he'll stick around to hold shit together when I inevitably fuck this up.

Stasi collects our plates and carries them into the kitchen after Beau agrees to wash them. He lingers at the table with me.

I brush my thumb along the back of his hand. "I'm sorry."

He meets my gaze with heat. "For what?"

"For not replying. For hopping on a plane and never looking back."

Beau deflates with a heavy sigh. "You weren't ready."

"No, I wasn't," I agree, glancing up at the night sky. "I'm the most afraid of myself when I get close to others."

Beau flips his hand so our fingers entwine. "Does that have anything to do with your comment about not getting to be a kid?"

"Everything to do with it. I spent my childhood keeping an abusive, alcoholic father alive. In the end, I failed."

"*Shit*. Liam."

Sucking in a deep breath, I prepare to let it all out tonight. "I spent a lot of years convinced love didn't exist because I'd never experienced it."

He gives my hand a squeeze, and my gaze drifts back to him, my pulse thudding faster at the naked emotion displayed on his pretty face. That lock of white has curled funky over his brows, the ends sticking straight out to the side.

"And what do you think now?" he asks softly.

"I think it's inevitable that I'm going to fall in love, whether I deserve it in return or not."

The sight of a tear sneaking down his cheek stops my heart. I reach over with my other hand to brush it away. "Beau. I'm not sharing this to excuse my shitty behavior. I'm truly sorry for hurting you. I'm sorry for assuming you'd bounce back like I was nothing more than a way to waste time between shows."

He nods frantically, but then the tears really begin to fall. He pops up to his feet and paces. "Ugh, sorry. This is embarrassing. Here I thought I'd planned a perfect day, and I'm ruining it by crying."

Stasi appears in the doorway. "Screw that."

Her words are delivered with more force than I've ever heard from her. I fucking love it. I loved hearing her lay into Hail on the phone when he was having meltdowns about his performances. Her voice would take on a little southern twang she does her best to downplay.

Thinking about Hail has my jaw clenching. Is he going to understand any of this? I've been so adamant that a relationship wasn't in the books for me. Add in the fact that he's got a solid grasp on just how many one-night stands I've had...

I file away the troubling thought for another night.

Beau remains stunned in place as Stasi moves in front of him. "You didn't ruin anything. It was a perfect day."

He crumples, arms winding around her waist and head resting on her shoulder. They rock side-to-side for a while, soaking up each other's comfort.

"How do we finish this date, Beau?" I ask gently.

Sniffling, he eases away from Stasi. "Well, it's after midnight. Technically, I think the date is over."

"Only if you want it to be," I reply.

Beau glances around in confusion. "Is this real life or a dream?"

"A dream, for sure." I nod.

"Then I want to sleep forever."

Taking their precious hands in mine, I lead them through the kitchen, right past the mess we made preparing food to cook, and into my music room. Other than my giant bed, it's the most comfortable spot in my house.

Stasi sits with me on the floor, our backs supported against the couch. Beau doesn't move from the doorway. He hasn't quite bounced back to his normal, sassy, troublemaking self.

"You bought an 8-string acoustic," he comments.

I glance at the newest guitar in my collection—a sexy, mahogany piece finished in a midnight blue that matches his eyes. I know it's his favorite brand to play, and it'll accompany his voice beautifully when he finally decides to record a track.

"It's yours," I say.

Beau's brows knit together. "Oh, *hell* no. I don't care how much money you have. I'm not accepting this."

"Leave it here then. Doesn't change the fact that I bought it for you."

When we lock eyes, Beau looks adrift. I think about how Lithos was ripped out from beneath his feet. He looks like how I felt when I stepped foot in my townhouse for the first time and realized I was on my own.

No shows to get me through each day. No band manager telling me what to do. No tour dates or city hopping or structure to my life.

Thankfully, I've found a new purpose in helping artists. I'm able to wring out every drop of their talent by stripping back all the layers of bullshit keeping them from baring their souls to the world.

What's it gonna take to give Beau a new purpose?

I haven't reached the bottom of what's haunting him in the moments he thinks no one's looking. I'm assuming it has something to do with the rapid success of his first album. Imposter syndrome snuck in and wrapped ghostly fingers around his neck, tightening until he couldn't breathe under the pressure.

"Beau. You don't owe anyone anything. You can take as long as you need to work whatever this is out of your system."

Without speaking, he comes to some sort of internal decision. Flexing and curling his right hand a couple of times, he reaches for the neck of the guitar and carries it over to perch on the edge of the other couch facing us.

My chest swells with the same warm pride I get when I watch any of the members of Atonement play.

Beau tips his head down and starts to pluck at the strings. It's a soft tune to start. Nothing more than simple, resonant chords to embrace us.

And then he weaves a beautiful melody with quick, perfectly placed fingers and that deep, raspy tone that wraps around me like a summer breeze.

I'm not sure how to categorize him. Country? Blues? Folk? A little of all three blended together until you can't tell where one genre ends and the other begins.

Beau has no labels. He redesigns what it means to be an artist.

Shit, he's redefining *me*.

Stasi peeks up at me, and guilt claws at me as I come to understand the fear in her eyes. In a way, I took Hail from her. Held up his chin and showered him with praise. Booked him shows at grungy venues and kept him motivated to grind his way to the top of the charts, dragging Malek and Griff along with us.

And now there's Beau with this big, promising future stretching wide before him.

I want to tell Stasi I know the key to keeping him here. That I can hold him back. But I *can't*. Not when I've committed my life to elevating musical dreamers.

As his final note rings out, a heaviness settles in his bones, slumping his shoulders and weighing down his head.

He looks exhausted.

"That was so pretty, Beau," Stasi murmurs. "Did you write it?"

"Something I've been working on, yeah." He shrugs, returning the guitar to the wall.

She lets her head fall onto my shoulder. Gauging the way they're both struggling to keep upright, I call it a night. "Time for both of you to sleep."

I gather Stas up over a shoulder, pleased when she giggles. Beau looks at me, a smile curling on his face. "Gonna carry me, too, tough guy?"

I charge him, tossing him over my other shoulder. "Smart ass."

My plans to tuck them in and clean the kitchen go up in flames the second I lay them down together in my bed. I find myself physically unable to pull away. When Beau crawls in to spoon her, I lay down on her other side so she can snuggle against my chest.

Just when I think the two of them have drifted off and I can sneak out, Beau whispers, "Liam?"

"Yeah, trouble?"

He hesitates. "I think I'd like to record something, but if it ends up sucking, we trash it, okay?"

Shutting my eyes, I smirk. "It won't be trash."

"But if it is—"

"Beau."

After another pause, he speaks in a sleepy tone. "It would be nice to leave a piece of me behind that I can be proud of."

I hesitate, knowing it's not smart for me to drive. There's always the fear that a migraine will set in and my vision will fade to a mass of warbling gray.

But my headache is mostly gone... so I should be okay.

My blood beats a little harder beneath my skin as I pull out of the garage and hit the gas.

It's blissfully quiet when I enter the studio—an Eden of musical possibility opening its gates to me. No other eyes or ears.

No expectations.

I'm anxious to work on my song. I've never been solo. My career started in a sweltering garage in Phoenix with Noah and three other guys we met at a concert. I figured it would end with a group, too.

As I run my fingers along the curved body of the classical guitar I've come to know on a spiritual level in my time working here, I question if I'm ready. Am I giving into false confidence that I can climb my way back to where I was when Lithos released our first album?

I poured my heart into those tracks. Two decades-worth of want so potent, it was practically a living, breathing entity.

To think I have the success now but can't produce...it's a special kind of mental hell.

My confidence flags as I pick up the guitar and wander into the recording room.

No, we're not going to spiral out.

Planting my ass on a stool, I'm prepared to slaughter my worry for the future and fight for my dream.

I pick up where I left off in Liam's music room earlier, finding peace in the way the notes fill up the empty space around me. My right hand is in sync with my head for once as my left glides along the frets, tapping and bending strings.

It's going to be a good day.

Everything *feels* good.

I fall deeper into the sound, letting it guide me. I don't force anything, and what results is a song filled with more emotion than I ever thought possible for me to produce.

About to play through it again, movement in the studio has me startling. I glance up and see Liam braced against the recording room door frame. Natural light pours in behind him.

Is it morning already?

"It sounds good, Beau."

I drag a hand through my hair and blow out a breath I feel like I've been holding for years. "Maybe."

Dark eyes flash. "Will you let me prove it to you?"

My heart kicks with an extra beat. When I told him I'd like to record something, I wasn't expecting it to be this soon.

Liam strides into the recording room. Picking up two microphones, he positions one near the guitar and the other in front of my face. After fitting me with a pair of headphones, he moves behind the glass window in the control room.

This isn't the first time I've experienced the soul-deep burn of his gaze, but the pressure to perform for a man who creates absolute art has doubt sharpening its blades.

We haven't even started recording, and I'm already choking. It was so much easier to hide behind Noah and let him take the lead. Now, I'm up front and center. I'm exposed. A raw nerve for the poking.

"Beau." Liam's firm voice through the headphones snaps me to attention.

"Shit. Sorry. You wouldn't happen to have a pack of smokes lying around, would you?"

His frown is proof I'm fucking this up. Groaning, I tug on the roots of my hair. It's at an awkward length where it's curling at the ends, but it's not long enough to pull back.

I've been floating in this strange gray area of existence for a while now. Self-care things like haircuts have fallen to the bottom of my priority list.

"I'm wasting your time." I deflate.

When Liam vanishes from the window, I prepare for him to kick me out. It's obvious I'm not worthy of this opportunity.

The recording room door opens, and Liam walks in, no trace of irritation in his expression. He reaches for the guitar and sets it aside. Then he moves between my legs, gently sliding the headphones off me.

I forget how to breathe in his presence. I don't think he understands the effect he has on me. How he makes my hands tremble and my pulse race.

Guiding me off the stool, he maneuvers my body until my back is pressed against the wall. His mouth meets mine in a crushing kiss, and lightning sizzles through my body, waking my cock right the fuck up. I slide my hands up his shirt, doing my best to match his sudden, aggressive energy.

"What's it going to take to help you relax?" he murmurs, sinking his teeth into my jaw.

"This." I gasp. "You. *Us.*"

He works his mouth back to mine. Our tongues tangle as one of his hands moves down to grip my ass and tug me closer.

"Fuck. *Liam,*" I whine.

His other hand wraps around my neck, right under my jaw, tilting my head back. When he licks my Adam's apple, I almost slump to the floor.

Why is that so hot?

He slides a knee between my legs to keep me upright, but all this does is put more pressure on my erection. I moan and grind my hips against him as my hands explore the hard ridges of his abs. Gliding my hands higher, I tease his pebbled nipples. His answering growl rumbles through my entire body.

Suddenly, he tears his body away. I reach for him like I'm tumbling over the edge of a cliff.

His pupils have swallowed up the rings of dark brown. "Office. *Now.*"

"Office. Yeah. *Yes.*"

Breaking into a jog, I clutch a hand to my erection to keep it from bobbing in the loose fabric of my pants.

Liam's on me the second I make it to his office. With a hard shove, he sends me tumbling into his leather desk chair. I mumble curses as he drops to his knees in front of me.

What have I done to earn his attention? What planets or stars have aligned in my skies? Last night I snuggled with him in his bed alongside a beautiful, sweet woman. And now he's here, kneeling for me like I'm some kind of higher being.

Inked fingers slide up my thighs. He hooks them under my shirt, dragging it up just enough to sneak his fingers under the waistband of my pants.

"No underwear, Beau?" he murmurs.

My stomach muscles quiver, and I squirm in the chair. "Like to live dangerously."

"That you do, trouble." His hand dips under my waistband to grip my erection.

I drop my head back and shut my eyes. "That feels good."

Giving me a few more slow, decadent strokes, he tugs at my pants. "Ass up. Tired of waiting. Your pretty, pierced cock belongs in my mouth."

I buck up fast enough to have him grinning. He drags my sweats down to mid-thigh, and a touch of nerves hits me at the thought that this man could have anyone he wants. He has Stasi, for god's sake. Why would he want a failing musician with an aversion to the gym?

"Shirt, too," Liam orders. "You're too fucking sexy to be covered up."

"You first. Want to see you."

Liam raises a brow, and my heart stumbles over a beat, imagining him bending me over his desk and smacking a palm to my bare ass.

Yeah. I might be into that.

After he pulls off his shirt, I clumsily remove mine. As I lean back in the chair again, he stares down hungrily at the shine of precum leaking from my slit. I bite my lip, squirming as he lowers his head to lick it up. He runs his tongue slowly along my shaft before he sucks me into his mouth.

Chaotic words tumble out of me. Demands. Praises. Curses. I'm not even aware of everything I'm saying, only that he's sucking my dick like he doesn't have a gag reflex.

"Gonna come," I say through gritted teeth.

Liam hums around my cock, and I explode, pulsing into his mouth with several unhinged groans. He doesn't waste a drop. He swallows what I have to give him, leaving me boneless and breathing heavily.

Sitting back on his heels, Liam's dark eyes glint. I've never seen anyone so poised after a blow job. He gracefully rises, brushing his fingers along my jaw.

He could ask me for the world, and I'd do everything in my power to give it to him.

"Let me do you," I beg.

His hand moves to his belt buckle and unhooks it. "You've got ten minutes until staff show up."

I grin, licking my lips. "Love me a good challenge."

Are you coming???

"We have a pool party to get to," I remind him.

Beau groans and flips onto his stomach. "Or we could go back to sleep."

"Stas is already there."

Somehow, I slept through her sneaking out this morning to go help her brother prepare. The two of them must have worn me out last night. Can't say I mind.

With a sudden burst of energy, Beau pops upright in bed. "Stas in a swimsuit. Oh, *hell* yes."

"That's the motivation you needed?"

"One hundred percent. Can you imagine it?"

"You don't think I've been looking at her for years?"

"Liam." Beau's excitement falters, prodding at something uncomfortable in my chest.

Where I was irritated by the interruption of my phone previously, I'm grateful for it now, saving me from having to delve into a conversation about my pathetic lack of self-worth and how it's kept me from pursuing anything serious with anyone. Including him.

The shit you learn about yourself in your thirties.

I snort at Hail's unhinged text message.

> Try and bail on our party, Liam. I'll hunt you down.

My amusement is cut short when Beau steps out of bed and stumbles into the nightstand, barely catching himself from falling to the floor.

Eyes snapping to him, I ask, "You good?"

He rubs a hand to his forehead. "Yeah. Must have stood up too fast."

I don't return to my text until Beau makes it to my closet safely with no more signs of unstable movements. Should I have fed him more last night? Should I have taken it easier on him when I was fucking him?

Beau struts back out in one of my sleeveless black band tees and a pair of striped swim trunks we bought him at the store after work last night. He's got his hat on backwards, that little patch of overgrown white hair popping out over the snaps.

My concern for him recedes when he flashes me a dimpled smile and turns to wiggle his ass at me. "Could have been yours this morning. Too late now. Apparently, we have a pool party to get to."

I lurch out of bed, rushing to get my arms around him. I knock his hat off and delve a hand into his wild fluff of hair, gripping it hard enough to pull him into a kiss.

"No more teasing," I say against his mouth, then I push him away before I lose control and dick him down so hard he walks funny the rest of the weekend.

Snatching his hat off the floor and holding it out to him, I say, "Thought you were ready to go?"

Eyes glittering, Beau grabs his hat. "I swear I'm gonna be rocking a boner all day."

We move to the kitchen and fill up a newly purchased cooler with a mixture of Coke, fruity seltzers, and beer.

Somehow, the simple act of preparing for a lazy day under the sun has me questioning if this is what normal feels like. I thought I wanted silence when I retired from music. Turns out it was a lie I force fed myself during the unpredictable years of my life.

I end up doing more staring than helping as Beau tears open bags of ice and dumps them into the cooler. He glances up at me with a frown. "Oh *no*. You had your opportunity. And we agreed no touching during the party."

Probably should have fucked him this morning for good measure. If only I'd woken up earlier...

We'd discussed our arrangement last night while tangled up in each other in my bed. Stas isn't ready to go public with this. I don't blame her. I'm not sure I'm ready either. I don't want outside influence or my shit reputation to taint us before we've had a chance to solidify a foundation.

Leaning down, I kiss him slowly. "Doesn't mean we can't flirt. Let's go, trouble."

As I speed toward Hail's house in my Pantera, Beau asks, "Are we *that* late?"

"No. Why?"

"Your driving. It's...a lot."

"I like to go fast."

"No shit. How many speeding tickets do you have?"

Tightening my hands on the wheel, I gun it to switch lanes between traffic. "Three."

"Woah. I expected way more. Cops are slacking."

A few cars litter the cul-de-sac outside Hail's house when we roll up. His house is the only one built so far at this end of the neighborhood, but give it another year and the neighborhood will be bursting at the seams.

Beau looks over the small ranch with a frown. "For metal gods, you two don't really know how to live the lifestyle, do you?"

"I've known Hail most of my life and still can't say I understand the eclectic workings of his mind."

Then again, I'm the one who made the sudden decision to retire from playing music to start up a recording studio. Seems we're both pretty unpredictable.

Beau chuckles at the welcome mat. *No thanks, we're good.* Hail told me all about how solicitors swarmed his house when he first moved in. Wonder if the mat's doing its job.

I bring my tattooed fist down on the black door, hot from the sun beating on it. Muffled shouting commences. No one comes to answer, so I burst in like I own the place.

"Liam mother fucking Beckner in the house!" Malek shouts from the open living area, an Xbox controller in his hands. His long, tan, lean body is on display, broken up only by a pair of neon blue swim trunks.

Griff crouches like a gargoyle on the arm of the sectional. When he sees me, he tosses his controller aside and charges at me. Leaping up, he attempts to hook an arm around my neck. It's a far jump, considering our height difference. I've probably got fifty pounds of muscle on him, too.

Catching him, I hold him off the ground like a toddler having a meltdown. His flailing comes with a smile. Angelic little blonde curls peek out of his black beanie. He kept it buzzed for so long, I almost forgot what his hair actually looked like.

"You're gonna put holes in Hail's drywall, asshole," I mumble.

Once I'm sure his bare feet are planted on the floor, I release him.

I expect another attack from Malek. Instead, he fist bumps Beau. "Hey, man. Good to see you again. You livin' in the Dallas area now?"

Beau's eyes dart over to me. "Nah. Just...uh...here for an extended visit."

My teeth clench together. I don't want to linger on the idea of him leaving, but I have to remember he has a house in Phoenix. And as much as he might believe his musical career is over, he has the talent to get back out there whenever he's ready.

"Sorry to hear about Lithos. You were the heart of that band," Malek says sincerely.

I study Beau for the slightest changes in his expression. He simply shrugs off the comment. "The break hasn't been so bad."

Malek finally turns to me and extends a hand. I blink down at it, expecting some sort of trick. "What the fuck is this, maturity?"

He flashes a wicked grin. "Someone had to grow up when dad retired from the band. Still can't believe you dropped out."

"Don't make me walk back out this door."

"Liam, noooo!" Malek lunges at me. I snap a hand to his head, keeping him away without much effort.

Griff smacks Malek on the arm. "Quit it with the clingy shit. You know he'll ghost us."

I frown. Yeah, the reputation I've earned isn't something I'm proud of.

Malek stalks off with a feigned attitude as Griff turns his focus to Beau. "You any good at Call of Duty?"

"Don't think I've played that one..."

Griff tugs him down the hall by the arm. "Great. We're getting our asses handed to us by a bunch of ten-year-olds."

While Beau gets sucked into video games, I haul the cooler into the kitchen where more people linger.

It should come as no surprise that my eyes fall on my best friend's sister first.

Fuck me.

Stas is sitting behind the tiny kitchen island, waves of golden hair flowing down her bare shoulders. She's wearing a red sundress that hugs her curves like it isn't enough of a punch to my gut just to exist in her presence.

Her pretty brown eyes slide up to meet mine, and I know today is going to test my willpower. Would it be so bad if I told everyone I was involved with the two of them?

Considering it's no secret among my bandmates that I fuck around, I doubt the news would be well-received.

"Liam," she greets, offering a shy smile.

My gaze falls to her matching red nails, and I feel the phantom of them clawing at my chest and back when I fucked her last night, right after she rode Beau to her first orgasm.

I'm flooded with the desire to stride across the room and fuse our bodies together. I'd ease a hand behind her neck and bring those full, pouty lips to mine. Hoist her up on that kitchen counter. Spread her out and bury my cock so deep in her body, she'd be sore for days once I'm done with her.

"Stasi." I strive for an uninterested tone.

Must not be convincing enough because Hail's watching me with furrowed brows. Yeah, he didn't miss me checking out his sister. Wouldn't be the first time. I wish I could promise him it would be the last.

Like the solid fucking friend he is, Hail moves to embrace me. He's one of the few humans whom I allow to touch me like this.

When he hangs on a little too long, I squeeze him hard enough to pop his back.

"Ah, fuck," he wheezes. "Alright, I get it."

Drawing back, I look him over. He looks good. He looks *happy*.

Hail's eyes flick to someone behind me, and I know from the way they shine with love, it can only be one person. I turn to take in my best friend's obsession—a dark-haired, tall, pretty male.

"How's it going?" I reach out to ruffle Z's mess of curls.

He gives me a soft smile in return. "Good, thanks."

We catch up on his time in London teaching music to kids. I tell him about the artists I'm working with in the studio.

And then my gaze instinctively drifts back to Stasi. She's walking the length of the pool in the backyard, every now and then dipping her toes in the water.

"Do you want a drink *before* or *after* I force you to grill?" Hail asks, cracking open the fridge. "I stocked up on Coke just for you."

"Brought my own, thanks. How you gonna coerce me into free labor now?"

Hail looks to Z for help.

"I told you I'd grill," Z answers in a quiet voice.

I move to grab the tray of meat Hail pulled out of the fridge. "You know I've got it covered."

"Oh, so you'd make *me* grill, but if Z offers to do it, you immediately volunteer," Hail complains.

Shaking my head, I grab a drink from the cooler and slip out the back door.

"Beckner!" Cora, one of Atonement's guitar techs, calls out, raising her beer in greeting.

I nod in her direction, expecting another conversation, but she's too wrapped up in Maria to wander over. There might be a spark of something there. Or maybe a companionship formed out of necessity since they have to deal with the chaos twins—Malek and Griff.

Either way, I get to watch Stasi uninterrupted from behind the grill.

Her gaze flicks my way, and she graces me with a warm smile. Then she begins a risky game of torture, starting with her tugging her dress over her head to reveal a sexy dark blue bikini.

My mouth goes dry. I watch in agony as she ties up her hair and begins applying sunscreen to her shoulders. I'm tempted to stalk over there and help, but I know the second I touch her it'll be game over. Even twenty feet away, I'm barely clinging to sanity.

I glance back at the house, certain I'm going to be found out. I snort when I catch Beau gaping at Stas through the living room windows. Shaking my head, I point toward the game he's supposed to be playing.

Not two minutes later, Beau appears at my side with a beer in hand. "I got booted. Apparently, zero kills isn't what Griff is looking for in a gaming partner. Pretty sure a literal infant called me a shit, too."

A low laugh escapes me. "Too distracted to perform, huh?"

Beau swigs from his Shiner Bock and swipes his mouth with the back of his hand. "How did you resist her for so long?"

"I was on the road. And when I was home, I kept myself distracted."

He leaves the conversation there, well-aware of the ways in which I entertained myself.

We supervise the grill, pretending we're not admiring Stas as she wades into the crystal waters.

Eventually, more of Atonement's crew flood into the backyard. Between chatting with them, I sneak glances at Stas and Beau. We exchange secret flirtations when we can. It's not something I've ever done before, but I'm appreciating the novelty of it.

For the first time since I came home, I can say I made the right decision by stepping down from playing guitar for Atonement.

Once the burgers and hot dogs are cooked, I place them on the table with other dishes people brought. Baked beans, chips and dips, homemade Rice Krispy treats, assorted fruit and veggies, and three kinds of salads.

I move over to where Beau's dragging off his shirt, giving his body the appreciation it deserves. He's not cut from hard work in the gym, but I don't mind. I love his softness. Love how his ass fills out those trunks. Love every patch of lighter skin decorating his tan body, too.

"Tone down the sex eyes," he murmurs, though his gaze drops to my shorts like he wishes he had x-ray vision. I'm about to call him out on it when he launches himself into the pool, splashing water everywhere. Screeches from the women gathered on the edge of the deep end have Malek and Griff running out as if summoned by the chaos. They immediately cannonball into the center of the pool.

When the afternoon heat gets to me, I tug off my shirt and wade into the pool.

"*Jesus.* Would you stop showing off?" Hail says, looking me over.

He's standing in the shallow end between Z's legs dangling into the water. Z hasn't shed his clothing, but the fact that he's even willing to approach water after what Hail told me about his past has me wanting to hug him.

"What else is he supposed to do in retirement besides lift weights and *fuck*?" Malek says.

Ignoring their chatter about my sex life, I float over to Beau and Stas. She's sitting on the edge, dripping water from the splash attack. Beau's got his arms rested on the hot pavement next to her thighs as he kicks his feet behind him in the water.

"Food's ready," I tell them.

"Mmm, I'm good right here," Beau replies, cracking an eye open to look up at Stas. Smiling, she turns his hat for him to shield his eyes from the harsh sun.

At one point, Beau climbs out of the pool to make us a plate of food to share. It's these considerate little actions that have my chest aching in new ways. The smiles and lingering eye contact. The gentle touches when we assume no one's watching. The silent promises we're making about the things we want to do to each other when we're no longer in public.

If life continued just like this, I could be happy.

And that's something I never thought I would be able to say.

"We're...figuring things out. No pressure."

She narrows her eyes at me. "How can I leave this place without certainty that you won't slip back into your hermit ways?"

I purse my lips. "My hermit ways?"

"You didn't have plans before these hot men came into your life."

Technically, Liam's always been in my life, but I won't argue that fact with her.

"Maybe I never told you about my plans."

"You didn't have any, dear." Iris pats my arm.

I let out a laugh. "You are something else."

"And *you* are something special. Don't you ever forget it."

The hollow ache of loss expands in my chest. What am I going to do without Iris in my life? Yeah, she's my patient, but she's also become a friend. A *good* one. A supportive one.

"I'm going to miss harassing you about your love life," Iris says.

It's my turn to reach out and pat her hand. "My love life really shouldn't be the highlight of your day."

She makes a show of looking around the room. "You see any flowers in here? Any cards or visitors lined up at the door?"

I scrunch up my nose. I haven't actually, and that makes me sad. I wasn't on shift when Iris was wheeled in, but I haven't noticed a single visitor in the weeks I've been working with her.

Eyes itchy and throat tight, I ask, "Where will you go when your time here is done?"

"Back to assisted living with the rest of the forgotten old farts."

Her bony fingers smooth over the sheets of her bed as she pretends not to care.

"Would it be overstepping if I came to visit you there?" I ask.

She wiggles into a more comfortable position on her bed and shuts her eyes. "I'll take it personally if you don't."

Giving her hand one more little squeeze, I fetch her a cup of ice water and turn on her westerns.

As I'm logging notes and reviewing charts at the shared workstation, my phone buzzes with a message. I debate not checking it—I have a growing number of voicemails from both of my parents I refuse to listen to. I made the mistake of playing one of them a few days ago in which I was being lumped in with Hail as a sinner if I supported his "gayness."

Technically, he's bi. And technically, they're ignorant assholes who would disown me in a heartbeat if they knew I was dating two bisexual men.

It's an inevitability I'll have to face, but right now I'm playing the avoidance game.

After I skipped out on a recent family cookout, Max, my older brother, texted me to make sure I still had a heartbeat—a very uncharacteristic thing for him to do.

However, there are people I *do* want to hear from, so I give in to the persistent buzzing of my phone.

I break into a smile at the photo of Beau in the studio, his hair piled atop his head from running a hand through it and his dimples out to play. Liam's visible in the background, leaned over his digital mixer, attention focused on whatever track he's perfecting.

> Sleepover at Liam's tonight?

> I might be able to pencil that in.

I go to set my phone down, and it rings again, this time with a call.

"*Two* phone calls from Liam Beckner in one lifetime? I'm starting to believe you actually enjoy talking," I tease.

"Mmm. I enjoy conversations with the right people."

"So only me, my brother, and Beau?"

"There are a few others, but you three are definitely my favorite."

A soft laugh slips free.

"We'll see you tonight, then."

Like I would say no to anything that man offered. "I'll be there."

"And angel?" His voice drops into a huskier tone that speeds up my pulse.

"Yeah?"

"You had better be naked in my bed by the time we get home."

Hot blood rushes through me. I check around me, answering in a whisper. "What will you do if I'm not?"

"Punish you."

I've got my keys in my hand the second the clock signals the end of my shift.

To say I rush out of work would be an understatement. I don't bother stopping by my apartment. I kind of hate the place. I thought I'd feel better about it after shoving those unpacked boxes into closets to hide them. Turns out the empty space just makes me feel worse about the fact that I'm nowhere near being able to afford a house.

Hopping out of my car at Liam's townhouse, a loud bark startles me. Brown eyes stare up at me from a fluffy black body standing on Liam's grass. He looks like some kind of golden retriever mix, but I'm no expert. I've never owned a pet. My parents said they were too messy, and messes weren't permitted in the Koval home.

Seems my brother has been included in that category now.

Save a spot for me, big bro.

Truth is, I'm the messiest of my two siblings. And when I finally summon up the words I need to say to my parents, I fear it will be a twenty-year hurricane of emotions I've bottled up because I knew other kids had it worse.

Liam had it worse.

My fucked up idea of family revolved around that core thought. I had a roof over my head. I had food in the fridge. I had clean clothes and school supplies. I had parents who didn't raise their fists at me.

But now I understand that their support is conditional. It doesn't matter how many smiling family portraits hang on their walls. Ugliness can still fester under the surface.

The dog sits down next to my shoes, his thick black tail wagging at an impressive rate. Dried mud clings to its fur like it's spent some time rolling around in mud puddles.

I lower myself down to his level. "Hi, buddy. Where's your home?"

The dog enthusiastically pushes its head into my hand, and I laugh. "You attention-starved, too?"

I'm not sure how long I sat there petting the dog. Enough time to decide to clean him up and take him to a vet to see if he has a chip. Surely someone's missing this friendly guy. He's too sweet *not* to have a home.

When I open up the door to my SUV, the dog backs up and whines.

"It's okay. I'm just going to take you to my place so we can wash you."

He lies down in the grass, wedging his head between his front legs.

"Okay. *Shit*," I mutter, glancing at Liam's townhouse. We've covered it in mud once before, and he didn't kick us out. Plus, he told me to make myself comfortable while he and Beau finish up work. Don't think he meant bringing a random dog inside his house...but *semantics*.

Patting my thighs, I lead the dog around the side of the house to the back door where Liam keeps his spare key. "Come on, boy. We gotta be quick about this."

I usher him inside, cursing as he leaves muddy footprints on the wood floors. Not sure I've ever been accused of making good decisions. I'll speed mop later.

Nails clack on the floor as the dog chases me upstairs to the main bathroom shower. As I turn on the detachable shower head, he sits down and wags his tail, looking up at me with far too much trust.

"You're a good boy, aren't you?" I coo, scratching behind his ears.

I give him more pets and encouragement as I wash him. At one point, while I'm reaching for the bottle of Dawn dish soap I'd snatched from under the kitchen sink, he shakes water all over me. Bubbles get into my eyes, and I have to take the sprayer to my face.

"Stas?" Liam's voice echoes through the house.

Panic floods me.

"You weren't supposed to be here when he got home," I whisper to the dog. He simply nuzzles his wet snout against my arm.

I debate locking the bathroom door, but I doubt I'll be able to sneak the dog by Liam when I'm finished cleaning him up.

Before I can come up with a plan, the bathroom door opens. I'm met with Liam's confused face. I'm fully clothed, covered in mud and bubbles, hugging a random scruffy dog in his shower.

"What the fuck is that?" he asks.

It's the closest to upset I've seen Liam, but even with the evident annoyance on his face, he manages to speak in his normal, calm, low tone.

I'm not sure it's healthy that he rarely lets go. No one should hold everything in all the time.

"How did that get in here?" I say weakly, glancing down at the dog.

The dog wriggles out of my arms, covering me in another layer of bubbles. It pushes open the glass shower door and sits down in front of Liam, trembling with excitement.

That's right. Win him over, boy.

No, I shouldn't be thinking like that. With how well-behaved the dog seems, some nice family is probably missing him right now.

Liam stares daggers at the dog as it whimpers for his attention. "Why is this thing in my house?"

"I think he might be lost."

Liam continues his staring contest with the dog. With each little tap of its paws on the tiles, I see him losing his resolve.

"Do you think he belongs to one of your neighbors?" I ask.

"Haven't seen any of them with a dog like this."

He lowers into a squat, reaching out to scratch the dog under the chin. The dog launches itself forward, and Liam ends up catching him in his arms with a grunt. I bite down on my bottom lip to hide a smile.

"Hello?" Beau pokes his head in the bathroom door.

The dog clumsily jumps over Liam's shoulder to attack Beau with sloppy kisses.

"Woah. Hey there." Beau laughs as he pats the dog's bubbled head. "When did you get a pet?"

Liam's gaze cuts to me. "I didn't."

Shrinking, I mumble, "I'm sorry. I'll clean up. I was going to take him to the vet, but now that I think about it, there's probably not a place open this late…"

Liam steps into the shower with me, ringed fingers gripping my jaw and tilting it up. "Don't do that. Don't ever cower to me."

"I…" Swallowing, I nod. "Yeah. Okay."

"The thought of ever scaring you…"

I stretch up to cover his mouth with my own. "You don't scare me, Liam. Promise."

He pecks another kiss to my lips and stands up.

"I'm guessing we want this guy back in there?" Beau asks, barely containing the wiggly, soaked dog in his arms.

"I would prefer that, yes," Liam replies.

Beau places the dog in the shower. Liam acts as a barrier for the glass door, but the dog seems content to run between us and bite at the water.

By the time we've got him clean, we're soaked through. Liam peels off his shirt and drops it onto the floor with a loud smack.

"I vote for the dog to stay," Beau comments, drinking Liam in.

I keep my mouth shut since I'm not sure I'm in the clear with Liam yet.

"Let's go, dog," Liam orders.

The dog follows him willingly out of the bathroom, and Beau turns that bright smile on me, water dripping from the ends of his hair.

"Hey, sweetheart."

Butterflies take flight in my chest. "Hi, Beau."

He moves closer to wrap me up and kiss my neck. "We should probably get out of these wet clothes."

Smiling, I step away and lift my arms over my head. Blue eyes glitter as he grins back, moving his hands to the hem of my shirt. Heat spreads beneath my skin as he peels it from my body.

He caresses me with soft touches and kisses before dropping to his knees and helping me shimmy out of my shorts. His fingers sink into the soft flesh of my backside. He tugs me closer so he can kiss me over my lace underwear.

Once I'm naked, I return the favor. Undressing him, I kiss every patch of vitiligo and freckle I can find on his body.

Pressed together, we make out lazily under the stream of water until it runs cold enough to have us shivering. Then it's an all out race to Liam's closet to steal his clothes.

And to think, weeks ago I was afraid of this place.

A shadow falls over me as I'm rifling through Liam's dresser drawers for a pair of sweats with a string tie. When I look toward the source, my pulse skyrockets at the sight of a looming, half-naked, tattooed figure in the doorway, blotting out most of the natural light from the bedroom.

Liam's expression is ominous. "No clothes."

Beau gladly drops the towel barely clinging to his waist. I remove my hand from Liam's drawer, prepared to beg him for forgiveness and a little tempted to ask if he kicked the dog out. Somehow, I can't see him doing that, though.

"I was clear about my expectations," Liam says, fiery gaze searing into me.

My cheeks flush as I recall his words from our call. *You had better be naked in my bed by the time we get home.*

His eyes move to the hand I've got clutched around my towel. Slowly, he walks over and tugs it free. Cold air nips at my bare skin, but I'm hot all over from the way he's looking at me.

"On your knees, angel."

Wide-eyed, I ask, "Right here?"

"Right fucking here."

Swallowing, I lower my knees to the hardwood floor where I've left a puddle of water. Liam brushes his fingers along my cheek. Then he tips my head up so I'm forced to stare back into pitch-black, hungry eyes.

"Bottom drawer of my dresser, Beau. Take out the rope."

"Say the word mercy and this stops. Understood?"

She nods, blinking those thick lashes up at me. Fuck, she's so submissive. She *wants* to give up control, even with the nervous tremble of her body.

I offer her little touches to help soothe her. A stroke of my fingers through her thick hair. A touch of my rings along her goose bumped skin. A brush of my thumb along the cupid's bow of her upper lip.

No matter where my body is positioned, she instinctively leans toward me like I'm the sun she orbits.

Sweeping locks of hair off her shoulder, I lean down to bring my mouth to the shell of her ear. "You want to be good for me. Don't you?"

I smirk when she closes her eyes and shudders.

"Yes." She's even quieter this time, the word barely breathed into existence.

My gaze lifts to Beau as he grips his erection. The urge is there to tell him hands off. Tonight is about teaching *her* a lesson. Edging him in the process is just a bonus.

Moving to stand behind her, I tangle a hand in her hair and tug her head back until she's looking up at me from her knees. Her trust shouldn't be such a turn on, but I'm already achingly hard.

I stroke a thumb along her cheekbone. "But you misbehaved tonight, didn't you?"

Her lips part. No sound comes out. I lower myself to her other side and drag my mouth up her neck. She's so warm, and she always smells so fucking good. I can't help but feather kisses along her skin, enjoying the way her pulse quickens beneath my lips.

I want to crawl inside her veins and spread through every inch of her body. I want to *possess* her.

Looping the rope around her wrists, I pull them together behind her back and form the first knot.

"Angel. *Answer me.*"

She squirms in my hold. "I got distracted. The puppy dog eyes, Liam..."

"No admission of guilt, hmm?"

Wrapping a hand around her nape, I thrust her forward so her right cheek presses flat against the floor and her ass lifts into the air. I spend a moment in awe of her perfect body, smoothing my palm down her spine.

When I get to the dimples in her lower back, I gather up the extra slack of the rope and thread it between her legs, resting it along one lip of her pretty cunt. Leaning over to kiss her shoulder, I pull the rope snug. She gasps, and I grin wickedly.

"Say the word and we stop."

"Don't stop," she whispers.

I wind the rope around her left thigh and shin several times, securing them with knots in a bent position. I repeat the pattern on her other side, effectively keeping her face down, ass up.

"Come here, Beau," I instruct.

He wastes no time moving behind us where he can better appreciate the view of the rope spreading her. Groaning, he squeezes his shaft. "Sometimes you scare me."

I won't disclose how many times I've practiced this. That I could knot him from head-to-toe and make him come so hard he blacks out. We'll save that for another night.

Right now, an angel is begging to be ruined.

Stasi tries to wiggle as I flatten a palm on her back. "Are you ready to admit your mistake now?"

"*Liam,*" she pleads.

I slide my hand down the length of the rope to tease a finger over her clit. "I'm right here."

She moans and tries to writhe in pleasure, but the tight knots keep her secured in place. Slowly, I circle her little bundle of nerves. She cries out.

"...misbehaved. I'm sorry. Liam...just...*please*..."

Hauling her up onto her knees, I kiss the hinge of her jaw.

"Beau. I want you to fuck her mouth."

Beau groans. "Fuck, *yes*. Is that what you want, sweetheart? You want to suck me off?"

Her head bobs. "I want to."

Cradling one side of her face, he steps in front of her and feeds her his cock. As she moans around him, his head drops back. "*Fuck*. You are so good to me. Just like that, baby. You're doing so good."

I could sit back and watch the show. I get off on denying myself pleasure while others chase it, knowing I'll be the one to finish them off. To make their eyes roll back into their heads and their bodies go soft.

But I'm at my limit already.

Loosening the knots around Stasi's legs, I keep only her wrists bound. "Tell me, angel. Do you want to be fucked from both ends? You want both of us to fill you up?"

She moans again around a mouthful of Beau. I smirk at the way Beau tenses up, then position myself closer behind her.

"Undo my belt," I order.

Bound hands claw for me. Eventually, she gets my belt undone and works on the button and zipper. When she frees my cock, she pushes her ass toward me.

"Eager for something?" I taunt, smacking one round cheek.

Beau pulls his cock out. "Tell him, baby. Tell him what you want."

"Oh, *god*," she gasps. "*You*. Want you."

He fills her mouth once more as I grab her hips and glide my cock through her slickness. Lining our bodies up, I thrust deep inside her, basking in her choked off sounds of pleasure.

I had planned on dragging this out, but the whimper of an animal outside my locked bedroom door has me suddenly remembering there's a fucking dog running amok in my house, and that's a bit of a concern for me.

I pound into her hard, using a hand in her hair to force her to swallow more of Beau's length. Not once does she tap out, even when I pop her off his dick so she can gulp air.

Pressure builds in my spine at how wrecked they both look already. We're going to have to work on our endurance.

Keeping my strokes short and deep, I move a hand to Stasi's pussy, applying pressure with my palm as my fingers circle her clit. I know she's close when her body coils up.

"Come for us, precious," I murmur, biting her neck.

Her strangled cries on Beau's cock have his hips stuttering. I hold her head as their orgasms rip through them. The thought of her swallowing him down has my balls tightening up. I slam into her one last time before I spill.

"Fuckkk. That was...Stasi, sweetheart, are you okay?" Beau asks, taking her face in both of his hands.

She manages a weak nod while I free the knots binding her wrists. Beau's there to catch her wrung out body in his arms. He's entirely capable of giving her the aftercare she needs.

I hate that I wasn't able to give him that in the past.

Then again, he typically passed out cold after I'd had my way with him, allowing me to slip out like a ghost.

Beau carries her from the closet as I stow away the rope. I hear the splash of water in the tub I've never used and question whether or not to intervene on their time together.

What do I bring to the table besides sex?

About to sneak off to the guest room to shower, Beau appears in front of me. He attempts to scoop me up bridal style. I chuckle at his pathetic efforts.

Finally giving up, he reaches for my hand and interlocks our fingers. "We need you."

Something itches in my chest as I let him pull me into the bathroom. Stas is sitting in the half-filled tub, arms wrapped around her bent knees, and those big brown eyes tinged with sadness that wasn't there moments ago.

Well, that won't fucking do.

Switching into protective mode, I step into the tub. Hot water laps at my skin as I draw her between my legs, resting her against my chest.

"We've got you, angel," I murmur, petting her hair.

Beau nestles himself behind her, peppering her shoulders and neck with delicate kisses.

"Too much tonight?" I ask.

She's quiet for a while, tracing light circles on my pec with her fingers. "No."

"You're always in control, you know that? Even if you want to pretend you're not."

"I know, Liam. I trust you. I promise."

"Then talk to me. Why are you sad?"

She tucks her head beneath my chin to hide. I wrap my arms around her shoulders and hold her.

Is she lying about being pushed over the edge? It wouldn't be the first time she's shoved aside concern for herself to please others.

Beau's eyes meet mine, shimmering with concern. "Baby, you can talk to us."

"Yeah," she whispers, nodding. "I liked what we did. More than I should, I think. I've not felt...good with others like I do with either of you. I've not felt like any of what I wanted...*sexually* was normal."

Anger sparks in my chest. "Did someone say that bullshit to you?" I demand.

Her fingernails press into my skin, and then she taps her forehead against my collarbone a couple of times like she needs to regulate herself. "It's in the past. Kids in college were assholes. I thought they were friends. Turns out a few of them shared things about me. Private things. I got labeled. I believe the correct term is slut shamed."

My temper flares. "Is that why you transferred schools?"

"And switched majors. Obviously, I don't regret it now, but at the time I hated myself for running away. I let them get to me."

My temper flares higher. I knew something had been bothering her back then. Something beyond normal family issues. Hail and I had flown home to visit her over spring break when she stopped replying to his messages. We'd only had one day with her before we had to jet off to another city for a show. Now, I regret not drilling her for answers.

But if I had known how people were treating her, I'm certain I would have ended up in jail with multiple assault charges.

Warm tears splatter on my chest as she returns to tracing my tattoos. "I let everyone get to me. Not just when I was younger. I didn't stick up for Hail last Thanksgiving when my parents were being horrible to him. Did he tell you that? I invited him, pretending everything would be fine when I *knew* better. He's always protecting me from them, and I couldn't return the favor. Not even once."

Stroking her back, I let her keep venting. I want all of that shit from her past expelled from her. She's carried the toxicity long enough.

"I know I need to cut ties with my parents. This isn't what a family should be. I'm just being weak. I don't want to be a disappointment. More than that, I really don't want to end up alone."

Her words slice through me like a hot blade. I find some fucked up solace in the fact that I was never seeking acceptance from my dad like Hail and Stasi were from their parents. I knew *exactly* where I stood with him at all times. No confusion about it. Step out of line? Get beat. Breathe wrong? Get beat. Ace a test? Get beat for being a smartass.

The Koval kids were subjected to mental warfare. They were made to believe approval was the equivalent of love.

"You are far from weak, Anastasia," I say firmly. "You are not *wrong* for the things you like. And Hail has never blamed you for not speaking up. Most importantly, you will never be alone. Not when you have me."

Sensing Beau's stunned gaze on me, I add, "Both of you have me. For as long as you want me."

Stasi snakes her arms around my waist and squeezes me.

Beau lifts a hand to brush a tear from her cheek. "Next time we'll let Liam tie me up and make me cry, okay?"

This gets an exasperated laugh from her. "Okay."

A whimpering sound breaks the intense moment, turning our heads to the bedroom.

"The dog," Stas utters.

Freeing herself from my arms, she wipes away the rest of her tears and leaps from the tub with newfound energy. I have to laugh as she rips a towel from the vanity and rushes out of the bathroom.

Beau grins. "That dog isn't going anywhere."

"Unless it already has a home."

His expression crumples. "Suppose I should hang around a little longer. You know, for emotional support."

"Suppose you should."

But Stasi's words are stuck in my head. I don't want her to feel alone. Even if she decides she doesn't want to be romantically involved, that won't stop me from supporting her as a friend.

I want to be at her Saturday morning yoga classes. I want to drink overpriced juices and steal the strawberries from her plate. I want to snuggle on the couch with her and have her womansplain football to me while I fuck up the rules on purpose just to get a rise out of her.

I want to take her on more dates and fall asleep with her in my arms.

Swallowing becomes an effort. Why do we struggle with involuntary actions when we start thinking about them? Are emotions contagious? Because now I'm all up in my feels, and I don't know how to escape them.

Lifting a hand to my forehead, I rub at the spot that's throbbing. A hand catches my wrist. When I crack my eyes open, Liam's standing between my spread legs wearing a frown.

"Another headache?"

"Probably lack of caffeine or sleep," I mumble.

But there's the creeping suspicion that something more is going on. Something worse than migraines. The universe seems to enjoy kicking me while I'm down. Why not throw health issues on top of cutting my musical career short?

Liam drops down onto the couch beside me. I quickly close out of my phone, not ready for that conversation.

"Beau."

My pulse leaps. "Hmm?"

"Take the rest of the day off. Go home and rest."

"Nah. I'd rather hang out here."

Liam takes the shake cup out of my hand and sets it on the floor. He repositions me so my head rests on his warm thigh. Emma peeks over from her computer, flashing a quick smile at the two of us. She makes a heart symbol with her hands.

"You can sleep right here," Liam says. "We've got some downtime."

"What if I refuse?" I waggle my brows.

Eyes glinting with humor, he lowers his voice so only I can hear. "You just want to be punished."

I smile at him. "So what if I do?"

He strokes his thumb over one of my dimples. "Then you were made for me."

My heart stutters. I shut my eyes as he explores my features, brushing fingers along the line of my jaw and over the patch of lighter skin I hide under my hair.

I'm satisfied to lie here and let him touch me as long as he wants to.

One second I'm humming in satisfaction, and then next I'm opening my eyes in confusion to an eerily quiet studio, the only light source coming from Liam's open office door.

Fuck. Did I fall asleep? How the hell did I manage that with musicians coming in and out?

I press the heels of my hands into my eyes. *Why am I still so tired?*

When I drop my hands away, the room lurches to the side, and my entire body feels like it's off balance. I cling to the edge of the couch until the spinning sensation fades.

Must be the massive amount of sugar I consumed and the lack of dinner.

I pull out my phone to check the time. There's a missed text from Stasi.

> Did you know it's Liam's birthday today???

With a surge of anger, I shove to my feet. Another dizzy spell hits me as I stumble into Liam's office and find it empty. He left the spare set of keys on his desk with a note to lock up if I decide to come home tonight.

I type out a rapid message to Stasi and send it.

> WTF. No, he didn't tell me shit.

At least I bought him ice cream. Doesn't make me any less pissed that he didn't tell me.

I message Liam.

> Am I allowed to call you an asshole on your birthday?

He leaves me on read. My fingers fumble over the keys enough times that I get frustrated with a response and pocket my phone.

Snatching the keys off the desk, I lock up and storm toward the Porsche in the dark parking lot, prepared to give him a piece of my mind when I get to his house.

And yeah, maybe my mouth and ass, too.

Stasi's SUV is parked in the driveway when I pull up. A pang of longing hits me out of nowhere.

No one will be waiting for me at my house back in Phoenix.

Sure, I miss the dry heat and the mountains. I have fond memories there. And yeah, my dad's there...

But Phoenix doesn't have *them*.

Even if Noah called to offer me a second chance with Lithos, even if my headaches and numbness and dizziness magically went away, I don't like the idea of going back out on tour. I've felt that same rush of excitement working with artists in the studio and spending time with Liam and Stasi as I used to get performing in front of fans.

I should have a talk with Liam.

But first, I'm gonna kick his ass for keeping a secret about his *fucking* birthday.

The patio door is wide open when I stomp inside the house, a pleasant evening breeze rolling in. I spot Stasi out in the grassy area throwing a frisbee for the dog Liam agreed to house temporarily when no chip was found at the vet.

In other words, he's now the owner of a pet she's secretly named Cosmo.

Liam's absent from the outdoor activities, so I carry on with my search. Spinning around toward the stairs, I bump right into his hard chest.

"*You*," I spit out, squaring up to him.

"*Me*."

"You are a grade A asshole."

Liam's expression remains neutral. "Old news."

I try to stand my ground, but he manages to push me back a step. And then another. My ass bumps up against something hard. Whipping my head around, I frown at the dining table that wasn't there before, accompanied by six gray upholstered chairs.

Nope. I will *not* be distracted by his random furniture purchases. His recent behavior cannot be analyzed for trends at the moment.

I jab a finger at his chest. "Why didn't you wake me up? And why didn't you tell me it's your birthday?"

His eyes crackle with amusement. "Why does it matter?"

"Because we should celebrate."

Liam crowds me, and I struggle to hold on to my anger.

"Yeah? How?" His seductive tone has my blood racing and my cock stirring.

"Well, that's up to you to decide. What do you want?"

He seals our bodies together. My stomach muscles spasm as they struggle to keep me somewhat upright against his weight as he leans into me. "You really want to know?"

I swallow. "Yeah."

Lowering his head, he kisses my neck. "I want you to run, Beau."

My heart stops. When Liam steps back, it takes a few moments for his words to trickle through my sluggish brain. I can see the hard outline of his cock in his jeans.

Oh, hell yeah.

I take off, darting into the formal dining room, half expecting to bump into new furniture there, too.

Liam's house isn't big, but it's laid out in a square with connecting rooms, so I have somewhat of a fighting chance. And if he starts gaining on me, I can just slip out the back door and find somewhere to hide. Maybe in some bushes. Maybe behind Stasi or the dog.

The thought of Liam claiming me in the grass under the stars has blood rushing to my cock. But as much as I want to get caught, I'm enjoying our game of chase.

So much for my anger.

I manage to dodge Liam's capture for several laps, only because he's not ready to catch me. My breaths are heavy. My head is pounding, but my need for him to fuck me takes priority. I'll forget about the pain when he's pounding me into submission.

A dark laugh echoes through the house. "Sounds like you need to do some cardio."

"Yeah, fuck that," I shout back.

Glancing behind me, I stumble. Liam's stalking toward me without a shirt, those lethal muscles flexing. He's got one hand wrapped around his studded belt to rip it free from his black pants.

Shit. I'm half panicked I'm going to come without even being touched.

Liam breaks into a run, and my heart nearly explodes from my chest. I make it three strides before his arm hooks me. He cradles the side of my head with a hand as he takes me down.

Still, the sudden jolt of his body colliding with mine has my vision blurring. One second, I register that I'm on the floor.

And the next, everything fades to black.

I drop to my knees and help ease Beau onto his side. Stasi holds his head this time. He doesn't appear to be conscious as she runs her fingers through his hair.

Each passing second feels like an hour at this point. This can't be normal, right? I have to imagine Stasi would be freaking out, too, if this wasn't something she was trained to deal with.

"Can you call for an ambulance?" she asks.

I dig out my phone and dial 9-1-1. Soon, I'm rattling off details to the emergency responder, but the words feel all wrong. Almost like lies.

Can you tell me what happened?

I was climbing the fence in our yard and fell.

Told the little shit not to do that, but he doesn't like to listen.

I shut my eyes to force out the vision of my dad hovering over my hospital bed, spewing lies about my broken fingers.

"We have an ambulance on the way. Stay on the line with me. Make sure his airway is clear, and he's not at risk of hurting himself."

I register the words. However, I'm frozen to the spot. No amount of internal commands will get my body to move. To gather Beau into my arms and assure him that I've got him.

"How long has the seizure been going on?" the responder asks.

"I don't know."

I have no fucking clue what I'm doing. I didn't when I found my dad dead, and I don't now.

So, I continue to watch Beau suffer, his hands clenching and limbs jerking while the responder asks for updates I can't give because I'm not sure I exist in my body anymore.

Fear sinks its claws deep into my ribs and cleaves me open. I don't want to lose him. I never wanted to lose him.

What if he doesn't come back to me?

Beau's muscles finally relax, and his eyelids droop closed. He groans as he tries to lift his head off Stasi's lap. It drops back onto her thighs like it's too heavy for his neck. A simple command minutes ago that's now an impossible feat.

"...messed everything up," he slurs, fighting to push himself upright once more.

My lungs constrict to the point of suffocation. I did mess everything up.

"I'm so sorry, Beau," I murmur.

He blinks his eyes open, seeking me out in the dark, empty room. His lips part but words stick in his mouth, held there by a fog of confusion he's fighting to shake.

I don't move closer. I'm terrified I'll hurt him more. I'm not built for this shit.

"This is *not* your fault, Liam," Stasi says in a firm tone. "You were both playing."

My face contorts into a grimace. Fear is everywhere now. Reflected back at me from two pairs of worried eyes. Almost like they've been bracing for when I decided I couldn't do this anymore. Like they've been waiting for me to break them.

Beau's words circulate in my head. *Have you ever tried?*

Fuck. I'm trying, Beau. I'm here. I'm here, but I'm no good for you.

The doorbell rings. I have enough of a mind to rush over to open it. Paramedics flood in with a stretcher. I hang up with the dispatcher, realizing I haven't been responding to her.

I stand in the entry hall, unable to do more than exist in a cloud of self-disgust.

When they haul Beau past me, I avoid meeting anyone's eyes. Shouldn't they be questioning me about his injuries? That's what happened the first time the police showed up at my house and discovered me standing over my dad's corpse. They'd ushered me out onto the porch and wrapped a blanket around me until the shock wore off and I could speak. It was the first time I'd come clean about the abuse. I thought it was the worst moment of my life.

But this...this right here is so much worse.

A soft hand touches my arm, drawing my gaze down to a pair of watery brown eyes. Something twists inside my chest. Stasi was perfectly collected during Beau's seizure, but now I can see her calm start to unravel, slipping out from where I imagine she compartmentalizes things at work.

"Will you talk to me?" she whispers.

Jaw clenching, I take a step away from her. "You should go with him."

She doesn't budge. I don't want to argue with her over this, but the idea of climbing into the ambulance has me wanting to claw my skin off.

I curl my hands into fists, digging my nails into my palms.

What if I damaged him beyond repair?

Stasi moves into my space, determination on her face. She embraces me, squeezing me tight around the waist and placing her ear against my rapidly beating heart.

Caving to her touch, I burrow my face into her neck and let her hold me until I feel somewhat calmer.

"I'll follow in my car," I say quietly.

"Promise?"

I draw away from her. "Text me the hospital if I lose you."

She assesses me with a frown before kissing my cheek and hurrying out the front door.

I brace my weight against the wall, practicing deep breaths. I'm ashamed of how long I stand there with my car keys in my hand, debating locking the doors and staying put.

Ashamed I almost let fear win out like it always does.

found a small mass in your left frontal lobe. The culprit for your recent symptoms. I'd say your wrestling match was a blessing in disguise, Beau. Some patients don't realize they have a tumor for years."

Brows burrowing, I drop my gaze to a frayed string along the hem of the shitty hospital blanket. At first, I'm not sure I heard her right, but then I really don't feel like asking her to repeat herself.

A fucking *tumor*? When did I agree to let something like that take up residence in my head?

"So, what does that mean?" I ask, voice cracking.

"It means surgery, Beau. The good news is I've performed hundreds of successful surgeries just like this one. I'm hopeful I'll be able to remove all of the tumor."

My blood runs cold. "Surgery. Like...*now*?"

"As soon as possible would be preferable, yes," Dr. Malone replies.

Pressure builds behind my eyes. I shake my head. "I don't live here. I was just visiting some friends. Wait, what happens if you *can't* remove all of it?"

I haven't even had a chance to record anything. I don't want the last thing I produced to be a failed album with Lithos.

She gives me an encouraging smile. "Then we put together a treatment plan to take care of the rest. Sometimes we need a little help from chemo or radiation. We won't know for certain until pathology has a look at the tumor. Usually, it takes one to two weeks for them to get back to us after surgery."

I nod like I understand a single thing she just told me.

The doctor claps her hands on her thigh as if to disperse the bad vibes. "Where are you from, Beau?"

"Phoenix."

She perks up. "I spent a summer there during my undergrad. Actually, I may have a recommendation for a neurosurgeon in that area if he has availability. Why don't I give you some time to process while I make a phone call? You can rest or visit with your friends. They've been anxiously pacing the halls. The tall, dark, and handsome one is causing quite the stir with the nurses."

My heart stutters. That has to be Liam, right? I mean, I knew Stasi was here. She rode in the ambulance.

I guess I wasn't expecting Liam to come after the way he reacted to my seizure.

"Okay. Yeah. Do you mind letting them in?"

While I'm not ready to tell them any of this, I'd appreciate their comfort. Maybe after a quick visit, I can convince them to go home and go to bed. They both have work in the morning. There's no reason for them to stay.

"Of course," Dr. Malone says kindly, rising to her feet. "And Beau? You have every right to seek out treatment elsewhere, but I want to assure you that you would be in good hands if you decide to have the surgery here."

I can't even manage a nod. When she's gone, I cover my face with my hands and work to bottle up the messy emotions swirling around in my stupid, broken head. I don't even know what the *fuck* radiation is. It doesn't sound like something a human should be able to survive.

Soft fingers touch my forearm. I drop my hands and wince at the bright fluorescent lights. I didn't even hear anyone come in.

Once my eyes adjust, I'm greeted by the vision of a blonde-haired, beautiful angel.

"Hi, sweetheart."

"Hi, Beau."

Her smile makes me sad. I don't want her to be sad. Lifting a hand, I brush it along her cheek, ignoring the tug of the IV taped to my arm. She turns her head to kiss my palm.

"You know, you don't have to do this," I say quietly.

"Do what?"

My brows pinch together. "Be here."

"Why wouldn't I be here?"

I give a shrug while my heart begins to crumble into tiny pieces. "Because this doesn't have anything to do with you."

Her expression twists into something pained. "How so?"

"You didn't ask for this. I just waltzed into your lives like I belonged there. I hung around because I wanted the two of you to be together. And then I got selfish. So unbelievably selfish."

Stasi recoils. "I'm going to blame this madness on the seizure. Otherwise, I might actually get mad at you."

I drop my arm onto the bed in defeat. Eventually, Stasi shakes her frustration and drapes her warm body over my chest. I do my best to soak it in, breathing in her citrus scent. I want to remember every detail of the summer we spent together when I'm back in Phoenix on my own.

To have fucking surgery.

She doesn't need to share the weight of this burden. She doesn't need to hear about how jacked up I am on the inside.

"You're so sweet, you know that?" I say, kissing the top of her head.

She sniffles. "You both keep saying that."

"No tears, baby." I squeeze her tighter, the burning sensation behind my eyes growing. As much as I want to curse some higher being for this situation, I made the mistake of coming to Texas. I brought this sickness into their lives.

Choked up, I ask, "Is Liam here?"

"He's taking a walk through the hospital. He's upset, Beau. I don't know what to do. I don't know how to reach him."

Something like a rock sinks in my gut. Liam's terror was the first thing I saw when I regained consciousness on the dining room floor. He clearly blames himself, but had we not collided, I would have gone on longer not knowing what was going on in my head.

I get the sense Liam wants to cast himself as a villain, even though he's done nothing to earn the poisonous crown. For anyone brave enough to stare into the dark pits of his eyes, they would see the truth of his nature. The tender soul he hides away.

"Beau. Do they know why you had a seizure?" Stasi asks.

The door opens once more, saving me from having to lie. My stomach turns over as Liam hesitantly approaches my bed, a duffle bag clutched in one hand, his shoulders hanging low.

He looks miserable. Like a metal god who fell off his throne.

I can't put them through this, even if I'm scared of battling a tumor on my own.

"This is not your fault," I tell him.

His eyes skim over the machines I'm hooked up to. "Looks a hell of a lot like it to me."

"I've been having head issues for weeks. You *know* that. The seizure was probably inevitable. People have them, Liam."

A muscle in his jaw ticks. His chin drops, loose tendrils of inky hair hiding his face.

"Please don't be stubborn about this. *Fuck*, will you come here?"

He doesn't move, and all the worry I'd been fending off comes rushing over me. Why would he want me like this? Why would anyone want to take care of me after I have my head cut open? No one is gonna sign up for all the appointments and whatever shitstorm of symptoms "treatment" might bring.

Liam has a business to run. Stasi has real patients to tend to.

And then there's the possibility that I won't get better. What if one surgery isn't enough? What if this becomes an uphill battle for the rest of my life?

Will it even be a long life?

Ugh. I wish I could get high. Even if I could sneak it into the hospital, I'm not sure I could trust my mouth under the influence. Look at how my conversation with Noah turned out. I ruined that friendship.

Liam drags a chair across the tile floor and parks it on the other side of my bed. He collapses into it.

When I hold out my hand to him, he brings it to his mouth and presses a quick kiss to my knuckles.

"I'm shit at this," he says, refusing to meet my eyes.

"Hey, I get to be the moody one right now," I tease softly.

He sighs and reaches a hand up to comb it through my hair. "Still a handful, even when you're laid out in a fucking hospital bed. I bought you some things. A change of clothes. Toiletries. An extra blanket."

I shut my eyes to keep tears from spilling. I *want* to regret coming here. I really do. But I've enjoyed my time with them more than I could ever put into words. I got to see a new side of Liam, the man I've been in love with for years.

I got the opportunity to fall in love with Stasi, too.

For that, I have to be grateful.

Now I just need to find a way to kick them out with kindness and summon up the courage to call my dad.

"Fuck the timing of this. Seriously," I mumble.

Stasi eases off my chest. I miss her warmth immediately. "Is there anything we can get you? Are you hungry or thirsty?"

I peck a kiss to the tip of her nose. "I have two favors to ask."

"Anything," she replies.

"I'd like an ice cold Diet Coke."

Liam stands up fast enough to make the chair screech on the floor, an inked hand already digging for his wallet.

"And two. I'd like for both of you to go home and get some sleep."

Stasi shakes her head. "I'm fine right here."

"Sweetheart." I tuck a lock of hair behind her ear. "I'd like to sleep, too."

Her little "oh" puts more cracks in my heart. I ache to comfort her, but Dr. Malone could return at any second, and I don't want them here for that conversation.

Stasi hesitates, chewing on her bottom lip. "Okay, but you'll call or text if anything happens?"

I sense Liam's intense gaze on me.

"Promise." The lie tastes bitter on my tongue. Still, it's the right thing to do.

Minutes later, they return to my room—Liam with the Diet Coke and Stasi with a styrofoam cup of ice chips. She kisses me quickly, then makes room for Liam at my bedside. He leans in to kiss my forehead. I can tell by the tension in his body and the distant look in his eyes that he's in the process of shutting down.

My heart breaks for Stasi. Have I doomed them?

I watch them leave with a sinking feeling in my gut. Death might as well have its skeletal arms around me because suddenly I can't breathe.

Something on a machine must trigger a nurse to come in. As soon as she sees the tears on my face, she gives me an understanding look.

"Emotional pain can be just as bad as the physical stuff, huh? Anything I can do for you, sugar?"

Practicing a deep breath, I glance over at the duffle bag Liam dropped on a chair. "You mind checking if my phone is in that bag, please?"

She fishes through it and hands my phone over. Then she removes a fluffy blanket Liam packed as well, arranging it over my feet. "You've got some good friends."

"The best," I choke out.

I wait until she leaves to make a phone call, guilt rising in my chest at the thought of dumping bad news on my dad when he's already experienced so much hardship in his life. Burying his wife should have been the end of it.

The phone rings several times, and I begin to lose hope that he'll pick up. I remind myself that it's still light outside. He's probably working.

"Beau? Is that you?" A gruff voice answers.

My pulse trips up. "Hey, dad."

"What's goin' on, son? You still out on the road?"

"Nah." I shut my eyes and take a deep breath. "I'm gonna be home soon. For good."

The pause on the other side has my throat tightening.

"Music thing not working out then?"

"You could say that."

"Well, I'm sorry to hear that. You've always had a talent for it."

I'm sucked back into memories of all the times he asked me to play for him, either on the back porch or in his office where we'd kept my mom's upright piano. He's been so supportive of everything I do.

We sit in silence for a bit as I work up the courage to tell him about my diagnosis.

A male voice sounds in the background of the phone. Something about loading up a trailer.

"I'll let you get back to work, dad."

"Hold on now. Roy can stand to learn some patience. I haven't talked to you in seven whole months."

God dammit. Now the tears are pouring down my face. I guess I didn't realize my dad cared. Seven months flew by. He didn't try to reach out once.

Then again, I didn't either. I assumed the ball was in his court, but I'm an adult, too. I'm just as capable of opening a line of communication.

"Dad." My voice trembles. "I'm kinda not okay."

Another pause. "What do you mean, Beau? Where are you? Do you need me to come get you?"

I cover my face with an arm like a kid trying to hide. "I'm in the hospital. And no, I can manage a flight home on my own."

Boots crunch on gravel. I assume my dad must be pacing or putting distance between him and his hired help. "You're scaring me, son. Why the hell are you in the hospital?"

"I'll explain in person. I think they're going to release me tomorrow."

"You'll fly home then? Can I pick you up from the airport?"

"Yeah. That sounds good. I'll text you."

"I love you, Beau."

"Love you, too, dad."

I hang up and submit to grief as it crashes over me and takes me under.

My bond with Liam took *years* to form. It was confusing and lonely and often felt hopeless. With Beau, it's been a whirlwind of butterflies and laughter and shared affection from the very start.

Both men have brought me such happiness these past months. If only I could lift their spirits in return. If only I could be their rock, capable of weathering storms.

But I don't know that I'm strong enough to be that person when I can't even stand up for my twin brother.

I'm too lost in my head to notice the elevator doors dinging open.

"Stas." Liam's stern voice snaps me to attention.

He's several strides down the main hall already. I rush to catch up to him as he walks out the automatic front doors.

I hadn't checked the time in Beau's room, but the sky has turned a dusky blue, and crickets chirp from the manicured bushes, oblivious to the fact that their season is over. If you can even say Texas *has* seasons.

"I'll give you a ride back to your car," Liam mutters, cutting toward his Pantera parked under a streetlight.

I watch him walk away without sparing a glance back. He hasn't looked at me since he got here. It's like he's already rebuilt his walls, no footholds or weak points detectable this time.

My heart begins to crack. Pain slithers along the fracture lines, threatening to split me into jagged pieces right here on the sidewalk of a busy hospital. I doubt even the best surgeon could put me back together.

This is the end of all good things, isn't it?

This isn't how Liam's birthday should have gone.

Forcing my legs to move, I shove down every sick feeling churning in my gut and hurry after him.

The silence in his car is deafening. Forget the fact that I couldn't form sentences without bawling right now. I don't think anything I say will reach him. He just wants to stubbornly drown in his guilt.

I reflect on our conversation at my apartment the first night he came to me. How he's clinging to the past, convinced his existence revolves around causing pain, all thanks to a horrible man who had no right parenting him.

Our time together should be proof that he's capable of loving not just *one* person but *two*.

Actually, fuck that. Liam Beckner takes care of *everyone*.

Why can't he let us take care of him for once?

When Liam pulls into the garage, he's quick to get out. He opens the passenger side door for me, but he makes no attempt to touch me. With his head held low, he tucks his hands in his pockets.

He looks small. *Fragile.* More like the boy who would climb through my bedroom window late at night.

Would he push me away if I tried to hug him? I wish I had an instruction manual for his moods.

Tears sting my eyes. Before they can spill, I break for my car and lock myself inside. I'm breathing heavily as I struggle to jam the key into the ignition with blurry vision.

"Don't cry. Don't cry. Don't cry," I chant.

By the time I get my stupid old car started and look up, Liam's garage door is closed, and he's nowhere in sight.

It's okay. Everything will be okay. He's not going to let this separate us.

But I can't say that with confidence. Liam has a history of pushing people away. He's done it once before with Beau.

It hurts to think we've come this far, and he might succumb to the twisted belief that he doesn't deserve to be loved in return. That he's somehow bad. Wired *wrong* on the inside.

With shaking hands, I call my twin.

"Hey, sis. What's up?"

An accented voice speaks softly in the background, and I instantly regret calling. I have to remember that his boyfriend is living with him now. Hail can't be at my beck and call when I get like this.

"Stasi? Did you butt call me?"

Eyes squeezed shut, I tap my forehead on the steering wheel. "No. I'm here."

"Why do you sound like that?"

Of course, my twin knows something's off. I shouldn't have called him. With Z fully back in his life, I don't want anything to pop his bubble of happiness. He worked so hard for it.

It's just... I don't have anyone else to comfort me right now.

I want my twin.

"Are you home?" I ask.

"Shit. What's going on, sis?"

I push out a shaky breath as tears continue to fall. "I don't know, Hail."

It's partially the truth. I don't know what's wrong with Beau, and I don't know what kind of storm is raging in Liam's head right now. I don't know what the future holds for us. Everything feels like it's coming apart at the seams.

"Hurry up and get over here," Hail replies.

After crying in my car until my head pounds with its own heartbeat, I drive to my brother's house.

I'm torn between feeling like I'm interrupting and also a little curious to get to know the man who wrapped my brother around his finger. Ever since the pool party, I've done my best to give them space to put down roots.

More like, I've had enough going on juggling two men that I haven't had time to bug my brother.

Hail flings open the front door as I raise a finger to the doorbell. One look at my puffy red face, and he's yanking me into a crushing hug.

I nuzzle my face against his worn shirt. "Missed you."

We break apart as Z pads toward us from the dark hallway. He's dressed down in joggers and a t-shirt that shows off his long, pale arms. He's arguably the prettiest man I've ever seen with his inky curls and crystal blue eyes.

Don't get me started on his voice. It was wild to piece together his quiet, unsure personality with his incredible, deep vibrato.

"Hello," he greets in that shy, accented voice.

"Hi, Z. Sorry for intruding like this." I try for a self-deprecating smile.

"No apology needed. You're always welcome here."

Hail tugs me inside and shuts the door, plunging us into darkness. "We were too tired to get freaky, anyway."

I scrunch up my nose as I toe off my shoes beside the door. "That's information I didn't need in my brain."

"Yes. Please stop traumatizing your sister."

With my eyes adjusted to the darkness, I catch the disapproving look Z gives Hail. It quickly turns into something tender. My brother stares back like he doesn't believe Z is real. Like he hung the very moon in the sky.

God, they're cute.

My parents assume their relationship is some young-life crisis hitting my brother or a middle fingers up response to their strict beliefs, but it's easy to see they love each other.

Hail found his human.

While Z drifts off in the house, Hail guides me to the couch. "Alright. Spill."

I wrap my arms around a throw pillow and rest my chin on the top of it. "It's just...been a long night. I might be overreacting."

As much as I want to delve into what happened, mentioning Beau's seizure would bring up questions on what I was doing in Liam's house. I know my twin would be the last person to ever judge me, but I'm not sure I'm ready to disclose everything that's happened between us.

Because what if it's all over?

"Is it mom and dad?" Hail asks.

"No. It's...relationship related?"

My brother's amber eyes grow wide. "Wait... are you dating Beau Whitaker? You guys were pretty damn flirty at the pool party."

"Sort of. Yeah."

I'm also sort of seeing your best friend. You know, the one who never dates...

Hail frowns. "Did he do something to hurt you?"

"No. No. It's not like that."

Hail rubs at the back of his neck as he processes this information. "Wow. Okay. A musician, huh?"

I wince, and Hail leans over to ruffle my hair. "Hey, I get it. Shit can be real fucking hard, but it's worth it."

God, I'm glad I cried out everything in my car or I'd be in tears again. The last thing my brother and his boyfriend need is to deal with a complete meltdown from me.

"Well, I'll listen if you want to talk. Or if you just want to hang with us tonight, that's cool, too."

I squeeze the pillow tighter. "You really won't mind if I crash for a while?"

"Z and I both want you here. He's just as worried about you."

I sigh. "He's something, isn't he?"

"Yeah," Hail agrees dreamily. "I'm kinda obsessed."

I chew on my lip as I dredge up the things I should have told him almost a year ago. "Hail, I'm sorry I didn't stick up for you at Thanksgiving."

"Hey. It's not your responsibility to protect me, sis. Anyway, you're built sweeter like Z."

"That doesn't mean I should let mom and dad treat you like that."

"They're bigoted, narcissistic assholes." Hail shrugs. "I may have made things worse by calling them out for not showing up to any of your graduations."

I purse my lips. "They kind of suck, don't they?"

"Real hard."

The bedroom door in the short hallway off the living room opens, and Z walks out with his bangs tied up, revealing the full extent of his stunning features.

Hail leans closer to me and whispers, "Gonna ask him to marry me."

I hide my smile in the pillow. If that's true, I'll need to start thinking about wedding details. Hail's organization skills stress me out in that they're practically nonexistent. And I know for a fact my parents won't be willing to help.

"Everything alright?" Z asks, his concerned gaze falling on me.

I nod. "All good."

The rest of my emotional baggage can wait for later.

"So what movie do we wanna watch?" Hail pops up from the couch to rummage through the kitchen cabinets.

Readjusting on the couch, I watch him pull out a collection of junk food—boxes of every variety of M&M's, popcorn, pretzels, and Cheetos.

"Does he ever eat anything other than carbs and sugar?" Z questions, positioning himself on the couch next to me so our knees touch.

"Hey, nothing else would keep in the house while I was on tour," Hail complains.

I snicker as he wanders back over to the couch and drops down on my other side. When he holds the bowl out to me, I pluck a Cheeto and pop it into my mouth. "Can this be considered dinner?"

"We're grown adults, right?" Hail throws a piece of popcorn into the air and catches it in his mouth, making me giggle.

"Can we watch the one with the proper soundtrack again?" Z asks.

Hail starts up a movie, no further convincing needed. I spend the evening squished between them, blanketed in comfort, and provided snacks and drinks whenever they saw fit.

I don't know what tomorrow will bring. All I know is I'm going to do my best to be strong for both of the men holding my heart.

After all, he lied about having a hotel reservation when I picked him up from the airport, he wasn't forthcoming about getting kicked out of Lithos, and he kept his feelings to himself during our hookups.

How many times has he tried to save me from uncomfortable situations I wasn't ready to deal with?

Now's not the time to wallow. Hail and Z are about to show up to lay down some new material.

I should have rescheduled with the mood I'm in, but what kind of professional would I be if I turned away artists because I'm struggling with personal shit?

Fans have been frothing at the mouth to hear more of Z and Hail ever since they reunited publicly on stage. So, I do my best to adjust my attitude and dismiss my staff early to save some face for having to deal with me today.

Emma hesitates on her way out. "Hope your day gets better, boss."

I release a heavy breath when she's gone.

What a fucking disaster.

Hiding in my office, I glare at my phone on my desk, willing Beau to call. He has every right to be done with me. *Both* of them do. But if he is done, I just want to know that he's going to be taken care of wherever he ends up. That someone will be waiting for him back in Phoenix.

Bells above the entrance jingle. Shortly after, Hail peeks his head in my office. "I don't think I'll ever get used to seeing Liam Beckner behind a desk. When do you pull out the suit and tie?"

Sighing, I tuck my phone into my pocket. "Didn't you come here to record something?"

So much for my attitude adjustment.

Hail's brows knit together. "Yeah. You okay?"

"Fine." I brush past him and nod in greeting at Z clutching his guitar bag in the lobby.

As they warm up in the recording room, I'm sucked deeper and deeper into mental quicksand. I start to question if the summer even happened. Was it all a dream, and I'll wake up alone?

Hail lays down his recordings first. When he's finished, he comes to sit on the stool next to me as Z cycles into the recording room.

"You're just as experienced with the equipment as I am. You don't need me here," I mumble.

"Do you even know me, Liam? I need you like I need oxygen."

He fiddles with something in his pocket, sneaking me a glimpse of a small velvet box. "Don't think I can wait any longer."

My jaw clenches. Unfortunately for Hail, I might be the worst person to support him right now.

The front door opens, and my gut sinks further as I glimpse long blonde hair in my peripheral vision. *Fuck.* If I look at Stas and see one ounce of sadness reflected back at me in those pretty brown eyes, I'll lose my shit.

Would she blame me if Beau decides to leave? How the hell did I think I could handle a relationship with two people when I've never even had one?

Hail bounces a knee on the footrest of the stool at a rate that has my blood pressure spiking. I reach over to stop him. "Quit. You're making me want to smoke."

He throws me a heated look. "Proposing's a big deal, Liam. Not like you'd know."

I snort. "Damn right."

The words don't feel right coming out, especially with Stasi nearby. I don't know that I'll ever change my mind on the idea of tying someone to me after witnessing how my dad treated my mom.

But if that were something Stas or Beau wanted...

Pulling a cigarette from the pack Beau left in my house, I prepare to light it. Hail snatches it from my fingers. "Don't start that up. You'll stink up the place."

"S'my studio," I grumble, tugging out another cigarette and lighting it up.

We fall into silence as Z strings together another song that will dominate the charts. These boys don't fucking miss.

When Hail slips into the recording room to check on Z, Stasi finally speaks. "I brought you something to eat. I wasn't sure if you had lunch."

Fucking hell. She would be worried about me. She's built that way. Thoughtful and sweet.

I run a hand along my jaw, struggling to keep my composure. "You didn't have to do that."

"I wanted to."

Words of apology dance on my tongue, but then Hail interrupts, asking if I can listen through the track one more time.

As much as I want to kick him out, I can tell he's biding his time while he gathers up the confidence to make a life-changing decision. I told him there's no reason to be nervous. Z's not going to say no.

But I know how my twins are.

I mutter a 'hold on' to Stas before hitting play on the track and doing my best to focus on the music washing over me. Once my perfectionism is satisfied with the mix, I turn around, prepared to grovel for forgiveness.

Only, Stas is gone.

Damn it. Why do I keep fucking up?

The thought of losing her, of losing *both* of them, has me standing up and knocking on the recording room window, breaking up Hail and Z's little make-out session. I drop a comment about them paying me by the hour, and Hail flips me off.

Thankfully, he takes Z's hand and guides him out of the recording room. His amber eyes meet mine. "Call you tomorrow, yeah?"

I give him a tight nod. "Yeah."

The tension in his body eases slightly. With rosy cheeks, Z adds a shy half-wave as they slip out the door.

The moment they're gone, I pull out my phone and call Stas. It goes straight to voicemail.

I call the hospital next, and a receptionist connects me to the neurology unit where a nurse informs me that Beau is no longer in their care.

What. The. Fuck.

Fear drags hot claws through me. Immediately, I hang up and call Beau.

"...you've reached Beau Whitaker. I'm probably on stage shredding right now, so leave me a message—"

"Damn it!"

Why didn't he tell me he was released? I could have picked him up.

Is that why Stas left? Do they not want me anymore?

Rushing to lock up, I speed home to find a random car parked in front of my porch. I knock on the driver's window. The guy apprehensively rolls it down.

"Who the fuck are you?" I demand.

Alarmed by my aggression, he holds out his phone with the Uber app displayed. "Uh, I'm here to pick up Beau?"

My pulse hammers in my ears as I storm into my house. I nearly collide with Beau coming down the stairs, his backpack slung over his shoulder. There's still fucking tape residue from the IV on his arm.

"Liam."

His panicked tone shreds me. I think about how wrecked Hail was last year when Z left him for Ireland. How I'd held him in a hotel room while he collapsed and cried until he was nothing more than a husk.

My heart rate spikes. "Explain."

Dropping his head, Beau slips past me. No matter how much I want to grab him and demand answers, I refuse to lay hands on him like that. I have no right to be upset if he wants to leave me.

I left him once.

His hand rests on the doorknob, and then I'm breathing too fast.

"Fucking *really*, Beau? Will you *talk* to me for a minute?"

I have no right to be mad at him. I know that. But I'm not in control of my feelings right now, and it's a terrifying thought.

"Did this summer mean nothing to you?" I ask in a softer tone.

The hand not clutching the doorknob balls into a fist. "*Fuck*. It meant everything, Liam."

"Then stay. Don't break her heart. I'll step aside."

He turns around and brings his body flush against mine, tears glistening in his eyes. "What's it gonna take for you to forgive yourself?"

My breaths are coming in short, hot pants. "I don't know."

His head falls to my shoulder, and I give in to the need to slide my arms around him. "I don't want to lose you."

Beau chokes on a laugh. "You don't know how badly I've wanted those words from you."

"Then stay," I repeat.

He buries his face in my shirt. "Liam. I *can't*."

"Is it the house in Phoenix? I'll fucking buy it off you if you have a mortgage."

"It's not the house," he murmurs.

"What is it then?"

He shakes his head. "You don't want me."

Anger snaps through me. "I want you."

"You don't. I swear you don't."

I ease back and lift his chin. "Why wouldn't I want you, Beau?"

He drops his arms to his sides in frustration. "Because I'm a mess!"

"I fail to see how that would change my desire for you."

He steps away from me. "Okay, then. How about the *fucking* tumor in my head? Would that do it? Is that something you want to sign up for? Surgeries and treatment and caretaking? Because that's not how I imagine a relationship going. That's not something I want to dump on anyone."

I'm not proud of my silence, but I'm afraid if I open my mouth at that moment, all that will come out is more anger. I'm pissed at this entire fucked up situation. Pissed that someone like Beau should have to suffer from something so far outside of his control.

"How long have you known?" I finally ask.

His gaze drops. "Found out yesterday."

I should have paid closer attention to him. I should have caught the symptoms. The morning he stumbled out of bed. The headaches. How he sometimes shakes out his right hand in-between strumming.

He's been so tired. He's been sick for *months*.

"I didn't mean for this to happen." His shaky words hit me square in the chest, robbing me of air and snuffing out my rage.

Suddenly, I feel empty. Achy on the inside.

Beau leans in to brush his lips to my cheek. And then he walks out my front door without another word spoken.

Gone from my life just like I vanished from his years ago.

In my nightmare, I'm standing in my spare bedroom in the dark, my gaze locked on the lump under the blankets on the bed.

I approach Beau with heavy steps. He looks so peaceful sleeping, his overgrown hair a poof of frizz and his lips parted just enough that they would perfectly fit my own.

The words I spoke to him the other night play on repeat in my head.

I want you to run, Beau.

Ripping off the blankets, I grab his ankle and drag him off the bed. His body hits the floor with a solid thump. He groans as he comes to, and then he tries kicking out at me in wild abandon.

I stare down at him struggling. Nothing stirs in my chest.

Beau claws at the floorboards as I drag him into my bathroom, indifferent to his cries.

Crying doesn't do shit. You should know that by now.

Our surroundings warp into a more familiar scene. Vintage tile. Green walls. A porcelain tub with a stubborn ring of dirt I was never able to scrub away. How much pain did that earn me?

Enough to create this monster inside of me. This vicious anger I can't seem to shake. Even in death, my dad still has a crushing hold on me.

Curling a hand around Beau's neck, I haul him over the edge of the tub. His deep blue eyes plead for mercy.

Did I look this pathetic when my dad punished me?

I shove Beau's head under the hot water and watch him squirm, knowing what kind of terrified thoughts are running through his head.

Nails hook into my forearm and scrape along my flesh. I startle awake in a cold sweat, the dog whimpering with his paw on my arm.

Somehow, I ended up laid out on the couch in the living room, darkness engulfing me.

Lurching upright, I sprint up the stairs, my heart beating too fast. No sign of life in the spare bedroom. No Beau here to hurt.

But it's not enough to reassure myself.

I rush into my bathroom, only sucking in a full breath when I don't find a body.

Slumping down against the cabinets, I cover my face with my hands.

I used to sleepwalk when I was a kid. I'd wake up under my bed or in my closet. Sometimes outside in the backyard. Those moments when I realized what happened—realized I had no control over my body—were almost worse than anything my dad could ever do to me.

Pulling tricks from therapy to calm my racing heart rate, I practice box breathing and focus on my surroundings. The cold tile beneath my feet. The faint smell of lemon cleaning solution. The quiet blanketing me.

A small, fluffy black shadow appears in the doorway. I've heard Stas murmuring the name Cosmo when she's loving on him.

"Come here, Cosmo."

He hurries over and lays down next to me, resting his head on my thigh. I run my fingers through his silky fur. I pet him for a while, but it's not enough to calm my ragged nerves.

Rising up, I snatch Beau's forgotten pack of cigarettes from the spare bedroom. As I head to the patio, it's impossible not to see Stasi and Beau everywhere I look. Lounging in the music room. Pressed against the hall as we succumbed to lust the night of the party. Sitting at the kitchen island eating dinner. Dancing and laughing in the rain outside.

It's only been hours since I've seen both of them, and I already miss them. I want their warm bodies next to me in bed. Want their smiles in the morning and kisses when we get home from work.

No lights shine from the interior of my house as I drop into a patio chair, a cigarette propped on my bottom lip. I've always been more comfortable in the dark. Easier to hide that way.

I've moved through life the same way. Silently. My only call to attention the sound I create with an instrument and the pleasure I summon from my partners in the bedroom.

Lifting up on one ass cheek, I tug the lighter from my pocket and singe the end of a cigarette while breathing in. I suck the smoke deep into my lungs, hopeful it'll shave a couple more years off my meaningless existence.

Which is *fucked*. I haven't had a thought like that in years.

I check my phone. No returned calls from Beau. My gut twists.

One missed call from Stasi.

Does she know Beau's gone? Does she even want to talk to me? She'd rushed to her car so fast after we'd arrived home from the hospital. She'd rushed out of the studio earlier, too.

Then again, I made no move to comfort her.

Can I be any more unreliable? Almost two decades of therapy, and I still don't have my shit together.

I hit the call button. Stasi answers on the first ring. "Liam?"

"Yeah," I push out. "It's me, angel."

"Are you okay?"

Pinching the bridge of my nose, I debate how much to tell her. Even with how close I am to Hail, I've kept him mostly in the dark about my life outside of music. I didn't want to bring him into my fucked up world.

Over the years, I never shook that need to shelter others. No matter how torn up I was feeling on the inside, I'd convinced myself that was always a *me* problem.

"No, I'm really not. Beau's gone."

She's silent long enough to have my blood pressure rising. "I know."

"He talked to you?"

"If you call a goodbye text at lunch talking to me, then yeah."

My chest constricts. Is that why she dipped out at the studio earlier? Was she upset? Why wasn't I there to take care of her?

"Liam. Can I come over?"

Dropping my head between my legs, I rub at my brows. "I'd rather you get some sleep."

"And I'd rather take care of you," she replies firmly.

Fuck. I think I love her.

"Alright. Stay on the phone with me while you drive over."

Keys jingle, and a door shuts. I listen to her breathing as her footsteps scuff over pavement. I'm half-tempted to tell her to stay put. I should go to her. My car's faster. She could be in my arms in no time.

We don't talk while she drives, but our silence has never been awkward. If anything, she's one of the few people I can let go with. No need to be professional.

No need to be unfailingly strong.

"Three minutes away," she says.

I fetch the keys to the Porsche and move it. "Pull into the garage when you get here."

Should I sell the Porsche to free up a permanent spot for her? Beau liked driving it, though...

The moment she parks, I unbuckle her from the seat and pull her against me. I lean our bodies against the side of her car and hide my face in her neck. "I'm sorry I left you alone. I told you I wouldn't do that shit."

Her fingers stroke along my nape. "It's okay."

Brushing my mouth over her skin, I focus on the connection of our bodies to help keep me grounded. "Tell me I'm not fucking this up. Tell me I'm not going to lose you, too."

"Oh, Liam." She guides me back a few inches with firm palms on my chest so she can look at me fully. "How about I tell you how worthy you are of our love? How I've never met a more caring soul?"

I lean into her hand as she brings it to my cheek. "You always prioritize others. You've done it with me and Hail. You've done it with Atonement. You took care of the entire backline crew when you were on tours, Liam. And *don't* you try to say you didn't because Hail and I talked."

Her sass would have me smirking if the situation weren't so shitty.

"That was work, Stasi. I was being professional."

She narrows her eyes. "Call up any of them and see if they wouldn't be willing to drop everything to help you. If someone thought your phone call was a burden, then they don't deserve you."

My eyes fall shut. "I appreciate your pep talk, but it doesn't change the fact that the only man I want to answer right now won't take my calls."

"*Fuck* calling him. We're going to hop on a plane to Phoenix and knock on every door until we find him, because that's what you do when you're in love."

I'm stunned by the fire burning in her eyes. There's no denying she's resilient. A quiet force not to be discredited. It's something I've envied in her ever since she held out her hand to me through her bedroom window the night I met her.

She'd told me she wouldn't let me fall.

Only I *did* fall.

I fell in love with a remarkably strong woman.

Sealing our bodies together, I kiss her. It's nothing more than the slow melding of our lips, steady and sweet like her, but it ignites a fire in me.

Drawing back, I brush my thumbs along her cheeks. "I think I can get his address. Let me make some phone calls."

I can't say it won't take me time to believe I'm truly worthy of either of them, but I'm going to do my best moving forward to make sure they know exactly how I feel about them.

I bring the heels of my hands to my eyes and press, like I can vanquish the pain in my head. It's got nothing on the fear of what I stand to lose with this tumor.

What if I never play music again? And if I'm done with music, what do I have left in this world?

The doorbell rings, interrupting my morning huddle on hopelessness. Frustration snaps through me like hot lightning. I told my dad not to come around until my appointment tomorrow with the new neurosurgeon. He's going to have his hands full with me after surgery. I'd rather he spend the time working the ranch while I'm still capable of taking care of myself.

I haven't broken the news that I plan on hiring home care. Not sure if he'll be offended, but that's a conversation best left for pancakes tomorrow.

Walking toward the security pad in the hallway, I have to laugh at myself for buying such a large house for one person. It was a stupid purchase after Lithos's first album took off. Honestly, I thought it was the next step on the rockstar checklist.

Big ass house? *Check.*

I'd hoped to fill it with people, but I haven't been home enough to throw parties or host cookouts, so it feels like a vacant, echoey cave with its bland walls and cold tile floors.

We're not going to talk about the monthly payments. I'll look into selling it for real once I deal with the tumor situation. Offloading that debt might relieve the pressure to produce something of quality with my music.

I glance at the camera on the wall system, and my heart stalls.

It can't be.

Did I have another seizure? Did I hit my head on something? Am I already six feet under and no one's told me yet?

There's no other way to explain why Stasi and Liam would be standing outside my privacy gate, suitcases at their sides. Pretty sure I didn't give them my address, and Phoenix isn't exactly a small city.

A surge of anxiety rushes through me that my address got leaked somewhere on the internet. I'm not that popular, right? *Definitely* not after this last album.

Hitting the button to unlock the gate, I walk to the front door like I'm in some sort of fever dream. When I open it, Stasi runs toward me. The instant she's in my arms, I'm overcome with relief. My missing pieces aren't lost. They're right here. They're in Phoenix with me.

I haul her off her feet and spin her around in a circle. I fill my lungs with her scent. Then I kiss the soft, warm skin along her neck and shoulder over and over again.

Fuck. This feels right. This is how I should have woken up this morning.

"What are you doing here, sweetheart?" I ask incredulously.

She breaks out of my arms, dropping to her feet. "Talking some sense into you, Beau Whitaker."

I frown at the little furrow lines appearing between her brows. She points a sharp black nail at me. Haven't seen those wicked things on her before. It screams Emma's influence.

"A text message? How dare you! Were you honestly planning on leaving things this way?"

Shifting my weight on my hips, I tangle a hand in my hair. "Maybe. Yeah."

Liam walks down the driveway with the two small suitcases, drool-worthy muscles in his arms flexing to distract me. He sets the suitcases aside on the porch and tucks his hands into his pockets almost awkwardly.

I'm not sure Liam Beckner has ever had to chase anyone before. Yet here he is, a thousand miles from home.

Chasing after *me*.

If I wasn't so concerned about them getting involved in my depressing life, I'd bark out a laugh at the absurdity of it. Maybe even poke fun at him until he threw me over a shoulder and tossed me on a bed to teach me a lesson.

At least he looks less miserable than the last time I saw him. No tension in his jaw or shoulders. I have to wonder if that has anything to do with the beautiful, angry woman staring me down.

I shift my gaze back to Stasi. "How much did he tell you?"

"Doesn't matter," she replies firmly.

"It *does* matter. It's a lot to sign up for."

She cranks up the heat on her glare. I swear, she's burning hotter than the desert sun. "Well, if you had cared to *ask*, you would know that I'm signed the fuck up. If you think we're about to let you go through this on your own, then you haven't learned a *single* thing about us."

Shocked, I soak in this new side of Stasi.

"Would it be inappropriate for me to get hard right now?" I ask sheepishly.

Her anger flags, the corner of her mouth quivering with a smile. "You're unbelievable."

Feeling more confident that she won't cut me up with those killer nails, I surge forward and kiss her. I kiss her like it's been more than a day since I've seen her. Like we've experienced a lifetime of summers together.

I kiss her like I love her.

Even when we part, I keep her close enough to melt into those rich brown eyes. "Are you sure about this?"

She nods. "I am."

"I don't get it. Why would you want this?"

"Because when you love someone, you support them. You take care of them. I want to take care of you. I want to take care of that stubborn man, too." She stabs a finger in Liam's direction. "No matter what comes our way."

She speaks with so much strength, I can't find it in me to question her further. This wasn't the plan, but I'm all mush on the inside. Research should be conducted on me because I'm pretty sure my insides are made out of marshmallow.

After she plants a kiss on my cheek and steps away, I'm left with no barrier from the considerable presence that is Liam.

Was I too cocky thinking he came here for me? Maybe he's only here to support Stasi. Maybe I'm scared to hope he could actually love me when I know for a fact he'll hold a piece of my heart forever.

Liam approaches me slowly, his dark eyes glinting with resolution. I stop breathing as he brings his hands to my face and gently tips my head back. My pulse skips.

And then he brings his mouth to mine.

It's the softest kiss Liam's ever gifted me. It leaves me in a daze when he pulls back.

"Is this real? Are you really here?" I ask breathlessly.

He brushes his lips along my jawline. "I'm here. Not going any-where this time. Not if you still want me."

"*Want.* Fucking want you so bad."

He runs the tip of his nose along my neck. "I'm sorry for the way I've been acting. For my failures. As much as I want to say that terrified man who witnessed your seizure isn't me, it is. I've worked hard to hide him."

I scoff. "You telling me Liam Beckner's human?"

"Human as fuck." He kisses my jaw.

Chest tightening, I dare to ask, "So... how long are you staying?"

Easing back, Liam glances over at Stasi perched on one of the suitcases. "Stas has to fly back in two days for work."

A needy pain blooms in my chest. I just got her back. I don't want to let her go again.

But where would I stay if I followed them back to Dallas? I can't continue bumming off Liam. I can't juggle a house payment *and* rent. Not when I have no set future income.

Liam pinches my chin between his fingers, turning my head to him. "I'm here for as long as you want me."

"But your studio—"

"Runs flawlessly under Emma's reign. I need to be better about taking time off."

He slides his hand up my neck and into my hair, stroking fingers over my scalp.

"Fine. You both win," I say weakly.

"No more running away."

"Too tired."

Sucking in a breath, I straighten up and look over at Stasi, still sitting on a suitcase, waiting to be invited inside my house.

It's not going to be easy balancing relationships with two people, but I can't imagine this working any other way. I've always been quick to hand out love. I have enough for both of them.

And for once in my life, I think I might be loved in return.

"Do I need to cancel hotel reservations for you?" I smile smugly at Liam.

"Figured we'd mooch off you for a change," he replies.

Liam retrieves the suitcases, pecking a kiss to Stasi's temple. I hold out a hand for her. "Come on, sweetheart."

Without instruction, Liam goes on the hunt for the main bedroom when we enter my house. I have to appreciate him taking charge. I don't have the energy to make decisions or entertain them with a tour.

"I'm curious. How did you know where I live?" I ask Stasi, leading her down the hall.

"Liam reached out to his previous band manager, and she contacted your band manager, who had a guy named Noah call him."

My stomach rolls over. "Liam talked to Noah."

"Yeah. Noah mentioned calling you..."

Irritation prickles under my skin. Did Liam tell Noah about my health?

Regardless, he hasn't called. I guess years of friendship don't mean anything to him.

Stasi's eyes move to my sandwich graveyard on the counter. "Should we order something to eat?"

I tug at the roots of my hair, burning with embarrassment over the fact that I couldn't do one small thing on my own while fighting off an emotional breakdown.

"Chinese food sound good?" Liam's deep voice carries through the house. His phone is already in his hand when he walks out of my bedroom.

My shoulders slump. "Yeah. That sounds great."

It shouldn't surprise me how quickly we fall back into a normal rhythm. We came together so easily. Sure, we haven't had much conversation about what our future looks like, but it seems to be an unspoken agreement that we'll make it work. Somehow.

We end up sprawled out on the Adirondack chairs in the backyard, surrounded by empty takeout boxes, as the sun dips below the concrete wall bordering my property.

They don't comment on my lack of landscaping. The yard is a dirt pit, spotted with a few cacti that were planted when the house was built. Saved me from having to pay for lawn care while I was touring.

I don't want to be happy about their decision to stay with me, but secretly, I'm relieved they're here. Not only do I low-key feel like shit, I've been overwhelmed by the amount of research I've done on tumors since my release from the hospital.

It's hard to determine what my recovery will look like when we won't know what kind of tumor I have, or if it's even cancerous, until a biopsy is done.

All that anxiety fades away when Stasi crawls onto my chair to snuggle with me. We're sluggish after the amount of fried rice and honey chicken we consumed. Perfectly lazy with our conversations.

I rest my chin on the top of Stasi's head. "I don't think I'll ever be able to thank you enough for being here. For choosing me."

Stasi repositions herself so she's sitting on my lap. "I'm gonna say something greedy. Just know this is entirely your choice. I think you should come back to Dallas for your surgery. Dr. Malone is a remarkable neurosurgeon, Beau. And you would have us there to help with recovery. But if you're more comfortable here, then we'll be here to support you as much as possible."

I run my palms along her back. "I'll...consider it. I have an appointment tomorrow with the surgeon she recommended here."

She nods, tucking herself against me. We stay like that even after the stars come out to play.

"So... my dad's planning on coming over for breakfast," I comment nervously. "Should I reschedule?"

Liam rolls his head to the side to look at me. "Your decision. I don't exactly win parental approval."

"My dad hasn't met a stranger," I assure him.

Liam's gaze moves to Stasi. I rub light circles over her shoulder blades, noticing her breathing has evened out.

"Is she sleeping?" I smile.

"Yeah. She expended a lot of energy lecturing me yesterday. Spent a lot of time today researching brain tumors."

I sigh, clinging to her tighter. "I don't want to let her go."

"I know." Vulnerable, deep brown eyes meet mine. "I don't want to let either of you go."

"*Ugh.*" I slam my eyes closed. "My head hurts too much to cry."

"Do you need something? Tylenol?"

I shake my head. "Just... stay with me, okay?"

"Yeah. I'm here."

Liam turns his gaze up at the sky. "If you think your dad will be open to us..."

"I wouldn't ask if I thought he'd hurt either one of you."

"Then I'd like to meet him."

My chest swells with happiness, and a touch of nerves for what tomorrow will bring.

A cheesy smile spreads across my face. "Big bad Liam Beckner is going to meet my dad."

He chuckles. "I'll turn on the charm."

"You know damn well you can."

"Don't know what you're talking about."

"No? That wasn't how you had me on my knees for you after one make out sesh behind a venue?"

My heart skips when I catch him full-on grinning. "Took a few cities to get you there. I had eyes on you from the start."

"Trust me, I was fighting not to cave and suck you off day one. Figured that would make for an awkward tour."

He falls silent, so I relax further into my chair. I could sleep out here under the stars, Stasi as my blanket and Liam's protective, soothing presence at my side.

"Bedtime, trouble," Liam murmurs.

When he scoops Stasi off me, I stretch my arms out, whining at the loss.

"You can have her back when you get into bed."

It's motivation enough to have me gathering my weary body out of the chair. I pop another dose of Tylenol from the kitchen cabinet, swallowing them dry. Then I hurry to the bedroom and tuck myself in beside her.

Liam follows suit, stripping down to his boxers and covering me with his warm body.

I feel comforted. Safe. *Loved*.

Maybe the universe was listening to my silent cries for help after all.

Beau brings his mouth to mine as our hands explore, slowly easing off clothes and tossing them onto the floor. Even when we're naked, Beau doesn't rush things. He seems content to take me apart one molecule at a time.

Eventually, he shifts his body to my side so he can watch his hand trace along my curves. He caresses my breast. My ribs. My stomach, the muscles there quivering at the ticklish sensation.

My breath hitches when he cups me between the legs. He teases me with light strokes of his finger, enough to have my hips moving, eager for more. More sensation. More pressure. More of him. *All* of him.

I bite down on my bottom lip. He's barely touching me, but the admiration in his gaze alone is enough to send me.

"So pretty," he praises, slowly sinking a finger inside me.

I whimper. "You are."

Dimples pop as he fills me with another finger.

"Beau." My eyelids shudder closed.

"Yeah, baby?"

I reach a hand down to wrap it around his hard cock, giving it a leisurely stroke. "Need this. Need you."

Nudging my thighs farther apart with his knees, he settles between them. I run my hands up his beautiful forearms, admiring his gorgeous veins and faint smattering of hair. My touch stops at his biceps when he starts to push his cock inside me.

"Beau," I say again.

He thrusts the rest of the way in, capturing my moan with his mouth. He kisses my throat. My jaw. My lips again and again as he begins to roll his hips. We stay in the position for a while, lost in ragged breaths and sensation.

When Beau sits up, I have to hold back a laugh. He looks wrecked, hair disheveled from my hands running through it and tiny crescent marks over his skin where I'd dug my nails in.

"How do you want it? How do I get you there?" he asks.

I place a hand flat on his chest and shove him, dropping his ass onto his heels. I climb onto his lap.

He chuckles. "Should I be scared that you're stronger than me?"

"Probably."

He grins up at me, stretching to bring our noses together. "Hi, sweetheart."

"Hi, Beau."

Gripping my thighs, he helps move me up and down on his length. Combined with the stretch of his cock, the press of his piercing inside me, the friction on my clit as I grind against him, and his sexy, throaty praises, it doesn't take long for me to fall apart.

His lips lock onto mine as he swallows my sounds. Another couple of deep thrusts and he comes, too. His arms band around my waist, holding me firmly in place while he spills inside me.

"So fucking good," he murmurs.

The rumble of the garage door spurs him into motion. He sweeps me off the bed, hauling me into the bathroom.

I giggle. "You scared Liam will be mad?"

Beau sets me in the shower and pecks a kiss to my cheek. "Nah, I can handle him. Gonna see if he needs help bringing stuff in."

He shuts me inside the shower with the hot water running.

After rinsing off, I slip into a slouchy cream sweater and light brown joggers. Wet hair tucked in a knot through the back of the snapback I officially stole from Beau, I'm lured out of the bedroom by the savory smell of bacon and sausage cooking. There's a platter of fluffy scrambled and fried eggs already prepared on the kitchen counter, along with a tray of cantaloupe and honeydew beside a tower of buttered toast.

Mid-flip of a pancake, Beau turns to flash me a big grin. I laugh as the pancake lands on the side of the pan and gooey batter droops onto the stove.

Liam gently pushes him out of the way. "Your kitchen duties have been revoked. *Out.*"

"Do you think we're going to eat this much food?" I question.

Beau wastes no time coming over to wrap his arms around me. "You fell asleep before I could ask last night. Are you okay with my dad coming over for breakfast?"

Panic drags my heart down into my stomach. What will Beau's dad think of me? Of *us*? I know how my parents would react.

"I told him about both of you last night. He's gonna love you," Beau tells me.

"Okay." I nod, brows kneading together.

He plants another kiss on my cheek. "Gonna shower quick."

As Beau slinks off, Liam digs out gourmet coffee grounds from the grocery bags on the counter.

"Oh, thank god," I utter.

"Think I don't know you, Anastasia?"

Warmth rises to my cheeks. As I brew a pot of medium roast, Liam's dark eyes peruse my body, spreading that heat all the way down to my toes.

I'm considering distracting him from his perfect pancake making when the doorbell rings.

My gut lurches. Should I wait for Beau? Who knows how long he's going to be in the shower, though, and Liam's busy at the stove.

Which leaves me to greet Beau's dad.

Steeling myself, I go to open the front door. The man standing on the porch doesn't resemble Beau much. He's got fair hair curling out from beneath a brown cowboy hat, and he's deeply tan with heavy creases around his mouth and the corner of his eyes. He smiles wide, showing off two dimples.

Okay, so there are *some* similarities.

"Well, hello there. I'm Dave."

I offer a hand, which he politely squeezes rather than shaking it. "Hello. I'm Stasi. Beau's friend."

"Now, he told me girlfriend last night on the phone. What's he done to lose a precious woman like you already?"

Laughter bubbles out of me. Just as Beau had put me at ease so quickly the first time we met, I find myself relaxing in his dad's presence.

Dave holds up a sack of groceries. "Beau asked for strawberry mimosas. I wasn't really sure what that meant. Strawberry juice or fresh strawberries with orange juice. I don't think I bought the right champagne either..."

His expression shifts into something that looks so helpless, I move in to loop my arm through his. "I'm sure whatever you bought is perfect."

Light blue eyes twinkle back at me. "Wow. You're really something, aren't you?"

"Wait until you meet Liam."

We walk in on Liam holding Beau hostage by a belt loop, his mouth hovering right over Beau's. He hesitates, gaze cutting to Dave.

If this were my parent's home, we would all be kicked out already.

Teeth clenching, my defenses snap into place. I may have failed to protect Hail, but I won't allow anyone to make Beau feel less for who he chooses to love.

"Good lord. Pictures don't do you justice," Dave says.

Liam steps away from Beau, and Beau lets out a groan. "You looked him up?"

"Uh, well... you said he was famous. I got curious..." Dave trails off.

"He doesn't care for fanboys, dad."

Liam smirks, ruffling Beau's hair. "Who says?"

Leaving Beau in a state of disbelief, Liam walks over to shake Dave's hand. "Nice to meet you, sir."

I have to blink back my own shock. It's not that Liam isn't respectful. I'm just not sure I've ever seen him dish out respect to a parental figure.

Dave claps his other hand to Liam's forearm. "Look at *you*, son. If you ever decide you want to change things up from producing music, you're welcome to come work on the ranch." He tosses me a wink. "You too, sweetie."

A flush covers my cheeks. Now I see where Beau gets his charm from. Liam's gaze cuts to me, brimming with amusement. I roll my eyes in response to his silent taunt.

After setting the wooden table in Beau's giant dining room, we sit down to eat. I expect the conversation to be dominated by Dave, but he asks questions about our lives instead. How we met. What my job entails. What we do in our free time. Where Beau and Liam traveled with their bands.

Either he genuinely cares about us as people or he's good at faking it for Beau's sake. Knowing Beau, I'd place my bet on the first one.

Dave rests his silverware on a syrup-drenched plate and pats a hand over his stomach. "What time do we need to head out, Beau?"

Beau's eyes flick nervously around the table. "So... I may have canceled the appointment."

Dave's expression crumples. "Why would you do that, son?"

"I want to have surgery in Dallas. I want to move there," Beau explains.

My heart skips, my fingers curling in the loose fabric of my pants.

Dave glances at me, followed by Liam. "That's where you all live, right?"

I nod. "We'd be there to help him."

After a few moments of silence, Dave's head bobs in understanding. "It's your decision, Beau. Can't say I won't miss you. I always miss you."

Beau rises out of his chair and throws his arms around him. "You're a good dad, you know that?"

"I can do better, son." Dave's eyes water, and he clears his throat. "You bet I'll want all of your numbers to keep in touch. And you'll need a spare bedroom for your old man to come visit."

Tears spring to my eyes as I watch the two of them hold each other like it's a normal thing. It probably was for Beau growing up.

"Well," Dave clears his throat. "What do you all plan on doing with your free afternoon, then?"

Beau cracks a devilish grin as his gaze moves to us. "You two up for another date?"

I glance at her starting down the trail again, dressed in one of Liam's sleeveless black band shirts over a dark green sports bra and matching green yoga pants. I'm glad it's a quiet day on the trail because my pants are feeling a little too snug.

Pushing aside filthy thoughts, I do my best to soak in the scenic landscape. The fluffy blanket of clouds moving above the rocky earth surrounding us. The tickle of a cool breeze against my skin, so fresh when I breathe it into my lungs.

I haven't hiked this trail since my mom was ripped from this world by a drunk driver. I can almost hear her yelling for me to pace myself because the first part of the hike is misleadingly tame.

When we reach the steep, rocky incline that makes the average human reevaluate their life choices, I sense Liam's gaze on me. While he doesn't say anything, he keeps close behind me as we start scaling the giant rocks in case my body decides to forget what balance is.

I have to accept the fact that he might always harbor that worry for me. It's not something I can tell him to shut off. He's programmed to care for others. I've seen it in the way he treats people in his studio and how he interacts with his friends. It's one of the many reasons I fell in love with him.

I pause atop a rock to suck in a deep breath. We're only halfway up the steep incline, and I'm already tired. This was a stupid idea, but I'm not sure when I'll get to do this hike again.

Or *if* I'll ever get to do it again.

There's so many unknowns with my upcoming surgery, it's hard not to get caught up in the possible negative outcomes.

Will I be *different* when I wake up from anesthesia? Will I lose mobility? Will I be able to talk? Will I continue having seizures? What if the mass is cancerous? What if my life revolves around survival, and I've just dragged Liam and Stasi into my depressing ass battle?

Stasi joins me on my rock. Snaking her arms around my waist, she kisses my cheek. "We've got you, okay?"

My throat tightens, nearly choking my words. "You could have anyone in the world. You two could be happy without me."

"Beau. Don't you understand? Without you, we're incomplete," Stasi says.

I have to force a smile to keep from crying.

Liam steps onto the rock next to us, perfectly unfazed by the climb.

"Do you want to keep going?" he asks.

I suck in a deep breath. "I'm not quitting."

We push onward, our combined pants the only sound in the air. It used to freak me out how quiet it was out in nature. How alone in the world you could feel.

And then I'd go home and sit down with a guitar or touch my fingers to the keys of my piano and remember how much life we're capable of bringing into this sometimes frightening world.

When we crest the top of the flat peak, I break into a grin as Stasi does a full spin to take everything in. Phoenix sprawls out around us, skyscrapers visible in the distance.

"Now you know how I feel every time I look at you," I say.

Stasi eyes me boldly. "You're ridiculous."

"You like it."

Her entire face lights up. "I do."

Mesmerized, I watch her for a couple painful beats of my heart. Then I find a good spot to lie down, propping my hands under my head.

Birds circle over our heads. I fall under their trance for a while, fascinated by how quickly they adapt to changes in the wind.

Eventually, Stasi and Liam settle on either side of me to watch the sun set, washing everything in perfect tones of salmon pink, melty orange, and baby blue.

No matter what the rest of the week brings, I can say it's been a good life.

I dig out my phone and snap a picture of all of us without asking, catching Liam in a scowl.

"Instant favorite," I say, saving it as my lock screen.

Stasi giggles. "Send it to me?"

"You know I will."

She snuggles closer. "I've never done anything like this before."

"Wait. *Seriously*?"

"The only time I've traveled outside of Texas was for tennis matches when I played competitively."

"Is this something you want to do more?" I ask.

She scrunches up her nose. "I haven't really thought about it."

I glance over at Liam. "How about you?"

He runs a big palm along his stubbled jaw. "I've traveled enough in one lifetime, but I wouldn't mind taking a few vacations if that's what you both want."

I blink at him in awe.

"How about you, Beau?" Stasi asks in a soft tone. "Do you want to travel more?"

I picture us vacationing together. Hiking snow-capped mountains. Kayaking through crystal pools of water. Tearing up desert terrain in an off-road vehicle.

Liam would draw all sorts of attention, especially if we go somewhere hot and he's stripped down to a t-shirt and shorts or swim trunks. Not to mention how many heads Stasi would turn.

And yet, I would be the one on the receiving end of their love. No one else.

"Little trips would be fine. I think I'm done touring. Not that anyone's knocking down my door to sign me," I say.

"Not yet," Liam counters.

"If that ever happened, it would be thanks to your production skills, not my talent."

"Bullshit. I've listened to you play for years, Beau. It's not a matter of *if*. It's a matter of when you're ready."

Too drained from the day to fight back, I shut my eyes. Secretly, I love that he believes in me, even when I don't believe in myself.

"You know what I'd prefer over a fancy vacation?" I say.

Stasi hums in question.

"Camping. Give me a tent under the stars any day of the week. S'mores. Noisy bugs. Coffee made over the fire. I used to pitch my tent out in a field on the ranch every summer. There was one afternoon with bad winds... my tent ended up in the trees with a giant hole in it. I cried about having to sleep in my bed that night. My mom teased me that I'd become part animal. My dad bought me a new tent the next day."

Stasi smiles. "Of course he did. I've never been camping, but I don't think I would have enjoyed it with my family."

Reaching for her hand, I entwine our fingers. "I'm getting the sense that your parents aren't very kind people, sweetheart."

"No, they're really not." After a pause, she asks, "Is your mom..."

"Gone. Yeah."

Liam rests his hand over mine, giving it a squeeze.

"I'm sorry, Beau," Stasi says. "I'm glad we got to meet your dad."

"Yeah, me too. Hope you don't mind him calling you now."

For some reason, this earns a snort from Liam. "I don't think she'll mind."

I pick up my dish scrubbing pace, trying not to think about how much time I've let slip through my fingers, wasted on meaningless sex I believed would fix the black hole heaving in my chest, when I could have been spending my days in bliss with them.

This right here is my fix. What I needed all along. And I'm committed to doing whatever I can to keep them around for years to come.

A lifetime if they'll have me.

I give the heavy thought a minute to sink in. While I'm not sure I'll ever learn to trust myself—not after what I had to become to survive under my dad's roof—I trust the two of them fully.

If they believe I'm someone worthy, then I'll just have to learn to love myself.

Pushing out a deep breath, I dry my hands on a towel and make my way toward Beau's bedroom. Judging by the sheer volume of clothes tossed onto the floor, they must be naked already. It's hard to tell with no lights on in the room.

However, I can *hear* them. Whispered praises and whiny, broken moans that have my cock filling.

I switch on a floor lamp, my blood heating at the vision of them tangled up in the bed. The sexy roll of Beau's hips as he grinds his erection along Stasi's toned thigh has me questioning what it would feel like to be on the receiving end of that long, beautiful, pierced cock.

Now that's a curious fucking thought.

Dropping my shirt onto the floor, I prowl to the side of the bed. Big brown eyes flick up to me and drink in my exposed ink with desire.

When Beau doesn't break away from trailing kisses along Stasi's collarbone, I run a hand through his hair and tug him up onto his knees. He groans in pain-filled pleasure.

I tease my mouth along the sharp cut of his jaw. "You that desperate to fuck her pretty cunt?"

His Adam's apple bobs under my lips. "*Yesss.*"

"Mmm. Would you like that, angel? You want Beau to fuck you?"

"Please," she gasps, reaching for him.

I flash a smile. "Such sweet beggars."

Beau tries to nod, but I'm still gripping him by the roots of his hair. I pull him into a hard kiss, gliding my tongue along the hot seam of his mouth until he opens for me. I run a palm over his bare chest, stroking his pebbled nipples and then moving down quivering stomach.

I skip right over his cock to grip his balls, earning a nip from his teeth on my bottom lip.

"Careful, trouble."

Beau growls. "Need to come."

Moving my hand from his hair to his jaw, I hold him under my gaze. I'm half expecting to see fear reflected back at me. My pulse thunders, my brain flashing warnings that I'm taking things too far. That I'm too aggressive. That I'll end up hurting him again.

Beau's eyes soften. His fingers brush along the inside of my forearm. "You know I love this."

After a quick nod, I release him. "Move to our angel's side. Show her what those wicked teeth and tongue can do."

A dimple pops as he repositions himself along her side. With a gentle hand, he guides her into a sensual kiss that has me forgetting my worries.

As I climb onto the bed, I graze my hands up Stasi's bare legs, pushing them wider to accommodate my larger size.

When she's spread out for me, I press my clothed cock against her pussy and let her *feel* what they're both doing to me.

"Liam," she murmurs.

She's already in a hazy state, eager to be used so thoroughly that everything clouding her brain fades away.

"Stasi, why does he get to keep his clothes on?" Beau asks, those gem-blue eyes glinting.

"Not fair," Stasi agrees, hooking her legs around my waist. With some effort from Beau, she flips me over onto my back. It's possible I let it happen, but I'll give them the win because I don't fucking mind the new position one bit.

I grab her by the thighs and haul her up until her pretty little cunt is right over my face. Flattening my tongue, I drag it along her slit. I chuckle as her hands smack out to the headboard.

Meanwhile, Beau's settling between my legs. He tugs off my shorts and boxer briefs in one go. I'm about to laugh at his desperation when he descends on my cock without hesitation.

Between the way he's sucking me into his hot mouth and the noises and curses Stasi's spilling as I devour her, I'm struggling to remember my own fucking name.

Stasi shatters on my tongue, and I have to snap my hand down on Beau's hair, yanking him off my cock before I come.

"Not what I had planned," I pant. "Want to try something. Something that will make both of you feel good. Come up here, Beau."

He obeys, and I fit Stasi between us, facing Beau. His lips glisten with spit from sucking me off. I'm tempted to let him keep going, but the desire for something *else* wins out.

Stasi leans forward to run her tongue along Beau's wet lips. I grip her hip hard, pushing my cock into the crease of her full ass.

"Naughty woman," I rumble.

She wriggles against me, rocking her hips back as she kisses Beau.

It still surprises me that I feel no jealousy watching another man take from her what I've been dreaming of taking for years. But witnessing the two of them together, the only two people to ever make me feel something *more*, is a thing of pure beauty. I'm high off it.

Addicted.

I don't think I could ever give this up. I want to be the only one to orchestrate their pleasure. I want him secured to me. Safe with me. Comforted by me.

Only ever me.

Rolling away, a low laugh breezes from me as Stasi whines in protest. "So needy. Don't worry, gorgeous. Beau and I are going to fuck you at the same time."

"Oh, god," she utters.

I slide out of bed to retrieve the lube I brought. When I move behind her once more, I lift her leg up over Beau's hip, opening her enough that I can tease them both. I kiss her nape as I run a finger along her slick, hot sex. Slowly, I pump it in and out of her. "So wet, angel."

Then I wrap a hand around Beau's cock and run it through her slickness, occasionally flicking and tugging on his piercing.

"She feels good, doesn't she?" I murmur.

"Fuck. *Yes*."

I push the tip of his cock inside her. Stasi whimpers. I catch her nails curling into his shoulder as he bottoms out.

I'm hooked on the way they're trembling and heaving with breaths, already overwhelmed with sensation.

It's about to get a hell of a lot better.

"Relax for us, angel," I instruct.

She tenses up for a second when I press wet fingers against her hole. I circle her little rosebud nice and slow as Beau fucks her gently.

"You feel so good, sweetheart. So fucking good. Want to stay buried here forever. So perfect for us," Beau rambles.

While he showers her with praises, she begins to push back against my fingers. I take that as a sign to ease a finger in.

"Ah. *Liam.*"

"See? One cock isn't enough for you, is it? You're greedy for two big cocks to stretch you."

She rests her head back against my shoulder. "Liam...I've never done this..."

Beau pauses the movement of his hips and cradles her face with one hand. "We've got you, Stas. Trust us. You want to stop, we stop, okay?"

She nods. I lube up my fingers once more and slowly work two of them inside her. I give her time to adjust before I push in a third. It's not nearly enough to prepare her for my size, but she starts begging anyway.

"*Please.* More, Liam. It's good. I need more."

Beau's barely holding it together, and I break into a smile. "Let's cause some fucking trouble. On your back, Beau. Our pretty girl is going to ride you while I fuck her from behind."

He moves fast enough to summon a dark laugh from me, flipping both of them into position. I brush Stasi's hair aside, smoothing my palms down her back and pushing her forward until I can see her body swallowing his cock over and over again.

After lubing up my cock, I grasp her round cheeks and start to sink my crown into her hole. It's such a tight fucking fit. My fingers clench her skin hard enough to leave marks.

"No tensing, Anastasia. Open up for me."

I blanket myself around her, pressing kisses to her shoulder and neck as my crown breaks through that tight barrier of muscle. I have to fight the urge to slam the rest of the way inside her. It's a test of self-control

I often fail when it comes to sex, but I refuse to put my own pleasure above hers.

Moving in fractions, I draw out slightly and push in a little deeper on each thrust.

"Liam. Liam. Liam." She chants my name in reverie.

"Fuckkk," Beau utters, his legs quivering on either side of me. "I *feel* you."

"Good. No coming. Not until I give you permission."

My eyes shut when I bottom out, but I force them back open. I need to see them just as much as I need to feel them.

"So fucking tight, precious. This hole is mine. Mine to fuck. Mine to *breed*."

She moans, her head dropping forward. Beau wraps her up in his arms, pulling her flat on his chest.

"We're good, sweetheart. Fuck, we're so good, right?"

"So good," she repeats.

"Goddamn, there's so much pressure." Beau pants, his knuckles turning bone-white as he clings to her.

I chuckle. "Beau can't handle us, angel."

"Shut—"

I thrust hard, snapping my hips against her ass. Two different moans echo through the room. My mouth curls up at the corners.

Yeah, there's no way in hell I'm ever giving this up.

We move in rhythm, turned off from reality. Lost in a world of pleasure meant just for us.

The moment Stasi leans her back against my chest, nearly boneless, I know she's close. I brush a palm up her body, cupping her breast and toying with her perky nipple as I rock into her with deep punches of my hips. With my other hand, I take her jaw and bring her mouth close to mine.

"Give me those sounds, beautiful."

I swallow her moans as she comes undone, clenching around both of us.

"Coming," Beau gasps. "Fuck, I'm coming."

The thought of filling her up has me spurting, too. We collapse into a heap of limp arms and legs, pressing lazy kisses to any skin within reach.

"Beau," I murmur.

"Yeah?"

"You should stay with me after your surgery."

I'd been thinking about it since the flight over. We can keep a better eye on him that way. Get him to his appointments. Make sure he's actually resting.

Two pairs of beautiful, hopeful eyes fall on me.

"Would be better that way, don't you think?" I ask.

"Definitely," Stas agrees.

Beau's not as quick to jump on board.

"What's it gonna take to convince you, trouble?"

His dimples slowly appear, his mischievous nature activated. "I don't know. What are you willing to give me?"

I grip his jaw in my hand. "I think the answer to that would scare you."

His smile falters as his eyes shine with emotion. "Doubtful. But yeah, I'll come bum some more at your place."

"Good." I give his cheek a little pat. "Shower time."

They both groan in protest. Ever the provider, I gather them up over a shoulder and carry them into the bathroom to wash them.

"Thank you," she murmurs, setting a notebook aside with details on Hail and Z's upcoming wedding. After tearing into the wrapper, she takes a big bite and slumps in satisfaction.

Just as much as I'll be monitoring Beau, I'll be doing the same for her. Stasi will take on the weight of the world, willing to let it crush her if it means keeping it off the shoulders of others.

I took her phone two hours into Beau's surgery so people would stop hounding her for updates. I've been communicating with Dave personally.

I'm not gonna lie, it would be easier to relax if I had a cigarette, but I decided to quit that shit on the flight to retrieve Beau, terrified I would contribute to the growth of that stupid fucking tumor if he was exposed to more smoke.

I pace the neuro waiting area for a little while, only taking a seat when I notice that I'm distracting the nurses at the station.

Stasi leans against my side, resting her head on my shoulder. "You're a good man, Liam. You're good for us."

I lace our fingers together and give her hand a squeeze. Right as I'm about to tell her all the ways she makes me better, Dr. Malone strides into the waiting room. She claps her hands together, breaking the tension in the air.

"He did fantastic. Surgery went as expected. I believe we were able to remove all of the tumor, but we need to wait for pathology results to confidently say we got it all."

Stasi releases a breath and nods. "Thank you."

"I do want to set some expectations," Dr. Malone continues. "We've got him in the ICU for monitoring. When he wakes up, we may see some speech and mobility difficulties with the swelling in his brain. Maybe even into his recovery at home. He's going to want to sleep, which is a good thing. His body needs to heal. We'll make sure he's set up with all the care he needs once he's stable and ready to be released."

"Of course," Stasi replies.

I can practically hear the gears whirring in her head, ready to make a battle plan to get Beau back on his feet and smiling again.

"We'll let you two come back as soon as possible."

With that, Dr. Malone leaves us. I wrap an arm around Stas and pull her against my chest.

"Our Beau is safe," I murmur, kissing her temple.

And as soon as we're able to confirm that his tumor is fully gone, no trace of cancer, we'll all be able to resume normal life. That's the hope, at least.

"You need anything?" I ask.

Sucking in a deep breath, Stasi sits up and looks at me. "Yeah. For you to stop drinking coffee. Your entire body is vibrating."

I chuckle. "Fair enough."

Gently, she pushes at my chest. "Go do another lap. Leave my phone."

Sighing, I hand it over and escape outside. I shoot off a text to Hail to check in on the dog currently under his care. Then I scroll up through his barrage of older texts I left unanswered, unable to give reason to my recent, strange behaviors.

I respect that Stasi isn't ready to explain how I fit into the puzzle with her and Beau. I have no right to push anything when I spent most of my life terrified of relationships.

When the fuck did you get a dog???

Is this a mid-life crisis?

Is dog a code word for something else?

Yes, I'll watch your dog.

A new photo pops up of Hail holding Cosmo in one arm. The dog's pink tongue is pressed against the side of his face.

He's deprived of your love, just like me.

Snorting, I pocket my phone.

After a brisk walk to burn off some of my anxious energy, I reenter the hospital. By the time I make it back up to the neuro floor, a nurse meets us in the waiting area. "He's awake if you want to visit for a few minutes."

Stasi pops up, and I let her lead. Each step towards Beau's room takes effort. A conscious decision not to bolt.

I didn't feel this torn up when my dad died. I didn't feel anything at all watching as he was lowered into the ground.

I'm mentally preparing myself for what we'll see when we walk into Beau's room. Still, one look at him laid out in the bed, head wrapped like a mummy, wires practically dripping off his body, punches the air from my lungs.

Again, I'm overcome by a sense of loss for the years we could have shared together.

Why did I wait so long to make him mine?

It's hard accepting that I needed so much time to realize what was within my reach. Beau's recovery is going to take time, too, and I can't say that doesn't scare the shit out of me.

With unsteady legs, I approach his bed as his closed eyelids twitch. Stasi takes his hand, careful not to touch his IV or disturb any of the tubes or cords.

"Sweetheart?" he mumbles.

"It's me. Liam's here, too."

His head rolls in my direction. He cracks open his eyes, winces, and immediately shuts them once more. "...bad is it? How bad...do...look?"

His words are coming slower than usual. I suppose it could be worse. At least, that's what I'm telling myself so I don't lose it. I don't like seeing him like this. Not when I've grown used to his energy and the spark of mayhem in his blue eyes. He's the one that brings color to my days. The one that makes Stas smile.

"Good," Stasi says, a tear rolling down her cheek. "You look perfect, Beau."

His brows furrow as he strains to push himself into an upright position. I quickly touch a hand to his shoulder. "Don't. Just... rest. I got her."

His chest rises and falls with a heavy breath. "Yeah. Tired."

In a matter of seconds, his heart rate monitor slows as sleep claims him.

I post up in Beau's hospital room for five straight days once he's moved out of the ICU. No fucking way I'm missing his release this time.

Stasi wasn't pleased about having to return to normal hours at work, but she's grateful I have the luxury of flexibility. When I offered to hire her, I got a lecture about foolishly throwing my money around. So, I started funneling money into research organizations for brain tumors.

I also promoted Emma. She tried to fight me on the raise, claiming the title alone was enough since she's now officially able to boss Hail and Walter around. Not that she wasn't already doing that. But I managed to convince her that she's worth every bit of the bigger paychecks I'm sending her way.

Honestly, I'm looking forward to the comical outfits she's about to show up in after a healthy shopping spree. And if she doesn't go shopping, I'll "foolishly" throw some more money her way.

"This feels unnecessary," Beau complains as I wheel him out to Stasi's awaiting SUV at the hospital entrance. "I can walk just fine."

I glance down and catch the muscles in his right arm straining as he tries to move it. My chest tightens.

"Still not cooperating?" I ask.

He tips his head back to look up at me. The stripe of rebellious white in his hair was unfortunately lost to the trimmers to prepare for his surgery.

"It'll be okay," he says.

But there's no conviction in his voice. Unease rushes through me. Beau will lie all day long if he believes his true feelings will be a burden on someone else.

How the fuck did I end up with the two sweetest people in this world?

He's definitely more concerned about regaining sensation in his arm than he's letting on. Stasi has him set up with the best PT in the area, and she'll be monitoring his exercises at home as well. But he's already gotten a stern talking to from the nurses for rubbing his wrist and hand raw, like he can will the feeling back into his damaged nerves.

Mindful of his stitches, I ease my sunglasses onto his face, knowing he's still sensitive to the light.

Thankfully, Beau's pathology results came back benign. Even with that victory, his health will require lifelong monitoring. Neurologist follow-ups and continual MRIs, checking for regrowth. I also took Dr. Malone's suggestion and got Beau set up with therapy sessions to help mitigate any changes in his emotional state that may spring up over time.

As I push him up to the passenger door, Stasi hops out and rushes over. We both hover, hands poised, as Beau climbs into the car.

"Is this how it's gonna be for a while?" he grumbles.

"Go ahead and try to push us away," Stasi fires back, brown eyes heated.

We both watch her stomp over to the driver's side in awe.

"I miss sex already," Beau murmurs.

I avoid adjusting my semi. "Focus on recovering."

Sinking deeper into the seat, he shuts his eyes. "I'm gonna recover *so good*. Get ready."

With a huffed laugh, I tuck myself into the seat behind Stas so I can have eyes on Beau the entire drive home.

As soon as we pull into my garage, I hop out of the car. "Hold the troublemaker hostage for a minute."

I wrangle the excited dog into the backyard before returning to help walk Beau inside.

"Bed or couch?" Stasi asks.

"No more bed. I beg of you," Beau replies quickly.

She prepares him a spot on the couch, dragging down pillows and blankets from the spare bedroom. When we get him comfortable, she arranges his paperwork and medications on the kitchen island.

I pull an end table beside him, setting him up with a bottle of water, fruit snacks and chips, electronic devices, and the remote for the TV.

"I appreciate both of you more than I could ever express, but we're going to have to tone this shit down. I'm exhausted just watching the two of you rush around. Will you come snuggle with me, please?"

Stas and I exchange a look. Dropping onto the couch, I lift Beau's socked feet and set them on my lap. Stasi curls up against his side, half draped over his torso.

Beau turns on a football game and ends up passing out in the first quarter. Neither of us wants to move, fearful of waking him.

"Friday night. You staying over?" I glance at Stasi.

She bites her lip. "I could…"

My pulse hitches. "You could stay every night until he's through recovery. You make him happy."

Big brown eyes lock on me. "Are you serious?"

"Do I joke much, Anastasia? Yes, I'm serious."

Her fingers curl into the fabric of Beau's gray hoodie. "Do I make you happy?"

I lean over Beau's body to brush a lock of hair behind her ear. "You already know the answer to that, angel."

"Mmm." She gives me a soft smile. "Just fishing for compliments."

"Then yes. You make me happy."

She nuzzles her cheek against my hand. "Yeah. I'll stay until he's back on his feet."

Beau stumbles out of the dark hallway, his hood pulled over his hair. It's hard watching him fumble around like a lost soul, doomed to haunt the townhouse.

Ten minutes.

I know Beau's losing faith that physical therapy will help him. It's something I see too often with my patients when they're only partially through our time together.

Honestly, I think a part of him expected to regain full function of his right hand after the tumor was removed.

I keep encouraging him. These things take time. He's made good progress with PT.

But when his eyes glaze over and his responses turn into mumbles, I question my ability to support him.

Beau shuffles over to kiss my cheek before wandering into the dark dining room where Liam purchased and stowed a keyboard in hopes of luring Beau down from the second floor of the house.

Hearing Beau's melancholic chords chips away at me. He struggles through a song, and from my position on the couch, I glimpse his shoulders caving inward with each fumbled note.

My phone buzzes with a message. Assuming it's Liam letting me know he's almost home, I grab it and immediately realize my mistake.

It's my dad.

> I would like to make this very clear, Anastasia. Your mother and I will NOT be attending your brother's wedding. We are NOT in support of his marriage. Mark us off the list.

My hands shake as I read over the message again, like it might change his mind about the invitations I sent out last week. Like it will correct a lifetime of verbal insults from a man I used to want to impress.

I've spent too many years striving to win the title of the golden child. I was the one who didn't suck up their precious resources. I required little time and money from them. And while I lost most of my scholarships due to major burnout in college, resulting in a lot of regrettable partying that further propelled the cycle of my self-disappointment, I never once asked them for help to pay a tuition bill.

As an adult, I've come to the sad conclusion that I'll never win anything from them. Especially not with my current situation.

Doesn't matter that I'm so fucking happy.

I think about Dave, and how accepting he was of us sharing space in Beau's life. Why can't parents just be happy for their children?

Are my parents even proud of Max?

I haven't heard from my older brother in a while. Our relationship has always been shaky at best, but I'm a little concerned I've lost him in the war dividing our family. That he's been poisoned to the dark side.

So then what do I have to lose telling them off?

I sink my chipped nails into my palms, my emotions further twisted by the broken song Beau's fighting to play on the keyboard, occasionally hitting a sour note with his uncooperative fingers.

Cosmo pops his head up at the rumble of the garage door.

Thank god.

My worries ease at the jingle of keys and the heavy thud of boots. Liam appears, pausing at the end of the hall to listen to Beau. He gives nothing away in his body language.

When Liam finally glances at me, I must be wearing my emotions on my face because he strides over to scoop me up into his arms and carry me into the kitchen. He places me on the counter and moves between my legs.

"What do you need, angel?" he asks.

I run my fingers along the collar of his t-shirt, willing my voice to stay strong. "Beau to feel better."

Liam smooths his big, inked hands over the sides of my face and into my hair. How he could ever believe he wasn't cut out to love someone infuriates me. It makes me want to look up his dad's plot and spit on his grave.

"He will. You're doing so good taking care of him," Liam replies in a soothing tone.

I nod, hating the prickle of tears in my eyes. I don't want to cry. I don't want to make Beau more upset. So, I have to do better. I have to keep my chin up. I have to ignore the shit my parents are trying to stir up and be strong for my men.

"You need a break. Why don't you get out of the house? Make a coffee run," Liam suggests.

I glance in Beau's direction.

"I've got him."

"He's due for his anti-seizure meds in an hour," I reply.

"I know."

"He hasn't eaten much today."

"I'll start grilling pork chops as soon as you walk out that door."

"You're going to grill out in the cold?"

Carefully, he slides me off the counter and molds our bodies together. "The cold doesn't scare me. And I'll have you back here soon enough to warm me up."

Biting down on a smile, I push up on my toes to kiss him. He trails his mouth over to my ear and murmurs, "Stay right here."

Confused, I watch him disappear down the hall. Keys jingle, followed by the garage door opening. He returns a few minutes later with a black Atonement hoodie.

"Car is warming up," he says, motioning for me to lift my arms.

When I do, he tugs his hoodie over my head. I breathe in the fresh scent of his laundry detergent.

"Thank you. Cold brew or latte?"

"Surprise me."

Slipping into the dining room, guilt prods at me as I take in Beau's sad form. He hasn't moved from the keyboard.

I wrap an arm around his shoulders and kiss his cheek. "I'm gonna run a quick errand. Liam's home, okay?"

He turns to kiss me fully, and I almost cancel my little adventure. This is stupid. I've been waiting hours for the three of us to be together. Why does it feel like I'm running away?

Because I'm no good to either of them in this state.

"Be careful, sweetheart," Beau breathes on my lips.

Before I can change my mind, I hop into my toasty car and drive to the nearest coffee shop.

As soon as the drive-thru employee hands me three giant caramel lattes, I pull into a parking spot and take a long drink.

I wait for a rush of dopamine to hit, but when that first sip feeling never comes, I drop my head into my hands and force a couple of deep breaths.

Everything feels heavy right now. Beau's mental state. The inevitable break up of my family.

The thought pops in my head to call Hail, but I don't want to keep bugging him when I'm having a rough day. Especially when I know I'll just end up venting about dad's text, and he couldn't care less about our parent's opinions.

Ryan might entertain my mood. However, I'm not sure we're at that level of friendship yet. We haven't done anything outside of brunches, which we've missed since Beau's surgery.

And Emma's busy running a studio like a badass. Though she did manage to sneak out one afternoon to get another manicure with me.

There *is* one person who might be able to snap me out of this, if she'll even open her door to me.

I haven't visited Iris once. She probably assumes I abandoned her like everyone else in her life.

I shoot Liam a text that I'll be a little while longer and swing into a grocery store parking lot to pick out a bouquet of flowers and some basic groceries. Then I drive to Iris's assisted living facility.

Soaked to the bone, I stroll inside with the extra coffees and pass them out to residents sitting in the lobby. I'll get new ones when I head back to Liam's townhouse.

The speed at which Iris whips open her door in a flowery dress and a fresh perm has me wondering if she had her eye glued to the peephole or if her therapy worked that well and she ran to the door.

I wish I could say I've had that much of a success with Beau's recovery. Wish I could fix him, too.

"You seem to be getting around well." I smile.

"Good lord, you look like shit. Do I need to call these boyfriends of yours and yell at them to let you get some sleep?"

I know better than to start apologizing. She'll just lay into me harder.

"I'm getting plenty of sleep," I reply.

Iris grabs my arm in a surprisingly strong grip and tugs me into her cute little apartment decorated with lush green plants and hand-painted teacups. "How unfortunate for you. When do I get to meet them?"

Besides the brunch crew, I haven't shared Beau and Liam with anyone.

"Soon," I tell her, intrigued by the idea of Beau charming her and Liam making her swoon.

Flipping through Iris's kitchen cabinets as she takes a seat in her recliner, I stow away the milk and eggs I bought her and dig out a vintage vase to put her flowers in.

"You think that's going to make up for you not visiting?"

I roll my eyes and laugh. "I know you're not that easy."

"So, what's the status on the boy toys?"

"I'd much rather hear about how you're doing, Iris."

"Boring. You do the talking first."

I drop into one of the creaky wooden chairs at her little dining table. "Things are...a little difficult right now. Beau had a craniotomy to remove a brain tumor. He's healing, but there's only so much I can help with on the physical side."

Iris mulls this over, her icy eyes locked on me. "Being cooped up while having to accept changes with your body ain't easy."

"No, it's not," I agree, lowering my gaze.

"Well, you're the gal to get him through it."

Sadness bleeds into my chest. "I don't know. I'm not sure what else to do to help him."

Iris is quiet for a while. "I still remember the first date I had with my Emil."

Eyes wide, my head snaps up to her. I watch her shaky fingers stroke over the gold band hung around her neck by a thin, smooth chain.

"He was the first friend I made when my family moved down here during my junior year of high school. Showed up at my door with a bow tie and a picnic basket. He remembered I'd mentioned my love for brownies during lunch at school one day. Told me he spent the morning in the kitchen with his mom, learning to bake them."

"Iris, that's incredibly sweet."

"We sat beneath the willow tree in my backyard for hours talking about everything. Two years later, we were married in front of that same tree."

A smile eases onto my face. Iris waves a hand like she's trying to dissolve the memory. "My point is the small things you do every day can make a big difference in someone's life."

I reflect on the months I've spent with Beau and Liam, noting the things that made them happy. Cookies, fresh strawberries, stars and sunsets, dates, camping...

Glancing out the windows, I frown at the sheet of rain falling from the gray sky.

Definitely gonna have to get creative with this one.

I chat with Iris for a bit longer, catching up on her dominating victories during bunko hours.

Promising to return soon, I say goodbye and rush back to the grocery store for additional supplies before swooping through the coffee shop drive-thru again.

Only this time, I'm in much better spirits as the same employee hands over another tray of drinks and a frequent customer punch card.

I can tell my moodiness is wearing on both of them. Shit, it's filling up the house like some dark, infectious cloud, poisoning everything it touches.

I miss being fucking *normal*.

Odd clinks and swishes of fabric from the dining room have me pushing up to a seated position on the couch.

"What is she doing in there?" I ask.

Liam leans into my sightline. "She threatened to cut me if I let you peek."

I crane my neck further. "Have I mentioned how much I approve of spicy Stasi?"

Liam forces my head back to him. "Do I need to distract you?"

I'm about to tell him yes, as long as he promises to do it in a sexually entertaining way, but then I remember I haven't showered or changed my clothes in over a day.

"Can I rinse off?"

"Why are you asking, Beau? This is your home."

Home. That fucking word. It might be my kryptonite hearing it come from his mouth. I'm not sure I've ever wanted anything more. I thought music was it for me, but now I've found something infinitely more important.

Them. *Us.*

Liam grips my bicep, hauling me to my feet and walking me to his bathroom. When he starts up the shower, I lift my arms in anticipation of him stripping me down.

Grinning, I ask, "Is this where I call you daddy?"

He tosses me a look of warning.

"Have I mentioned I miss sex?" I add.

"You've only been cleared for light activity."

I waggle my brows. "We can go easy."

Another dark look spears through me. "When have I ever fucked you easy, Beau?"

Blood rushes to my cock, but when he doesn't make a move for me, I frown and tug my hoodie over my head.

I catch a glimpse of my reflection in the mirror, and my confidence dissolves. No wonder he doesn't want to do anything with me. I'm a mess. Soft-bodied with dark bruises under my eyes. My hair is different lengths. The hospital staff only shaved the patch where the surgeon cut into my head. I've kept my hood up and avoided mirrors as much as possible ever since.

Thankfully, the bruises on my arms from being poked and prodded have disappeared.

Liam catches me assessing myself and closes the space between us. His warm lips touch my neck. "You're beautiful, Beau."

"Liar," I mumble.

His hands clench tighter around my waist. "Don't even try to tempt me into punishing you. Recovery comes first."

Turning my head to the side, I capture his mouth in a slow kiss. We get stuck there for a while, his palms running over my bare skin as I bring a hand to the back of his neck and sink my fingers into his hair.

His mouth leaves mine, and I groan in protest. "I swear my dick's gonna fall off."

"Trouble." Liam nips at my ear. "Tell you what. As soon as you're cleared for normal activity, I'm all yours."

My jaw drops. "Wait. What does that mean?"

"Exactly what I said."

"Nuh uh. I need you to explain."

He turns me in his arms and kisses the corner of my mouth. "Use your imagination."

"Holy *shit*. But… have you ever bottomed?"

"I'm willing to give up control for you."

Groaning, I palm my hard cock. "You can't just say shit like that and expect me to remain calm."

Liam strides out of the bathroom, leaving me in a mood.

I hastily wash my body. By the time I step out of the shower, I'm still hard and even more irritable. Liam isn't phased when he returns to drape me in a fluffy towel straight out of the dryer.

"Still an asshole," I mutter.

He spins me around and pushes me back against the vanity. My towel drops in the process. I leave it on the floor, needing him to prove to me that I'm still desirable. Needing *something* because I feel like I'm about to hit rock bottom.

Liam's eyes do a slow perusal of my naked body, flashing with a dark sort of hunger that heats my blood. My breath hitches as he drops to his knees, bringing his mouth level with my erection.

"If you're just gonna tease—"

I shudder as he sucks my cock to the back of his throat to shut me up. He pops off only for a second. "Any dizziness or other abnormal symptoms, and you tell me immediately."

"Yeah. Sure. You got it."

He circles his tongue around my piercing, summoning another groan from deep within my chest. "I'm serious, Beau."

"*Fuck*. So am I. Don't stop."

His big hands grip my thighs as he licks his way down to my balls. He spends some time sucking each one into his mouth. I'm not even aware of all the sounds I'm making or how loud I'm being.

He works his way back up to my shaft and curls his tongue around me, laving it up and down and over my crown as he draws me back into his sinful mouth.

I'm fighting to keep from coming in thirty seconds, but the fact that I haven't come in *weeks*, coupled with the thought of getting to top him and the vision of him on his knees, has me bursting down his throat.

Trembling and panting against the vanity, a foggy, blissful sort of calm overcomes me.

Liam smacks a hand to my ass cheek. "Get dressed. Stas is waiting for us."

When I step out of his closet dressed, Liam's sprawled out on his bed with Stasi perched on top of him.

I wander over to pull her off the bed and into my arms, snuggling my face into her warm neck. "Sorry for being moody earlier. Liam sucked me off, and now I feel much better. What do you have to show us, sweetheart?"

She lets out a soft laugh, her cheeks flushed. "Okay, so I'm apologizing in advance if my idea is stupid."

"You take those words back," I say.

Big brown eyes shine up at me—decadent pools of rich bourbon that warm my veins just as much as a shot of liquor. "I'm not taking them back until you see what I've done."

Liam drapes himself around her backside, his hands sliding into the pockets of my sweats. Or *his* sweats since I borrowed them from him.

"I might not be able to play rough with Beau right now, but I can still discipline *you*, angel," Liam warns.

Stasi slips out from between us and grabs both of our hands. "You can do that all you want when Beau's able to join in. Come on."

Liam chuckles as she leads us down the stairs. I'm struck speechless at the bottom of the stairs by the sight of golden starlight circling the normally dark, empty dining room.

"Did you...pitch a tent inside?" I ask, chuckling in disbelief.

The entrance flaps are tied back to reveal a spread of pillows, blankets, battery-powered tea lights, and a picnic basket.

"It was too cold to do a date night outside, but you had said you love camping, and I know Liam likes the stars—"

I crush my mouth to hers, my heart soaring to new levels. "I love it."

Beaming, she guides me into the tent, fluffing up a stack of pillows for me to lean against. Liam crawls in after us. As soon as he's inside, he wraps a hand around her calf and tugs her flat onto her back. She lets out a little yelp before he kisses her.

"Too fucking sweet," he murmurs.

Heat rushes through me as I watch them exchange tender kisses. I'm not sure if jealousy is supposed to be a thing in these situations. Sure, I'm jealous of the fact that he could claim her right now if he wanted to, and I'm stuck, unable to reciprocate physically thanks to my stupid health.

But that's temporary.

This—*us*—fuck, I really hope it's a forever thing.

Liam kisses his way down Stasi's body until she's giggling and pushing at him to sit up. She fixes her hair in a high bun before digging items out of the wicker basket. Cups of hot coffee from the shop she'd stopped at on her way home, mini sandwiches, fresh-baked cookies, strawberries, trail mix with little marshmallows, chocolate pieces, and graham crackers, and giant slices of watermelon—something we'd come to learn over the summer is a favorite of Liam's.

When I glance at Liam, he looks just as astonished by the woman we've managed to win over.

Keeper, I mouth.

She could have spent her evening with anyone the night of that album release party. For some reason, she chose us.

After eating through most of the food she packed, we sprawl out on our backs. Stasi's got her head and hand on my chest. Her breaths are coming slower and slower.

Closing my eyes, I smile. "She fell asleep, didn't she?"

"She did," Liam answers quietly. "Beau. Can I ask you something?"

I run my fingertips up and down her spine. "Anything."

"Did you tell anyone from Lithos about your symptoms?"

My hand stops moving. "Why does it matter?"

"Noah thought you'd gotten mixed up with drugs. I didn't tell him your business, but I made it clear that wasn't the case."

Words get stuck in my throat for a little while. "Ah. Well, thanks."

"If you explained what was actually going on, they would probably take you back."

I release a long breath. "I don't want to use my health as an excuse for my creative shortfalls."

"You absolutely fucking can use it as an *explanation.*"

I turn my head to look at him. Fake starlight illuminates his serious expression. He's such a dangerous looking man, and yet he couldn't be more selfless or caring.

"I'm okay, Liam. *Really.*"

More than okay with the two of them bleeding warmth into me.

"You ready to try coming back to the studio?"

I give a soft smile. "Do you want me to come back?"

"You work for me, Beau."

"You should fire me. I left without giving notice."

His dark eyes flash with anger. "I'm in charge. And you're not going to leave again, understand?"

I want to laugh at his command, but I'm still not convinced I'm living in reality. Did I wake up from anesthesia? If not, I think I'm okay staying right here forever.

"You're gonna get sick of me," I say.

"Maybe."

I make a pouty face at him. "You better be glad she's holding me back."

Surprisingly, Liam lets out a deep laugh that makes my heart skip.

"You called me a liar, so it doesn't matter what I say. You won't believe me anyway," he says.

"Nevermind. I believe you."

"Mmm. Good. Have I told you how perfect you are today?"

"No. Not perfect. I'm *happy*," I murmur sleepily. "Hey, Liam?"

"Yeah, trouble?"

"Thanks for chasing after me this time."

"Nuh uh, trouble." Liam curls a hand around the back of Beau's neck and bends him over so he has to brace his hands on the couch cushion.

My pulse leaps. Liam had me in a similar position last night, pounding into me from behind while Beau sat beneath me on the couch. After Liam took me over the edge, we both doubled up on getting Beau off with our hands and our mouths.

Liam grinds his hips against Beau once before releasing him. "We don't have time for this."

Beau glances at me, seeking weakness. "You both hate me."

Rolling my eyes, I stomp over to peck a kiss to his lips. "Restrict someone from vigorous sex for a couple months…"

He makes to grab me, but I feign his attack with a laugh. "I'm covered in powdered sugar."

"I don't mind. I wanna taste you."

The doorbell rings, interrupting what would surely unravel into a heated situation. Cosmo scampers into action, nails clacking on the floor, as I hurry to the sink to wash my hands and shed my apron.

When I make it to the entryway, Hail and Z are hauling in armfuls of gifts. Cosmo prances around their legs in excitement. Hail gives him a couple good head scratches, then glances around at the explosion of garland sparkling with white lights in the tight space. "What in the winter wonderland…?"

His amber eyes fall on me, a question dancing there. My heart pounds faster. I had planned on coming clean this evening about my relationship with Liam. Doesn't mean I'm not panicking over my brother's reaction.

I value my bond with Hail. I worry that he's going to think I'm trying to steal Liam from him. That, or he'll try to convince me of all the ways Liam will break my heart, and I already do a solid job at stirring up anxiety on my own.

"It smells amazing in here," Z comments.

I force a smile while trying to suffocate my nerves. "Spiced apple candles."

Beau and I went a little decor crazy, but I couldn't deny him his fun when this afternoon was the first time since our makeshift camping date that he seemed like himself again. I don't blame him one bit for our decision to skip over Thanksgiving like it didn't even happen. He wasn't feeling well, so we spent the day on the couch snuggling him instead.

Hail jabs a thumb in the direction of the front porch. "Found a cowboy in the driveway. I'd like to nominate him as our replacement dad."

I blush as a handsome, stubbled, middle-aged man appears in his cowboy hat and leather-booted get-up.

Hurrying out the door to collect some of his bags, I sling an arm around his neck to hug him. "Hi, Dave. We're so happy you were able to make it."

His light eyes sparkle back at me. "Wouldn't miss it for the world."

Liam strides outside to grab Dave's suitcase.

"Thanks for letting me stay," Dave remarks, patting Liam on the bicep.

"No reason for you to go anywhere else. We have the room," Liam replies smoothly.

A pang of longing spreads through my chest. Something about seeing Beau's dad and Liam interact so kindly has me wishing for more holidays together. More memorable moments like this in Liam's home.

I know the fantasy can't last. I've enjoyed staying here while Beau recovers, but I have my own apartment I need to return to, and Beau's planning on finding a place in Uptown. Our mornings waking up together will become sporadic. Our time together whittled down as regular life absorbs us once more.

Regardless of how much I tell my brain this, I don't think I've wanted anything more than to keep living with Liam and Beau.

Would it be too much of a leap for us?

I drop my chin when I catch Hail's gaze on me once more, a slight furrow between his brows.

Beau rounds the corner into the hallway. My eyes grow misty as Dave hurries to embrace him. He rocks Beau side-to-side, stroking a worn, tan hand over the back of Beau's hair.

"Missed you, son." Dave's voice cracks with emotion.

Beau swipes at a rogue tear streaking down his cheek. "Damn it, dad. You're not supposed to make me cry on Christmas."

Chuckles fill the entryway. As everyone drifts into the kitchen and living area, I ferry gifts under the tree. In my chaotic running around, the doorbell rings again.

Liam cocks a brow at me. "Were we expecting anyone else?"

I swallow. "Uh, yeah. I wasn't sure he'd come."

I'd been so busy making sure the holiday would cheer Beau up that I'd forgotten to mention I'd invited my older brother.

Max had called me a week ago to ask if Hail and I were going to mom and dad's for Christmas, to which I'd spilled about our alternative plans to have a get-together without them.

When I open the front door, Max stands on the porch awkwardly in pristine black slacks and a hunter green dress shirt, Felicity clutched in one arm and a bottle of fancy wine in the other hand.

I snatch up my niece, cooing at her cuteness in a red velvet dress and a matching bow over her wispy, ash brown hair.

When I turn around, Liam's standing in the hallway, watching me with a soft gaze.

And here I thought he'd be overwhelmed by the decorations and the people.

I carry Felicity into the living room, and Hail swoops in to get some belly laughs out of her. Z smiles affectionately at his side.

"I'm guessing this is your niece," Z says.

Dave holds out a finger for Felicity to wrap her little hand around. "What's your name, sweet thing?"

Queue the explosion of my ovaries. Something about a room full of grown men turning to mush over a baby.

"This is Felicity, and my brother, Max."

"Pleasure to meet you all," Max addresses the room.

Dave claps a hand down on Max's wide shoulder. "Right back at ya, son."

Max's eyes widen slightly, and then Beau moves in to further stun him. "Hey, I'm Beau. Stasi's boyfriend."

With a twitch of a brow, Max looks to me and then back at Beau. He catalogues the scar on Beau's head that hasn't quite been hidden by his hair, then the dimples in his cheeks. His assessment ends with the left hand Beau extends toward him. His right hand isn't quite up to par yet, but we're getting there.

I hold my breath, anticipating some smart-mouthed response from Max before he pivots on his loafers and marches from the house.

Except, he politely shakes Beau's hand.

See? Grass is greener on this side of the fence.

Not that I'm trying to get Max to choose sides. If he wants to maintain a relationship with our parents, that's on him.

We all turn our attention back to Felicity as she lets out a shriek of joy.

"You're a boisterous little thing, aren't you?" Dave laughs. "Beau was a loud baby, too. He wanted all the attention."

I break into a smile as my gaze finds Liam's for a few lingering seconds. I hope he knows how thankful I am for opening up his door to all of us.

I should probably tell him how much I love him.

Max takes Felicity so I can help Liam prepare the outdoor table for dinner. Christmas in Texas usually means mild weather, giving us the opportunity to eat outside as the sun sets.

We dine on glazed ham, scalloped potatoes, and seasoned vegetables. Even Max, my normally stuck up brother, finds comfort in Dave's easy dinner conversation, mingled with Hail and Z's wild stories from their tours.

After refilling our drinks, we collectively wander into the living room to open gifts. I wedge myself between Beau and his dad. Liam sits beside Hail and Z on the other couch. Max sits down on the floor with Felicity, shocking those of us who know him as he helps her open the gifts I bought her. She gets a kick out of crumpling the wrapping paper, ignoring the age-appropriate toys I bought her.

Beau bought me a Cowboy's football jersey. As I slide it over my cropped sweater, he beams up at me, a hungry glint in his eyes. Suppose he wouldn't be exerting himself too much physically if I rode him later.

Liam got me an Arizona snapback. Apparently, he likes it when I wear hats, so now I'm going to have a whole collection.

As I show him the new display of tiny cacti and succulents I bought him and stowed around the house, Beau mutters "plant daddy" under his breath.

"I have something else to show you later," Liam informs me.

My heartbeat stutters. He gives me a flat look, warning me not to get any wild ideas.

I watch everyone else tear into gifts—guitar pedals and accessories, goofy pajamas, a subscription to a wine distribution company for Max—and then my focus shifts to Liam as he opens up the envelope from me and Beau with a month's worth of gift certificates to our favorite brunch place. It's not enough, but what else do you buy a metal god who has everything?

Eventually, Liam coaxes me into the hall with a curl of a ringed finger.

"No dirty thoughts," he whispers, leaning down to kiss my jaw. "It's a practical gift."

Opening the garage door, he flicks on the light and moves over to nudge one of my tires with a black combat boot.

"You got me new tires?" I ask incredulously.

He shrugs. "Didn't think you'd accept a new car."

I storm over to shove at his chest, but he doesn't budge. "That's too much and you know it!"

"Not for me."

"Oh, yeah? You're just rolling in cash, aren't you?"

He steps against me, and I swallow, heat sparking beneath my skin. "Want me to pay off your student loans, too?"

"Don't you *dare*."

He chuckles, peering down at me with lust raging in his eyes. "Love it when you get all worked up."

I huff out a breath. I'm finding it hard to cling to my anger with his hot, hard body pressed against me.

"You're too tall," I mutter.

"Mmm, you're just short."

"I'm above average height for a woman, thanks." I reach up to twirl a lock of his inky hair around my finger. "Your hair is a distraction."

"A sexy distraction."

I purse my lips, fighting back my own smile. Suddenly, he lifts me up into his arms and crushes his mouth to mine. We're nothing more than heated kisses and desperate touches for a few perfect moments.

Liam drops me to my feet as the garage door swings open. Beau pops his head out. A knowing smile tugs at his mouth when he looks us over. "Ahem. We're here for the show. The car show, that is."

As Dave, Hail, and Z drift into the garage to admire Liam's old cars, I sneak back into the house to find Max, the only person missing from the group.

I'm not sure why he showed up without his wife, but I don't want him to feel like we're trying to leave him out.

Sometimes I wonder if Max's standoffish nature stems from feelings of being an outsider to me and Hail's twin bond.

"Hey." I sit down beside him on the couch where he's bouncing Felicity on his knee, his dress shirt sleeves haphazardly pushed up.

He attempts a smile, but it comes across as more of a grimace. "Hey."

"I'm really glad you came."

He fiddles with the hem of Felicity's dress. Sensing something wrong, I make grabby hands at her. Is he sleep deprived? Is it his demanding career working for our dad that's wearing him down?

Max pushes out a long breath and hands her over. "Heather and I are getting a divorce."

I freeze for a second, waiting for the punchline. Max isn't the type to crack jokes, though. He's as serious as our father.

"I'm sorry, what?"

"She's...involved with someone else." He holds firm to an expression-less mask. "I wasn't aware I made her so unhappy, but...I *do* work a lot..."

His eyes drop to where Felicity's playing with a dainty bracelet on my wrist. "I offered to cut back on hours, but Heather's not interested in working through our problems. Or *my lack of effort in our marriage* is how she worded it. I suppose we never really had chemistry. Not like Hail and his...fiancé. Not like you and Beau."

"Oh, Max. That's a lot for anyone to deal with."

He runs a hand over his slacks, brushing away dog hair. He's always been OCD when it comes to cleanliness. He would have had a heart-attack if he'd had to share a bathroom with me and Hail growing up. I'm not sure how he made it through years of football with close contact with man sweat and germs.

"I shouldn't be offloading right now. Not the time or place," Max says.

I frown. It's weird picking up on the similarities between us. Max always appeared so put together—almost unbothered by whatever life threw at him—and yet it's becoming clear he pushes aside and invalidates his feelings, too.

Felicity claps her hands together, and I have to bring her closer to kiss her cute little head.

"No matter what happens, you know I'm here for you," I tell him.

His chin wobbles. "You shouldn't be. I haven't exactly been great to you or Hail. I don't expect either of you to forgive me."

"We were all under a lot of pressure growing up."

He nods and clears his throat. "I just... I don't think mom or dad will understand, you know?"

I wish I could laugh at the situation. If it wasn't so fucking sad, I probably would. How long has he been hanging on to this secret, terrified of proving to our parents he's mortal?

We've all failed to live up to our parent's expectations in some form. And I'm going to be the biggest fuck up of all with my current situation.

Rage surges through me, fueled by the shame I still carry for failing to stick up for Hail all these years. I don't want to be that weak person anymore. I have a damn voice and my own views on what's right and wrong, and I'm bone-tired of us trying to cram ourselves into molds we were never meant to fit. It's not healthy, and it's not sparking any fucking joy.

"Hold on," I say, handing Felicity back to my brother.

I pull out my phone. My Hail moment has been building for a long time. As much as I should confront my parents in person, I don't want to give them any more of my time or energy.

Of course, my call goes straight to my dad's voicemail. He doesn't want to admit he's making a huge mistake. Doesn't want to take ownership of his failures with his kids.

"Hey, this message is for you and mom," I start. "I just want you to know that all three of your children are having a wonderful Christmas without you. A shame you can't pull your heads out of your asses enough to see what you're missing. Also, I'm in a relationship with two men. Yeah, at the same time. I don't plan on leaving either one of them, so save the lectures. I don't care what you think anymore."

When I hang up, Max's eyes are practically bugging out of his head.

"There." I toss my phone aside. "Now they'll be too distracted by my bullshit and Hail's 'big gay wedding' to care about your divorce."

My heart is racing, but I'm filled with pride. I'm making choices to protect myself and my brothers. I only wish I'd had the chance to lay into Liam's dad, too. Death wasn't punishment enough for that horrible man.

I brace for some condescending remark about my life choices from Max, but what comes out instead shocks me.

"So...uh... is the other guy Liam, then? I thought...with the way you were crushing on him..."

I break into a smile. "He's the other guy."

Max's brows shoot up. His gaze sweeps to the hallway as Beau and Liam reappear from the garage, one wearing a dimpled grin and the other doing his best to hide his feelings.

"Okay then..."

Bless Max for doing his best to come up with a proper response. I have to appreciate his effort. I think it's safe to say I've found common ground with my older brother through our supposed fuck ups. Guess that's what happens when you get older and life steamrolls everything petty out of you.

"They make me happy, Max. You deserve to be happy, too."

He frowns, glancing down as Felicity tugs at his silk tie. "She's my top priority. But... maybe in the future..."

Liam and Beau drop onto the couch beside me as Hail and Z wander into the kitchen with Dave to pick at the desserts. Max is doing his best not to act weird as he makes small talk with Liam about business operations at the studio.

Their conversation gets cut off as Felicity crawls over my lap to grab the lock of hair that escaped Liam's bun. Liam gives a low laugh. "Aren't you a strong one?"

She curls her chubby, sticky hands in his dark shirt, pulling herself up to a wobbly stance on his thighs. The moment she's fully in his care, the most incredible smile forms on his face. To threaten my heart even more, he starts talking to her in a soothing tone that has her captivated, me swooning, and Beau groaning.

"He can't get anymore perfect, can he?" Beau complains.

Liam ignores him, too wrapped up in the baby eagerly vying for his attention.

Eventually, Max packs her up and excuses himself to prepare for her bedtime. Liam escorts Dave upstairs to show him where his room is as Z tidies up the kitchen.

Hail plops down onto the couch beside me. "Hey, sis. Getting pretty serious with you, Beau, *and* Liam, huh?"

Blood drains from my head. "Hail—"

"Save it. You guys couldn't be more obvious with the way you've been looking at each other. But if Beau keeps drooling over my future husband, I may have to kick his ass."

When I open my mouth to scold him, Hail cuts me off with a melodic laugh. "Kidding. The accent gets everyone. Claws away, yeah?"

I scrunch up my nose in disapproval.

"Honestly, I can't think of two better men to love you."

Heart swelling, I settle my head on his shoulder. "I agree."

"You know, Beau's got the talent to get back out there..."

"I feel like you're about to tell me this isn't sustainable."

"Then I'd be a hypocrite. Dating a musician is hard. Dating *two*?" He pauses for dramatic effect, and I blow out an annoyed breath. "As long as the three of you are willing to put in the effort, everything will work out."

"You don't think Liam will wake up one morning and change his mind?"

Hail nudges me with his shoulder. "You kidding? Liam's never going to leave your side. Yeah, there may be times he needs a little space. Sometimes he ignores my calls for weeks. Just have patience with him as he works through his shit. He cares for you. He always has."

I snake my arms around his waist and squeeze a grunt out of him.

"Scary strong."

"Nothing wrong with that."

He pecks a kiss to the top of my head. "Strong on the inside, too."

"Love you, big bro."

"Love you, too, sis. Best Christmas ever."

"I'd say we should make it a tradition, but with you and your damn touring, it's probably not going to happen."

He ruffles my hair. "Oh, we'll make it happen. Long as you keep making gingerbread cookies."

I smack his arm away but then settle against him again, content to soak up the evening with the people I love the most.

Chest tightening, I peek over at him. Sadness still clings to him. "Then why do you look like that?"

He runs a hand along the back of his neck. A nervous tick of his. I know his every tell. Spent years cramped on buses and in hotel rooms with him, sweating and bleeding for our dreams. Well, *his* dream. All I ever wanted was for Hail to be on top.

But now, I have dreams of my own, and they involve waking up next to two beautiful souls every morning.

"I'm hurt you didn't talk to me. Like... how long has this been going on? As long as Stasi's been with Beau? I'm not trying to be needy or anything, but you're my best friend, and you've had some rough days recently, and then Beau's health... that must have been really hard..."

Surprising pressure builds behind my eyes, threatening tears I haven't spilled since god knows fucking when. "You're worried about me."

"Yeah." Somehow his reply is worse than a lecture or a fist to the jaw for fucking his sister. It leaves me reeling. I expected a little anger. At the very least, words of warning from a protective twin. He and Stas are a team. A packaged deal. If I hurt her, I hurt him, too.

Casting my gaze out at the night sky, I shake my head. "You're a fucking anomaly, Hail Koval."

He laughs. "Is that a compliment?"

"Always."

The mood settles back into something comfortable. A companionship formed over two decades of friendship. Something that runs deeper than blood.

"I spent a lot of years convinced I wasn't what anyone needed. Beau and Stas...they're showing me otherwise. I wasn't keeping secrets with the intention of hurting you, but I wanted to be respectful of Stas's wishes to stay quiet. Shit with your family isn't good. It's been stressing her out."

Hail sighs. "Discover you're bi and your entire family falls apart."

"Your parents suck," I mutter.

"We should form a club."

Snorting, I drop my head and rub a hand along my stubbled jaw.

"I get why you didn't say anything," Hail says. "Guess it's hard for me to process that there are things I don't know about you. I assumed you'd at least share the important stuff."

That one glances off my chin like a blow.

"I tell you things," I mumble.

His laugh comes out exasperated. "You bought a recording studio without telling me."

"I showed you two days after I bought it."

"Yeah. *After* you bought it. I didn't even know you had one picked out. And Z... you waited to tell me you found out where he'd run off to when we were having problems."

I lift my gaze to him. "I'm sorry, Hail."

"So, are you serious about them? Cause you know I'll go to bat for my sis, and I'm starting to really like Beau."

"I'm serious, Hail. I want to pursue this. You know that's not something I've ever wanted before."

Hail stares at me like he's trying to piece a puzzle together. Like he's sifting through memories to pinpoint when I changed my mind about commitment.

"Well shit, Liam. Stasi's had a crush on you since we were teenagers."

I sigh. "I'm an oblivious asshole."

"And Beau?" he prods.

"Beau's perfect for her."

"What about for *you*?"

I spin one of my rings around a finger. "I don't deserve him. *Either* of them."

Hail places a hand on the back of my neck. I lift my head up to meet his stern expression. "You are every bit worthy of their love."

His hand drops, and then he lets out a breathy laugh. "Jesus, you would end up with two partners. Just don't tell me any of the weird shit you three get up to."

I chuckle. "You know I'm good at keeping secrets."

"Oh, I *know*. Answer my calls more often."

"Stop touring so much. Then we don't have to rely on phone calls to keep up."

"Hey, I'll be home for a while after my honeymoon. Prepare yourself." Hail moves to the sliding door, throwing it open.

"Bullshit. You two can't sit still for more than a couple of weeks."

I follow him inside, overcome with comfort as I take in my decorated home. Garland and string lights hang from every doorway, and the scent of apples fills the air from dozens of flickering candles atop the new furnishings I bought.

Hail pauses. "I don't know. This domestic situation you've got going on is pretty appealing."

He slips off to join Z strumming a guitar on the couch.

Strange to think the comment doesn't bother me. Not when giving up the fame and the money and the screaming fans gives me the opportunity to see Beau and Stas any time I want. Not when I can feel the tattered pieces inside of me finally mending.

Proof I'm exactly where I'm supposed to be.

I glance over at Stas and Beau flirting in the kitchen and nearly lose my self-control. Beau's got her caged against the island, his hands gripping her exposed hips in that little cropped sweater she's wearing, his tongue licking up the trail of powdered sugar on her cheek.

If we didn't have company, I'd fuck them both right there.

No. I'd take my time with them. Take them upstairs to my bed and show them how much I've fallen for them.

Slipping my hands in my pockets, I continue watching their playful struggle in the kitchen. Beau lifts his head from Stas's neck and flashes me a blinding smile.

Can I be certain I won't fuck this up? *No.* But Stas and Beau are making me question everything I thought I knew about myself.

Maybe I can be what they need. Maybe if I work hard, I can be *more*.

I let my hands slide off the keys. "Or you recognize that this isn't working. My career's over. Just tell me straight up, Liam. I'm done being handled like I'm breakable."

Fuck the ups and downs of recovery, too. If I'd known I was going to feel like this, I might have opted to leave the damn tumor in place.

Removing it didn't *fix* me. It only made my arm worse.

Stasi keeps telling me to be patient. I think she's wearing herself thin trying to convince me everything will be fine. That things will get better. She's putting her all into date nights, most of which she ends up massaging my arm until I pass out on her lap.

It's so one-sided. I hate it.

I drop my head onto the piano, convinced Liam's silence is confirmation of my garbage playing.

It's been months since I've felt productive. Fucking *years* since I've created anything of quality to share with fans.

This is the career I chose. I've wanted it for as long as I can remember. I've worked so hard to get here.

And now I'm failing miserably.

Worry curls in my gut that I'm pissing Liam off. I wouldn't blame him for getting upset with me. I asked him to bring me here in the middle of the night just to waste his precious time. I dragged Lithos down. Now I'm dragging Liam and Stasi down, too.

I should have stayed in Phoenix.

The piano bench creaks beneath Liam's muscled form as he sits down beside me. Just having his thigh pressed against mine helps to relieve the invisible pressure crushing my lungs.

"Beau. Look at me."

I shake my head and squeeze my eyes shut. "Can't."

"Why?"

"Cause I'll cry."

Liam lets out a heavy sigh. "Then cry, Beau. Wish I fucking could."

My head pops up. When I look at him, his expression is stoic, but there's pain in his eyes. "Liam."

He shifts his position on the bench so he's straddling it. Then he pulls me into his arms.

Tears leak from my eyes. "I'm sorry. I had it all figured out. All the fucking notes. The tempo. I wrote lyrics, Liam. I haven't written decent lyrics in forever, but I've been rotting on your couch so long I wrote goddamn lyrics I'm actually excited about. And I can't do shit with them because I can't play through the song without making a mistake."

Liam rests his chin on top of my head. "You waited seven years for me."

"What?" I murmur, confused.

"It's been seven years since I left you in a New York hotel to board a plane for a European tour. You waited seven years for *me*, of all fucking people, and yet you can't give yourself a few months' grace with music after having your head cut open."

My chin quivers. "See? Knew you were mad at me."

He squeezes me tighter. "I'm not mad at you, Beau. I'm mad at the part of your brain that's making you think you need to wear yourself thin to get back to producing hits. Because you *will* produce hits again."

Throat swelling, I fight to swallow. "But what if I don't? What if I never get it back, even after all your support? I don't know who I am without music."

"You'll always have music. It's this pressure to produce you don't fucking need. You don't owe anyone anything, Beau. Not at the cost of your mental health."

The tears really start falling, and soon, I'm sobbing into his shirt. "I'm tired, Liam. I'm so fucking sick of being tired."

"Then rest, baby. Let me hold you for a while."

I would be embarrassed that I've slipped into those silly hiccup sounds from crying too hard if not for him telling me how perfect I am the whole time. How beautiful and sweet and funny I am.

How I'm everything he's been waiting for.

After I've soaked his shirt, he eases me back and tugs off my hood. I wince, hating being exposed to him when I feel like I'm at my fucking lowest, but he just leans in to press a kiss to my scar. "I'm going to support you no matter what, you know that, right?"

My chin trembles as I lower my head. "I do. I just...want to be me again. I don't want to be a burden anymore."

He grips my chin and lifts it. "You are *not* a burden. Your circumstances may have changed, but you are still you. You are still the man I love."

"*Fuck.*" More tears spill down my cheeks. "You know I love you, too."

His throat bobs. "Yeah. But it's nice to hear it."

My heart thuds painfully. I raise my hands to his cheeks, stroking my fingers over his stubble. His eyes are as dark as coals in the low lighting of the studio, but somehow they hold warmth as he stares back at me.

I lean in to kiss him. "I love you, Liam Beckner. Always have. Always will."

He nips at my bottom lip. "Good. Now, do I need to keep lecturing you, or are you going to be kinder to yourself?"

I chuckle. "Told you I'm a mess."

"Beau Whitaker's human?"

A smile eases onto my face. "Human as fuck, baby."

His fingers slide into my hair. "The only baby here is you."

The bells jingle above the door, and we both turn to see our girl walking in. My mood instantly improves. She's wearing our clothes, my sweats and his hoodie. Her hair is down in loose waves that tumble to her elbows.

"Couldn't fall back asleep without you two." She gives a shy shrug.

I hold out my arms to her. "Come here, sweetheart."

She hurries over, allowing me to pull her onto my lap. Her hand brushes along my damp cheek. "You were crying."

"Hole in my head left room for a lot of big feelings," I say with a smile. "Ah, shit. Don't do that. Please don't be sad." I do my best to kiss away her frown. "I'm fine. I promise. I appreciate everything you've done for me. I'm going to spend my life making it up to you, okay?"

"It's not a debt, Beau," she says solemnly.

"Okay. Yeah." I nod. "I'm sorry."

After I hold her for a while, I hand her over to Liam. My heart swells as I watch him kiss her tenderly.

Is this really the same man who was terrified of relationships?

Feeling inspired by his bravery to face his demons, I straighten up on the piano bench and stretch out my fingers. "I know it's late, but can I give it another go?"

Liam pecks a kiss to Stasi's lips and looks over at me. "As long as you're not doing it for fans."

I grin. "Forget the fans. I want to play for the two of you."

Your ass is mine, baby.

Yours.

Excitement rushes through me. That motherfucker came home early from work to prep for me.

Fumbling with the door lock, I kick off my shoes the instant I'm inside his home. Huffing a breath, I take the painful extra seconds to peel off my socks. The last thing I need is to wipe out on the stairs and cause more damage to my brain. Liam might not touch me ever again.

My blood turns molten when I find him in his bed, naked and dipped in ink, his damp hair flowing down over pecs carved from stone.

He's a god. A literal god. And he's on his knees for me in his bed like I'm the one in power. It's a potent fucking feeling. Adrenaline thrums just beneath my too tight skin as I'm overcome with need for this man.

"If I fuck you, I'm going to want more," I tell him, my fingers already dragging my zipper down. "I'll want to fuck you again and again like you belong to me."

Liam's expression remains blank. Almost *cold*. But it's in the burn of his deep brown eyes how much he wants this. How much he wants *me*.

"Then fuck me, Beau," he says darkly.

Swallowing, my hands shake with nerves, anticipation, and heady lust as I step out of my jeans and boxers.

His cock twitches. I give my own a few strokes for show, sinking a tooth into my bottom lip.

I want to make him feel good. I want to etch myself in his fucking soul so he carries me with him into the afterlife.

Climbing onto the bed, I bring our bodies together. We're skin-on-skin. Chests and cocks and thighs pressed together.

I settle my hands on either side of his face.

"Beau," he murmurs, body tensing.

I realize in that moment just how hard this is for him. How much he's struggling to give up control.

"Do you trust me?"

"You know I do."

"I'm gonna make you feel good. I promise."

His chest heaves against mine, and then he pushes out a deep breath before meeting my lips in a tender kiss.

We work up to tongues and teeth and wandering touches. Liam's dark eyes glint as they drop to watch my hand stroke over both of our erections.

After a few more slow kisses, I smooth a hand down to his ass and squeeze it, marveling at the strength in every inch of his body.

He rumbles with a growl when I sneak my fingers between his cheeks, stroking them against his hole.

"Mine," I say with a grin.

"For today."

Reaching over to his nightstand, I grab the bottle of lube and slick up my fingers. When I position my body behind his, his muscles tense up again.

"Liam, have you done this before?"

"I have."

I frown. "But you don't enjoy it."

"Did I say that?" He reaches back to grab my hand and slips it between his cheeks. "I enjoy whatever brings my partner pleasure. I get off when you get off, Beau."

Does he ever stop thinking about others?

Circling my lubed fingers around his hole, I take my time stretching him. I don't want him to have any regrets. Liam is trusting me with his body. If he decides he doesn't like something, then we stop.

I run my other hand over his shoulders. Along his scarred ribs. Down to the dimples in his lower back. Only when I've got three fingers sunk into his ass do I remove them and nudge my crown against his prepped hole.

"Tell me if I do something wrong. If you don't like—"

Liam braces his hands on the headboard. "Hurry the fuck up, Beau."

Breaking into a smile, I start to push inside his hot, tight body. Carefully working myself in and out, I let him adjust to my cock stretching his ass. He bows forward, head dropping.

"Okay?"

"Yeah."

I move my hands down to his hips and change the angle on my next thrust.

He groans. "Beau."

"Good?"

"*Fuck.* Good. Keep doing—"

I shove all the way inside his ass. His whispered curses and hitched breaths are all the encouragement I need to let go. I fuck him hard, paying attention to his body and the noises he's making.

Soon, we're both slick with sweat, our hot skin sticking each time we come together. I reach around to stroke his cock, spreading the precum beading along his slit down his shaft. I work him right up to the edge, and when his body shudders, I stop moving to deny him the orgasm.

"Gonna ruin you for this," Liam pants.

I kiss a burn scar along his spine. "Promise?"

He pushes back on my cock, summoning a guttural noise from me this time.

"Fuck, I'm so close," I gasp. "Damn it."

"We need to work on your stamina."

Liam's taunt has me pulling out. I try to flip his giant body over, but he ends up moving for me, propping himself against the headboard. He spreads his legs, his thick, hard cock on full display. His chest and abs rise and fall with heavy breaths.

The things I want to do to this man. The things I want him to do to *me...*

I reach for the bottle of lube with shaky hands and slick my fingers again. Then I shove two of them into my ass.

Liam chuckles. "A little desperate?"

"Not how this was supposed to go, but I haven't had you inside me in months."

I push in a third finger, but I can't get myself stretched quick enough, so I give up and climb onto his lap. My hands grip the headboard on either side of his head as I slowly lower myself down onto his cock.

"Fuck me. I'm so addicted to you," I mumble.

Liam's hands slide down my chest to grip my hip and ass. I'm all breathy moans as he thrusts deep inside me. His muscles flexing are a thing of beauty.

"So sexy, Beau. Love watching you ride me." Liam slows the snap of his hips as one of his big hands drifts to my cock. "Should I let you come before me? Or should I make you suffer, too?"

Pressure builds at the base of my spine, hot and tingly and utterly mind-melting.

"Holy fucking shit. Need inside of you again."

He releases his hold on me, and I readjust to line my cock up with his hole. Two hard thrusts inside his tight heat, and I'm losing control.

"*Look at me.* I want to see those gorgeous eyes when you come inside me."

That's it. I'm done for. I push my release as far as I can inside his body, only pulling out when I'm certain some of me will forever be left behind.

"Never in my life." I watch in awe as I ease out of him. "Never seen something so incredible."

Liam looks wrecked when I glance up at him. His cock stands proud, swollen and red. He's breathing hard.

I explore the rest of his body with my mouth and fingers. I trace his abs with my tongue. Suck on both of his nipples. Bite down on both ass cheeks as I push each heavy leg up to gain more access, mesmerized by the sight of my cum slowly seeping out of him.

Liam snaps a hand to my hair. When he tilts my head up, his eyes are burning with sexual frustration.

I smirk. "If you want me to stop, just say so. But I also think you need this."

His grip loosens on my hair, turning into a gentle scratch on my scalp that has me practically purring.

I work hard to unravel him. And when I'm done worshiping nearly every inch of his gorgeous body, I climb back on his lap and sink down on his cock.

His primal growl echoes through the room as he explodes in my ass. I drop my sweaty forehead to his chest, and we stay there in silence, drained of everything.

He brushes his fingers along my temple and through my hair. I reach up to wrap a hand around his wrist. "Liam?"

He rumbles in response.

"Would you cut my hair for me? Figure I should look somewhat presentable at the wedding tomorrow."

"Only if you release the song you recorded," Liam says.

I stiffen under his touch. "You think it's ready?"

"It's more than ready. Beau, you silenced the studio yesterday with your playing. I shared a clip with Hail and Z. They won't stop asking me when they can add the track to their playlists."

I rub my face against his hard chest. "They're just being polite."

"Well, I'm *not* polite. So take my word for it. I wouldn't let you release anything if I expected the world would crucify you for it."

Playfully, I nip at his skin. "What if it reflects poorly on your studio?"

"Beau," Liam warns.

"Fine," I mumble.

It's been a year since I've shared my music with the world. Pretty sure people think I'm dead by now. Is anyone even going to recognize my name? Should I care? I haven't been playing for anyone else. After months of physical therapy and encouragement from Liam and Stasi, I've been playing for me again.

Liam eases both of us upright. Chest to bare chest, he kisses me once more. "Let's take care of that hair, sexy."

Retrieving a wooden stool from the music room for me to sit on in the middle of the bathroom, his fingers gently comb through my hair. They're followed immediately by the buzzing clippers, and I watch as long locks of dark brown hair rain down on the tile floor.

New hair. New song. New chapter in a hopefully long, happy life.

"Good plan. See you in a few hours."

After he hangs up, I try to shake off the nerves for my twin brother. *God, is he really doing this?*

Snatching my dress, strappy gold heels, and make-up bag, I rush to my car.

It's an abnormally warm winter day. Perfectly overcast. If that's not a sign that this wedding was meant to be, I don't know what is.

After assuring the vendors know where to set up, I soak in my hard work. It's a beautiful venue. Balcony doors offer stunning views of the Dallas skyline, serving as the backdrop for the ceremony.

I talked the hotel staff into hanging sheer white panels of fabric in the open doorways. Wildflowers decorate every surface, bringing a pleasant floral scent to the airy space. Outdoor furniture has been rearranged around elegant stone fire pits for roasting marshmallows. And there's a dance floor under string lights that will glitter like a fairytale when the sun goes down.

Ugh. I'm not emotional. It's only my twin getting married. The person I played shadow to for so many years. The sweet human who lifted my head when I was feeling down. Who became my shield from the cruel words of our parents.

I grab some sandwiches from the lobby, dropping them at the room where Liam is helping Hail get ready. Then I head toward Z's room to deliver his lunch.

Ice-blue eyes open wide when Z answers his hotel room door. He's here alone, no biological family left to claim him, but there are so many guests coming today that love and accept him as their own.

"Thank you," Z says, easing his long arms around me. "Sorry for dropping a lot of this on you."

"I was honored you asked me for help. I'm so happy for you." I swipe away a rogue tear on my cheek and look him over. He's dressed in a dark suit with a crisp white shirt and a black bowtie. He's got winged eyeliner on and dark red nail polish that suits him.

"You are unfairly pretty, Z. Now what is there left to do? Your hair?" I ask, reaching for the mess of unruly black curls falling down over his inky brows.

He lifts both hands in defense. "Um. It's good."

"You sure?"

His gaze drops to the floor as his cheeks turn bright red. "Hail likes it this way."

"Oh, Z." I hug him again around the waist. "How many times am I going to cry today?"

His laugh is a quiet thing. Almost like a whisper. "Probably not as much as Hail."

"I'll leave you to it, then," I say, fixing his bowtie. "Call or text if you need me."

He nods. "Thanks."

I check in with Malek and Griff, too, but there's no taming the chaos that surrounds them. Their hotel room reeks of weed and spilled vodka. Red solo cups dot every counter, along with enough half-eaten snacks to feed an army.

"You have to button the dress shirt all the way up," Griff complains, approaching Malek with raised hands.

Malek slaps him away. "It doesn't look good that way, and it's uncomfortable."

"It looks like shit if you put the tie on over an unbuttoned shirt."

"Yeah, maybe for other people. I can pull it off."

Griff rolls his eyes. "Just because you *can* doesn't mean you should. It's a wedding, fucker."

A flash of a wicked smile from Malek. "So you admit I look good like this?"

"I didn't say that—"

With quiet steps, I slip out of their room.

"Stas! No! We don't know what we're doing!" Malek shouts right before the door clicks shut.

I book it down the hall, braid slapping against my spine.

It's a flurry of bubbles and frizzy blow-dried hair leading up to my transformed look. Soft beach waves spill down the open back of my long silk dress the shade of champagne.

Just as I'm sliding a bobby pin along one side of my head, a message buzzes on my phone, alerting me of Beau's arrival. My heart skips in anticipation.

I step back from the mirror and assess my reflection. The dress is classy, with a little peek of leg through the thigh to floor slit. It's nice and all, but it's no snapback and sweats. Honestly, Hail wouldn't care what I showed up in as long as I'm here for him.

Grabbing my dainty purse and heels, I perform a feat of athleticism by slipping them on as I race toward the elevator.

One look at Beau when the doors part, and I'm robbed of oxygen. He's dressed in black slacks that hug his thighs and a white button-up shirt with the sleeves rolled up his veiny, naturally tan forearms. The sides of his hair have been cut short, while the top was left in longer, pretty waves.

In a crowded hall of guests, I only see him.

My pulse pounds as I step out of the elevator and his head turns. I feel his eyes run down my body like a soft caress. He shakes his head in disbelief before striding over to me with a smile that shows off both heart-stopping dimples. He kisses me sweetly, right in front of everyone.

"You're breathtaking," he says.

If he wasn't holding me, I'd probably float away. "Right back at you, handsome. Love your hair."

His blue eyes shine. "Liam did it."

I'm stunned by him. He looks so good. So filled with life and energy. It took months to get him here, and while it was hard, now I feel like we can handle anything the universe wants to throw at us.

Looping his arm through mine, Beau guides me into the grand wedding space filled with musicians and friends of my brother. Some I recognize from video chats. Others I glimpsed at Atonement's shows when they played in the area.

Prickles of awareness spread along my skin as we step out onto the balcony. I turn to lock eyes with Liam.

And forget how to exist all over again.

"Beau," I utter.

Liam's a vision in his all-black suit, his long hair spun up into its usual messy bun, showing off the full extent of his strong features and neck tattoos.

Liam runs his heated gaze over both of us, conveying everything he wants to do to us in secret. Telling us we've only just begun. This is the tip of the iceberg, and there's so much more to explore.

Fuck suits for looking so damn good.

What is it about a bad boy that quickens my pulse? Is it because I used to hide my own rebellious nature? This craving for danger?

"Je-sus." Beau sucks in a gulp of air like it's a rapidly depleting resource.

Hail stands next to Liam, holding a beer and looking dashing in a crimson dress shirt with suspenders. He's more punk rock today than metal.

I snort. Suppose he considers that formal attire.

My twin strides over and pulls me into a side hug. "Thanks for all your help, sis. This day is perfect."

I sniffle and pat a hand over his stomach. "You deserve it, Hail."

He drags Beau into a full-on hug, and my throat tightens with emotion at the acceptance surrounding us.

"Still on for later?" Hail asks.

Beau grins. "Still on."

I peek up at Beau in question. He simply pecks a kiss to my cheek. "Patience, sweetheart."

He's lucky I became distracted by the staff appearing with trays of appetizers, or I'd hound him for answers.

The food is eclectic, a mix of fancy brunch items and dishes Hail and Z experienced while touring together.

Really, everything is mismatched in the best way possible. My brother wanted Z to be happy, and Z isn't one to ever vocalize his wants. So it was up to me and Hail to make the best decisions possible.

Judging by the smiles and laughter filling the venue, everyone is enjoying themselves.

After all of our low moments and disappointments growing up in a toxic home, this is more than I could have ever asked for to celebrate my brother's big day.

I can't say I've ever seen love. Smitten kids in high school and college, yeah. Marriages of convenience, yes. But as we file into the rows of chairs for the ceremony and I watch Z walk down the aisle toward my antsy twin brother, I can see the overwhelming love flowing between them.

Hail won't stop smiling like a goober. It has tears welling in my eyes, threatening to spill. I purposely went light on the make-up, knowing I would most likely ruin it.

I sense dark, intense eyes on me, but I refuse to meet them. I can't look at Liam. I'll be found out in an instant. It's not that I need marriage, but I *do* want forever with someone.

Two someones.

A whispered apology from behind has me turning to catch Max dropping into an empty chair, his daughter in one arm and a giant diaper bag in the other. He looks flustered. Almost as if he sprinted here on foot.

Beau interlocks our fingers and gives my hand a squeeze. "You okay?"

"Yeah." I swipe at the rogue tear dangling from my chin.

"Let 'em fall, baby. I got you."

When I glance up at Beau, tears glisten in his eyes, too. "Beau…"

"Ah fuck. Something about those words 'in sickness and in health'…"

The tremble of his chin nearly has me crumbling. He glances down at me, those mesmerizing eyes swirled through with contentment, love, and a little fear I think we'll all carry into every MRI scan coming our way.

After the ceremony ends, the married couple sneaks off for pictures. Their metalhead friends are set loose on the open bar, but nothing really picks up until Hail and Z return.

I'm pretty sure Z's cheeks will remain flushed the entire reception.

Max joins in the dancing with Felicity in his arms. She's all giggles and spastic arm movements, and his eyes are brighter than I've ever seen them. He looks at her like he's holding the entire world in his arms.

Hard times are coming for him, but it's evident he's going to rock this single dad thing, regardless.

Malek and Griff are nonstop energy. They spend the evening wrestling and piling their plates with an ungodly amount of food.

Maria slips into more Spanish with every cocktail she downs. We all nod like we understand her passionate words.

A woman named Selma flew in from London. She's perched at the bar with Atonement's band manager, Sondra. They're not related, though their names are similar and they both seem to have dominating personalities.

Before I can slip off the dance floor to rest my feet, Liam catches me around the waist and spins me around to face the DJ.

Only, it's Beau standing front and center, holding the guitar Liam bought him. His eyes fall on me, and a warm smile spreads on his beautiful face. My knees just about buckle.

I settle my weight against Liam behind me as we watch our man perform. His song is slower than anything I've ever heard him play, but I recognize pieces he's been tinkering with over the last few months, fighting through therapy, headaches, sleepiness, and depression. The harmony is so beautiful. I feel like I'm breaking apart. Splitting at the seams to spill out too many emotions all at once.

Beau was convinced he would never get up in front of a crowd like this again. Now he's winning over hearts with his performance.

And *good lord* can the boy perform. Listening to him play in a quiet setting is one thing, but seeing him manipulate a crowd of a hundred-some musicians with a single song is quite another.

An achy pain blooms in my chest. If Beau's back to where he needs to be, do I have any reason to stay at Liam's house?

Liam turns me in his arms and leans down to my ear. "What's wrong?"

I bite the inside of my cheek. "It's nothing."

"Anastasia." He nudges my chin with a knuckle, bringing my gaze to him.

I'm so fucked.

I'm so in love with both of them.

I don't want to leave them.

I don't want to move out.

"I should probably get my stuff from your house."

His dark eyes shine with something indistinguishable, and my heartbeat falters.

"Or you can break your lease tomorrow and move in. Permanently."

"Liam..."

His thumbs stroke along my jaw. "Is that what you want? You want all three of us together in my house?"

My fingers curl into his suit jacket. My brain tells me to shut down the offer. He's just being his normal provider self. I don't want to pressure him into an uncomfortable situation.

But then I remember Iris's words. *You need to speak up. Tell them what you want. Be brave. Make demands.*

I nod frantically. "I want it. I want it so bad, Liam."

"Then we're picking up your boxes tomorrow."

Liam presses his lips to mine, and we softly sway to the rest of Beau's song in a sea of other couples. I haven't felt this light on my feet since I can remember.

When Beau finishes performing, Liam gives me a nudge. "Go get him."

I rush to wrap my arms around Beau. I'd hop into his arms if this dress allowed it.

"You're incredible," I exclaim.

Beau grins, peppering me with kisses. "Wouldn't have gotten here without you."

Liam joins us with ice waters from the bar, and we wander over to an empty red couch by one of the stone fire pits.

As we sit, Beau rests his head on my lap and slings a leg over Liam's muscled thigh. I run my fingers through his shorter hair, loving the texture of the buzzed sides and back. I bend down to press my lips against his. When I lean back up, Liam takes my chin in his hand, bringing me into a soft kiss.

"Hotel room or our home tonight?" Liam asks, his other hand sliding over the bare skin exposed through the slit of my dress. Heat rushes between my legs.

"Um...I vote for hotel room..." I say, blushing.

Totally not already picturing us wrecking it.

"Want," Beau replies eagerly. "Want so hard."

Glancing around the party, I wonder when it would be appropriate for us to slink off. Probably not until Hail and Z take their leave.

I can be patient. I have forever with my two men.

Eventually, the old Atonement crew wanders over. Always one to ruin a mood, Malek sprawls over Griff's lap to get closer to us, a predatory jungle cat creeping on its prey.

"So, Liam. Let me get this straight. Or *not* straight." A flash of sharp white teeth. "You're fucking him, and he's fucking her, and she's fucking you?"

Griff jabs a hand into Malek's ribs, and Malek curls up like a centipede.

"What? Everyone knows I have no filter," Malek says.

"I wish you'd find one," Hail complains, absentmindedly playing with his husband's bowtie. Z's smiles have come freely today. I notice his fingernails are painted the same shade of red as Hail's dress shirt.

Relationship goals.

"My sex life isn't up for discussion," Liam replies.

"Yeah, asshole. Don't ask people who they're fucking." Griff smacks Malek's head. Malek reaches a hand up to pinch at Griff's nipple.

As soon as Hail ushers Z inside the hotel under the guise of resting up for their honeymoon flight out of DFW in the morning, the party starts to wind down.

Which means *our* night can begin.

Liam slides a room key into Beau's pocket, letting his hand linger there. "Room 708."

He leans over to kiss the hollow behind my ear. "I'm the only one allowed to peel that dress off you, understood?"

I nod desperately as Beau takes my hand and pulls me to my feet. "Let's go, sweetheart. Our boyfriend wants to play."

Reaching out, Liam grips Beau by the tie and tugs him down close to his mouth. "You can kiss her. You can touch yourself, but you don't get to come until I say so."

With Beau's tiny growl of frustration, he leads me away.

I glance back at Liam as he takes a seat at the bar for a glass of sweet tea, knowing he's about to make us wait for him.

Thankfully, it won't take years this time.

Epilogue
Beau

Five years later

Tiny feet patter on wood floors as I tug on a hoodie and lock up the music room and our bedroom. I leave Lilah's pink bedroom—what used to be the spare bedroom—open in case she changes her mind about letting Felicity play with her toys.

It's not that our daughter doesn't like to share. It's that she's particularly concerned about the cleanliness of her space after the last time Felicity came to play.

I pause at the bottom of the townhouse stairs, waiting for the culprits of all the ruckus to appear on what has got to be their hundredth lap around the house.

A miniature Liam comes skidding around the corner into the hallway, her thick curtain of black hair swishing around her round face. Cosmo skitters after her and thuds into the wall, causing me to chuckle.

Warm brown flick to me. Immediately, they burn down to my soul, ravenous for secrets.

I would say it's normal for all children to stare like that, but Lilah's on another level. She's the offspring of the metal god Liam Beckner, and I swear she was born with the idea that she was meant to protect me, too.

Daddy, you need to nap.

Daddy, you need to call your doctor.

Daddy, you need to drink more water.

I let her baby me, knowing if I refuse, it will upset her. She's the perfect mix of my two favorite people loving each other, and that's something special.

She's special.

She may not have my genes, but I wouldn't want it any other way. Now we don't have to be concerned about her inheriting my predisposition to develop brain tumors.

Honestly, there was no hope of her growing up normally. Not with three parents—two of which are well-known musicians. And not with me having to undergo surgery before her second birthday when my doc found another mass during a routine MRI.

My health has unfortunately had an impact on us all, but anytime I get in my feels about it, Lilah takes my face in her little hands and glares at me until I break into soft laughter because seeing that kind of fierce expression on a three-year-old is wild.

I can't say it's been all negative. Lilah is the most cautiously gentle and observant child I've ever come into contact with.

Chuckling, I watch her zip on by for another lap around the house.

Max's daughter skids into view seconds later, slamming into the hallway and rattling the collage of pictures we've hung over the years of our vacations. She's wearing a Halloween cheetah costume Max says she refuses to take off, even though it's several sizes too small.

"Super cat speed!" she yells, following this up with her best impression of a menacing growl.

We're not sure where her personality came from—I've never met her mom—but I have to put some weight on Max's inability to tell the girl no.

At six years old, she's running the show.

From somewhere in the house, Lilah squeals in terror. By the time I rush into the kitchen to save her, Liam has already scooped her up onto his broad shoulder.

When Lilah grabs onto his bun in what has to be a death grip, Liam just hums with laughter and secures a big, inked hand over her tiny leg.

My heart kicks my ribs hard. I don't think I would have fought so hard for each day if not for them in my life.

"The tiger got to you, huh?" I smirk at Liam's rainbow-painted nails. More polish covers his skin than anything else.

"Hey. It's an upgrade to go with his pretty hair." Felicity pouts for all of three seconds before launching herself at Liam's leg like a beast trying to scale a tree.

Max rubs at his brows. "I'm raising a feral animal."

I pat a hand on his back. On top of being a single parent, his workload as the CFO at a new company has him wound more tightly than normal. We've done what we can to help support him by babysitting Felicity when issues pop up with daycare or illness.

Liam chuckles as he peers at Felicity. "Down, kitty. You can't have this one."

Felicity roars again, drawing an airy laugh from Stasi as she sweeps in through the back patio door.

The friend group we've solidified over the years—our yoga brunch crew, Ascension Record's staff, and whatever members of Atonement are in town at the time—are gathered in the backyard for a cookout.

Stasi's instantly drawn to Lilah, arms reaching up to snatch her from Liam's shoulder. At first, he turns his body away, not willing to part with her. Then Stasi levels him with a fiery look that has my cock taking notice.

I'm almost tempted to join the gym to watch their power dynamic unfold there, too. But also, ew to working out.

Stasi dips Lilah in her arms and peppers her cheeks with kisses, earning some of the most heavenly giggles. Liam flips Felicity upside down and carries her outside, shutting the door on her growls.

Lilah reaches for me. "Want daddy!"

Syrupy warmth spreads through me. I'm not sure anything else could ever compare to being loved unconditionally by a child. It's an experience I'll cherish no matter the challenges that may come with my health in the future.

"Don't you want mommy, Lilah?" Stasi asks, rocking our sweet baby in her arms.

Lilah squirms harder. "Want daddy!"

Stasi pouts as she walks her over to me. "This isn't fair."

My grin spreads wider. "Maybe we should have another one."

She contemplates it for a moment, teeth sinking into her bottom lip.

"I'll watch." I waggle my brows.

She rolls her eyes. "Maybe if one of *you* carries it this time."

I chuckle, but it's cut off as Lilah tightens her arms around me in a chokehold. Loosening her hold, I sway her around the house, pausing in the hallway to let her look over the pictures.

She likes seeing us together hiking, kayaking, and dirt biking. She likes the pretty orange and pink sunsets we've captured and the flowering cacti from the garden at our house in Arizona, our holiday getaway home whenever Liam and Stasi take time off from being workaholics.

Lilah's little fingers creep up into my hair, seeking the raised lines along the left side of my scalp. It's become a habit for her to trace them. Almost like she needs to feel them healed.

"Are you gonna get another boo-boo?" she asks.

My chest tightens, but I keep my smile in place. "I'm not sure, baby."

I've been tumor-free for several scans now, but that doesn't mean I'm in the clear.

Lilah rests her palm over my scars. "I can heal you with magic if it happens again. Okay, daddy?"

If only that's how it worked, sweet girl. If only.

Gently taking her hand in mine, I kiss the tips of her tiny fingers. I'm not sure why they're always sticky. I do my best not to think about it.

The doorbell rings, and I wander over to it with Lilah as my passenger. She's constantly in one of our arms, so much so that she was late to crawl and walk.

When I open the door, Hail and Z greet us with hands full of chips and pop.

"Dude. Congrats," Hail says. "Your song is *still* number five on the rock charts."

"Is it? I hadn't checked..."

The little boy hiding behind them peeks his head around—their newly adopted son, Zack. He's eight years old, timid, untrusting, and yet his blue eyes light up with admiration any time he looks at one of his two dads.

Maybe we should adopt, too. We could fill this house with kids. We have more than enough love to give.

"Come on in," I say, stepping to the side.

Just as I'm about to close the door behind them, someone shouts my name from across the street. Peeking out, I catch Noah jogging up the driveway, a big smile spreading on his face. I wasn't sure he would make it with his busy schedule, but he's been putting in the work to mend our friendship after a heart-to-heart a few years back. Turns out we were sucky bandmates, but we're pretty good at being friends.

Noah keeps asking me to join Lithos as a special guest at a show, or even on tour, but I can't fathom ever leaving home again. I'm satisfied to create music under Liam's supervision in the comfort of the studio where my daughter can watch from his lap.

"Everyone's here," I call out behind me.

This is received with a "let's fucking eat!" from none other than Max's daughter.

"She's a troublemaker," Lilah says, struggling with the pronunciation of such a big word.

I break out into a wider smile. "Nothing wrong with that, baby."

A little bit of troublemaking is what got me here, surrounded by friends and family who love me.

After Ignite's release, I came back to RMU, though I honestly wasn't super excited to write a female character. We're complicated creatures, and I find I'm much more critical of FMC's than I am of MMC's.

I figured I could cure my lack of motivation by adding in another male character. Ironically, Beau ended up being my toughest character to puzzle out. He wanted to be all of the things. Stas wanted to be none of the things. And Liam was set on not having a relationship, which doesn't make for a very good romance book...

Add in an overlapping timeline with Drag Me Down, and I was ready to call it quits. I took another break, drafted Devour, and came back to Raise Me Up for a third time, determined to power through like a champ! I chipped away until I found my love for all three characters. Took me a whopping 315,867 words to get here. Not to mention the 65K I wrote for Devour within that time frame.

So there. I haven't been slacking. Maybe there was a tiny bit of slacking because a girl's gotta read too, okay?

But mostly, I was playing a mental game where I tell myself I'm not a real author and no one wants to hear from me. As much as I've always loved writing stories, this isn't something I'm professionally trained in. I barely made it through business school, damn it.

I also questioned if I was the right person to write about certain topics. I do my best to research and gather real life stories if I don't have direct experience in areas, but even then, I worry I'm going about everything wrong.

Add in the crippling fear of strapping myself back into the emotional rollercoaster of publishing a book, and yeah...I let things eat away at me. I won't continue on this sad tangent—I save those for family and friends (sorry, guys)—but I just wanted to share how difficult this book was for me to finish, and how proud I am to be releasing it into the world.

With that being said, I had a ton of support along the way! As always, I have to give a shoutout to my husband for pushing me out of the house to write when the mom guilt got too real. Thanks for supporting me writing queer books!

Nicole, words are not enough to express how grateful I am for your friendship. Besties for life. Good luck getting rid of me. If you hear rustling in your bushes, it's me. Hi. Anyway, you listen to me wallow about book shit on the daily, and for that alone, you deserve infinite gold stars.

Kersten, I'm so happy to have met you! Thanks for being a fantastic friend and author resource. We'll meet in person one day (Queers & Quills 2027?!)

Maria, you rocked the beta thing! Seriously, thank you for the solid feedback. I knew I could trust you with this manuscript. And girl, your spice suggestions had me blushing!

Julia, I can't thank you enough for volunteering to beta this one. Your constant updates and encouragement while you read helped me tremendously!

Nattie, thank you for all your help with ALL of my books! I appreciate you beta reading and ARC reading.

LaQuita, my second momma, thank you for sharing your recovery story about your uncooperative, evil brain, and thank you to Adam for talking neuro with me, not even questioning the fact that I needed that knowledge to write a poly romance book!

Jordan @euphoricpromotions_, you were a lifesaver during this process! Without your help designing graphics and managing ARCs, I might have melted down!

Emily, you get gold stars for answering all my doctor questions and for not judging me when I spent most of our vacations together writing instead of relaxing.

And to all the readers, thank you so much for taking a chance on me and reading my books. Much love!